# SECRETS

## A MOTORCYCLE CLUB ROMANCE

# UNVEILED

## REBECCA HAMBY

# AUTHOR NOTE

My dear readers, I beg of you to please read this trigger warning list to its entirety. While I love a good dark romance as much as the next, I always take the time to read through the trigger warnings. I encourage you to do the same. Your mental health matters. I do not condone any actions or scenes, while I have written them, yes, however, I do not condone them. I want to make that clear. Murder is bad. Remember that—murder is bad.

Please read the list below before continuing to the prologue.

Thank you to all my wonderful readers. I love you dearly.

---

### Triggers

Graphic violence
Murder
Mutilation

Kidnapping
Loss of a parent
Body dysmorphia
Breath Play
Alcohol use
Weapon use

———

**About Secrets Unveiled**

Told in Dual POV
OTT (Over the top) male
J/P (Jealous/Possessive) M
Brothers Best Friend Trope
A Motorcycle Club Dark Romance

# PLAYLIST

Chokehold – Sleep Token
You're Going Down – Sick Puppies
My Brother's Best Friend – Hannah Trager
Teenager In Love – Madison Beer
Favorite Crime – Olivia Rodrigo
Take Me To Church – Hozier
Sex On Fire – Kings of Leon
Older – Isabel LaRosa
Favorite – Isabel LaRosa

# DEDICATION

To my motorcycle obsessed mother, who loves a good morally gray male character, this one's for you. Thank you for loving my writing and always asking me when my next book will be released. You're my biggest fan.

SAGE

# PROLOGUE

## SAGE

### SEVEN YEARS AGO

It's so hot.

The flames are climbing higher up the staircase. I fear this is the end for me. I'm screaming out for my father, but the sounds of the raging fire overwhelm my ears. The flames are growing by the second.

It's so hot.

It sounds like a train rumbling down the tracks, out of control. It's painfully loud. My skin feels as though it's starting to melt. I'm stuck on the third floor; the stairs are completely engulfed in thick black smoke, making it impossible to see. My screams have faded into coughs as I feel my lungs constricting within me. Invisible hands are squeezing my esophagus. I try to force myself to swallow, but I can't. My chest is tight, and trying to suck in even the slightest bit of oxygen seems impossible.

"Help, someone, please!" My cries appear pointless

since I haven't seen or heard anyone. I remember waking up—today is my fourteenth birthday—and being overrun with billows of smoke seeping beneath my door. Sitting up, I swing my legs over the side of the bed and race to the door. Opening my bedroom door, I'm hit with a wall of heat that's so intense I can hardly open my eyes.

"Dad?" I call out, but I'm met with no response. Panic quickly consumes me, as does the smoke. I drop to my knees, trying to get below the black clouds. This is where I realize I won't be getting to the main level by way of the stairs. A blanket of black smoke conceals the staircase that I know is there but can no longer see. There's no other way out. *How am I going to get out of here?*

I run back to my room and straight to the balcony, swinging open the French doors. Instantly, I inhale a breath of fresh air. The sun has barely begun to rise. The sky is a pinkish hue as smoke crawls through my room and out the balcony, like I've just opened a vacuum to the outside world. The sky is beautiful, the colors dancing together as the warm summer breeze hits my face, blowing my messy blonde hair back. The forest below me is quiet.

It's beautifully quiet.

The leaves are rustling, and the branches are shaking just enough to make the faintest noise of cracking as they bend with the wind. As the sky touches the earth, the colors shift from pinks and oranges to vibrant greens as they collide against each other. It's beautiful, breathtaking even. If I die, at least this will be the last image I see.

Just then, the sound of glass breaking from the heat of the fire startles me from my trance. Turning to see the flames have now reached the third floor, tears begin welling behind my eyes. Closing them, I move until my back hits the railing and instantly think of my older brother. He's safe; he isn't home. He's been at his friend's house since last night. Saxon is safe with his best friend, Saint. They're probably still sleeping off the alcohol they drank last night, no doubt. A meek smile forms across my tear-stricken face.

I slide my body down the railing until I'm sitting on the tile floor, hugging my knees to my chest and resting my head over my forearms. Curled up in this ball, I start to feel lightheaded as the smoke in my lungs starts to feel heavier and heavier. Lifting my head and opening my eyes, I realize my vision is becoming blurry. I try to blink away the haze, but no matter how many times I do, my vision remains the same.

Objects that were clear to me with hard outlines look to be shifting into softer blurs of colors. I can no longer identify my bed, or anything from my dresser to the doorframe. I give up, no longer wanting to try anymore, and close my eyes as my head falls back to the railing with a hard thud. This is it for me. What a way to go out.

My eyes still closed; I hear a loud noise that sounds like a bomb going off. I snap my eyes open, but still, I can't see much, just blobs of furniture I know are there. Something is moving, and it's moving toward me.

"Sage, stay awake. Stay with me. I've got you," a voice says as my body is lifted from the cool tile floor. I'm instantly cold as whoever is lifting me presses my body to theirs. Droplets of water hit my face. The sudden shock of going from hot to cold is soothing. Their body is completely saturated in cold water. I can't move. I feel utterly paralyzed as I float through the air and back into my room.

The air is hot again, and I want to protest and go back to my balcony, but I can't. My brain is no longer allowing me to communicate what I want. Just then, a cold blanket, or towel, has been thrown over my body, shocking my system. God, it feels so good.

"You're going to be fine, Sage. I'm getting you out of here," the man's voice says as he continues to carry me through the house. Waves of heat hit me as we pick up pace, and I feel the familiar bobbing of stairs as our bodies move as one, taking each step one by one. How are we descending the stairs? Last I saw them, they were completely overrun by black smoke? Moans and grunts fill my ears as whoever is carrying me races us through the house. Who is this man?

I can't breathe anymore; the smoke is too much. Just when I think I've taken my last breath, a wall of fresh air makes its way into my lungs as something is placed over my nose and mouth. The clean air is forced down my throat and through my nose, making it so easy to breathe. I'm doing minimal work as the oxygen is filling my body, allowing my lungs to inflate with the good and release the bad.

"Is she going to make it?" I hear the man breathe heavily. My eyes are closed, but I want to see who's talking. I try to peel my eyelids open, but I can't. The heaviness is too much, and my exhaustion is taking over.

"You need to see the medic, son. Here, lay down," another voice says.

"For Christ's sake, tell me! Is she going to make it?!" the man yells loudly, but again, he receives no response. Am I going to die?

"I need another medic over here—this kid's burned pretty bad!" There's no more protest from the guy, just silence after the sound of doors closing and the rumble of pavement picking up beneath me. I let go then. I relax and allow the exhaustion to take over. I say to myself before I collapse, *happy fucking birthday, Sage.*

SAGE

# CHAPTER

# 1

## SAGE

"Frankie, how many times have I told you not to do the laundry?! You're supposed to separate the lights from the darks! You can't just throw everything in there together!" I scream to my uncle as he sits at the dining table, sipping his coffee and typing away at his computer.

"Calm down, witch stick. I was just trying to help. Now, stop doing the laundry—it's your birthday, for fuck's sake," he bellows, not once lifting his head from this computer. I cringe at the nickname witch stick. My brother and his best friend made it up one day when they saw me lighting a sage stick in my room. I was reading a book that explained how if you light a sage stick in your room or house, it's supposed to ward off all evil. I was ten and afraid of the dark at the time; little did I know the nickname witch stick would follow me around for the rest of my life.

Yes, today is my birthday. My fucking birthday. The day

I now have to share with the anniversary of my father's death. The fire fighters determined the fire was caused by faulty wiring that ultimately caused our house to burn down completely. I don't know how I made it out that day; I never found the person who retrieved me from my balcony. The fire fighters said I was carried out by a man, or rather a "boy," as they called him.

Still, a mystery of a boy, or an angel from above, felt as though I was worth saving that day, but not my father. He perished in his bedroom that morning, trapped and unable to escape through his window or bedroom door. This is where I have a problem thinking it was a fluke. How was his window and door so tightly secured that a grown man couldn't force his way out? I begged the police to look into it further, but I was told it had already been declared an accident and to move on. My only parent was stolen from me that day, ripped from my life in the most brutal of ways.

I never knew my mother; she died soon after giving birth to me due to extensive amounts of blood loss. My father raised me and my older brother, Saxon, by himself. He was a strong man, a loyal man, a loving man. I miss him every day. Every fucking day.

"Shut up, Frankie. You know she doesn't celebrate her birthday, you damn fool," my brother barks. He makes his way through the kitchen and to the laundry room, where I stand in front of the washer examining my now dingy-looking clothes.

"Morning, sis," Saxon whispers in my ear, kissing the top of my head. He takes my white shirt from my hands, turning it over to get a good look. The once bright white piece of cloth is now a hue of blue from my jeans that had been tossed in with it. "Go get ready, I'll take you shopping," Sax says to me, tossing my shirt back in the wash before turning on our uncle and leaving the laundry room.

Our uncle Frankie, our father's little brother, stepped in

and became our legal guardian when our father died. I appreciate him every day, but let's be real, Frankie was an adult child himself when he took on the fatherly responsibility. He was twenty-eight when he found himself in charge of two children. He was only just reaching a mature age himself and was forced to grow up really quick. Frankie didn't mind, though; he was equally distraught after losing his brother, his best friend, his boss.

Frankie and my father had been working together since before I was born. My family started a less than legal underground business some wouldn't approve of. Okay, no one would approve of. My father, Luther, is what most people called the real mayor of Golden Heights, which is not far from the California coastline. Luther, and his father before him, had been running a motorcycle club as far back as my great-grandfather, Lorenzo, who created the club.

Now, I know what you're thinking. We, as a motorcycle club, must be involved in a slew of illegal activity. To be honest, you'd probably be right; I couldn't give you a straight answer. I honestly have no idea what occurs behind closed doors within the club. Since my father was alive, I haven't been allowed to know the inner workings of what the club does on a day-to-day basis. What I do know is my family's club is not the kind you want to mess with. We, or rather the members, are ruthless, brutal, and, dare I say, barbaric at times. One time, I caught my father and brother brutally beating a rival motorcycle club member because he was caught snooping around the clubhouse. I couldn't even recognize the man after they were done with him. My brother's best friend, Saint, found me spying on them and told me to never discuss what I saw, or he would tell my brother. I haven't told a single person what I witnessed and never will.

As far back as I can remember, I've tried my hardest to sneak my way into the club's meetings, listen in on private conversations, and even drill my brother to tell me what actually goes on, but I have yet to know a single thing. Other than the one incident with my father.

I stand there in the kitchen a moment longer, listening in on the conversation while I drink the rest of my coffee. I've asked Sax if I could tag along with him on the club activities, or *secret activities*, if you will, but I'm always hit with a "no" before I can even finish my sentence.

*The world has bigger plans for you, sis, and I'm not allowing you to be something you're not meant to be. You're meant for so much more.*

I've heard this a million times. So, I've just accepted his answer and stopped asking. I understand that my brother wants to protect me from whatever the hell they do with the club. As hard as I've tried to pry Saxon and Frankie for information about the club, I've given up when I'm constantly rejected and told to stay out of it. I've accepted that I may never know what happens behind closed doors.

Saxon has now taken up the responsibility of being "the leader" for all intents and purposes. Frankie never wanted that responsibility, so when our father died, he took Sax under his wing and taught him the ways of the club. Frankie isn't a bad guy—I fucking love him actually, it's just he's more of another brother than an uncle in some ways. Yes, he cares, he really cares; he never let me date or see boys my age. He basically followed the same rules my father implemented. He's the father-figure, but also a friend and understands the pain we felt of losing our father because he also lost a brother.

I look over my shoulder and see Frankie throw a tangerine at Saxon, smiling as he calls him a dick, but Saxon is too quick. He catches the fruit with his left hand, giving him a smile back. Saxon makes his way over to the table sitting across from Frankie and pulls out his phone, setting it on the table. Saxon is a big guy, way bigger than Frankie.

He's twenty-seven years old, six years older than me, but our relationship has always been close. *Protect your sister,* my father would tell him, and he always does.

His large six-foot-three frame towers over Frankie's smaller build of five foot eleven that he swears is actually six feet even. Saxon leans back in his chair, his black leather vest, or "cut" as the club calls them, opens in the front, exposing his bright white shirt that hugs his muscular chest. Saxon's hair is a deep brown, not entirely black, but pretty close. He's pulled his hair back into a messy bun so it's off his shoulders. Liquid black eyes stare across at Frankie as they start discussing upcoming club activities that have been sent to Frankie's laptop. Their arrangement works perfectly, Frankie is the brains and Saxon is the brawns. Each doing what they like doing best, so it works out. They speak in a cryptic language when I'm around, to not give away too much information for me to hear.

We look nothing alike, Saxon and me. He looks every bit like my father, and from what I'm told, I look like the spitting image of my mother. I never saw her in person, but I have one photo of her holding me in the hospital, and it's true. I could be her twin. We both have long blonde hair, a smaller, slightly upturned nose, high cheekbones and unique gray-silver eyes that are so bright in the light, they're almost eerie.

"I'm getting dressed real quick, and I'll be right down, Sax," I call to him as I make my way up the massive staircase to my room that's still on the third floor. After our house burned down, we rebuilt the house right back up, just how it was before. It looks as though it was never a pile of ash on the ground at all. I was against it at first, not wanting the constant reminder of the place my father died, but once it was built again, it just felt right. It felt like my father was still here, in a sense. Frankie obviously moved in with us during that time but has since moved out into his own home right down the street from Saxon and I. It's been mine and my brother's home ever since.

"Happy second chance!" I hear someone bellow from the front door, and I know who it is without even turning around. I shoot him a middle finger; his chuckles echo up the foyer, and I roll my eyes. Saint, my brother's best friend and member of the club since he was seventeen years old, has made it his job to remind me every year that I've been given a second chance at life. So, instead of happy birthday, he says happy second chance. I used to hate it, and sometimes I still do, but there is something to be said about God giving me another shot at life. I hate the saying, yes, but I appreciate and thank God every day I get to continue walking this earth. As for Saint, well, I wouldn't say I hate him per se. Saint has always been present. I knew him and I would butt heads the moment he tried to drown my first boyfriend in the pool. On the rare occasion my father let me have a boy over, Saint showed up, as usual, and tried drowning him in the deep end. If you ask him, he'll lie through his teeth and say it was all fun and games, but I knew his true intentions. He didn't like the way my boyfriend looked at me in a swimsuit. He made that very clear when he threatened to stab his eyes out with his pocketknife. He's that second brother I never asked for, and to be honest, he torments me more than Saxon ever has.

Swinging open my bedroom door, I head for my dresser and pull out a pair of blue jeans and a loose black V-cut T-shirt. I don't bother doing my hair, I just pull it back in a low pony and fit my black ball cap on top—my go-to look. As much as I would love to be the girly-girl, I am definitely one hundred percent a tomboy through and through. Raised by my dad and brother, you could say it was inevitable. I go for comfort and that means my usual jeans and loose T-shirts, and I never forget my ball cap. Saint calls me a bro-girl; I don't fit in with the usual girl crowd. I prefer the motorcycle club and that means a lot of males. I've grown up in it, and it's my comfort zone. I love them all, and they love me like their daughter or sister. We're a family.

There's a tap at my door, and I turn to see a smiling Mira, our fake mother, if you will, but really, she is the glue to this house. Mira has been working with our family since I can remember. She is a fifty-five-year-old widow of the club that has been taking care of me and Saxon since before my dad died. She's here every morning, seven o'clock sharp, and doesn't leave until early afternoon when she finishes her work. We've offered to have her live with us since she's here all the time anyway, but she refuses. She likes having her own spaces, and I know she doesn't have the heart to sell her home that she shared with her husband.

"Good morning, my beautiful angel!" she calls out to me, stepping into my room and pulling me into a tight hug. Mira is all of four feet, ten inches, and I have to bend over to fit into her arms. I love it though; she calls me an angel, but in reality, she's the real angel. She's taken care of us and makes us feel as though we never lost a mother at all. Saxon says Mira is more of a mother figure than most others; sadly, I never knew my real mom, but I was told she was the definition of perfection. Saxon was extremely close to our mother, even though it was only for the six short years he got to spend with her. So, with that, we've started calling Mira "Mom," and she loves every bit of it; I call her mom more so than Saxon. Mira lost her husband when they were both in their twenties. The club was targeted by a rival motorcycle club across the border, and we lost a lot of good club members that day, Ronaldo being one of them. She's never married again or had any children of her own, so when we started calling her Mom, she was over the moon.

"Happy birthday, my sweet girl. I can't believe my baby is twenty-one. It was like yesterday I was changing your diapers, and now look at you, the epitome of beauty and grace." She grabs my face between her hands and kisses my cheeks and then the tip of my nose. Tears well in her eyes as she continues to hold me tight in her embrace. I laugh as she plants kisses all over my face, as if she doesn't see me every day already.

"Thank you, Mama,". Mira is the only person I don't mind telling me happy birthday. After my father died, I banned anyone from wishing me happy birthday, but Mira refused. She said it's important to celebrate the day of my birth; it meant that she was blessed with a daughter since she didn't have any children of her own. For that, I allow her, and only her, to wish me a happy birthday.

After the assault of hugs and kisses, she steps back and looks me up and down.

"Aye, so beautiful." She clasps her hands together, holding them under her chin as a few tears fall down her delicate face. I smile down at her as I brush away her lingering tears.

"Alright, Mama, no more tears from you. You've reached your quota for the day," I say to her, making her laugh her squeaky laugh, which only makes me smile wider. Her joy and positivity are so infectious I can't help smiling and laughing along with her.

"Okay, okay, but I was coming to tell you there was a package left for you at the front door. No name was left on it, but it's addressed to you," Mira says to me, but she's fiddling with her apron, looking in every pocket as if she's lost something. "Where in the world did I put—" She cuts herself off. "Aye, here it is." Handing me a card, she puts her hands up in the air before continuing. "You will take this without any fuss, you hear me?" I laugh because I know what it is. She gives me fifty dollars for my birthday every year. I've refused to take her money in the past, but it's no use arguing with her. I'll usually find the bill hiding somewhere in my room a few days later. So, I accept her gift with a smile.

I thank her, giving her another hug and kissing her cheeks before she turns to leave my room and get back to whatever she was doing before. She stops before closing the door and turns back to look at me over her shoulder.

"By the way, I've told Frankie not to touch the damn laundry before. I don't understand why he insists on doing so. No worries though, my dear. I can make your whites brighter than they were before. You have my word." With that, she closes my door and leaves me standing alone, with a smile pulling at my cheeks.

"Thanks, Mama," I say to myself.

SAGE

# CHAPTER

# 2

## SAGE

Making my way down the stairs, I swing myself around the banister, a habit I have, and back towards the kitchen. The guys are still sitting at the dining table talking in their secret language I can never decode, but I pay them no mind. Opening the fridge, I grab a water bottle, twisting the cap before turning to the white granite island and seeing the package Mira informed me about.

I take a big gulp of water before setting it down beside the package. I hesitate a moment, not wanting to open it.

"You going to open that, witch stick?" Saint asks. I turn to glare at him and notice his crooked smile as he leans back in his chair. I roll my eyes at the use of my nickname, as I always do. Saint is one of those annoyingly attractive men, but I'd never tell him that. He's massive, even bigger than Saxon. He's a towering 6'5" with an insanely ripped physique, golden tanned skin, and smoky grayish-silver eyes that intimidate a lot of people by how unique they are.

They aren't the same color as mine, but they are distinct, and Saint is the only person I know with those colored eyes.

Giving him a death glare, I watch as he brushes back his thick black hair, which falls right back over his forehead as soon as his hand leaves his head. His smile is unnerving and irritating as fuck as he fiddles with a toothpick at the corner of his mouth. Bright white teeth shine through his full lips as he twirls the stick from one side of his mouth to the other. Saint is dressed almost the same as Saxon: dark baggy jeans, a white undershirt, and his leather cut that hangs open in the front. A long silver chain dangles by his side that hooks to his belt and trails to his back pocket. Arrogant and cocky as hell, he sits there staring at me, raising an eyebrow as he waits for my response.

"Who's it from, anyway?" Saint asks, not waiting for me to answer his first question. I roll my eyes, which seems likes the hundredth time this morning already, before replying, "Every year since Dad died, I've been getting a package on my birthday. It never says who it's from. It just says, *Another day worth living, happy birthday*." I start opening the package as the guys now watch in silence. I lift open the top of the small box and stare down at its contents. I freeze.

"What's it this year, sis?" Saxon asks as he watches me frozen at the island in total shock from what I'm seeing.

"Well?" Saint chimes in impatiently.

"Oh my God," I whisper to myself. The guys must be curious because the sound of shuffling and their sudden hovering has me pulling out the present and placing it in front of me for everyone to see. Saint stands to my right and Saxon to my left, both of their tall frames now leaning over me to see what I'm gawking at. Frankie stands across the island, looking down as well before the silence is finally broken.

"Are those first edition Shakespearean playbooks?" Frankie asks. Like me, Frankie has a love for literature. His mother instilled in him and my father the joys of reading. Becoming lost in an alternate universe and experiencing other worlds all from the confines of one's own mind—it's a luxury she never let them take for granted. Growing up, my father always read to us, mostly Shakespeare, my father's favorite. My father was a sucker for love. He always said, *What's a life, living without love?*

"Yes," I whisper as I look up and meet Frankie's eyes. Frankie and I bond a lot over books, and I love that he knows exactly what this gift is without having to take a closer look.

"They're what?" Saxon asks, taking the small book from the island and turning it over to examine it. Saxon never liked reading like I do; he tolerated it since my father enjoyed reading to us, even though he never really enjoyed listening. It was the only time of day the three of us were together. I cuddled in my father's lap while Saxon lay on the floor in front of us. Just being together was what Saxon liked, and that was enough for him.

"They're first edition Shakespeare playbooks," I say to him, taking back the book so he doesn't damage it. "Romeo and Juliet, Macbeth, A Midsummer's Night Dream, and Hamlet." I stand there, admiring the small playbooks. The bindings and covers feel so old and fragile I'm nervous they may fall apart. How did this person know I loved Shakespeare so much?

"Well, whoever sent them to you is just as big of a nerd as you are," Saint says over my shoulder, nudging me with his arm and pushing me forward.

"Do you even know who Shakespeare is?" I ask him, knowing he has no clue. He shoots me a smile over his shoulder as he makes his way back to the table and sits back down, spreading his legs wide.

"He's probably a guy who died a long time ago and only became famous for his work once he was six feet under." Saint laughs under his breath as he pulls out another toothpick and places it between his teeth. "How'd I do?" he asks, cocking an eyebrow.

"Don't listen to him, sis," Saxon says, placing his hand on my shoulder. "He's just mad that he's a twenty-seven-year-old man-child who's still mad at our ninth-grade theater teacher for not casting him as Romeo in the school play."

A deep belly laugh comes from Frankie, and I can't help myself from laughing with him.

"Hey, I deserved that role! I would have been the best fucking Romeo they've ever seen," Saint retorts, lifting his hands to his sides, gesturing at himself as if he's God's gift to us all.

"Sure, you would've been, dumbass. You only wanted to play Romeo so you could kiss Sabrina Farley, who was Juliet." Saint laughs at Saxon, who nods his head in agreement as I shake my head at their stupidity.

"Better take good care of those, sweetheart. That's some gift," Frankie says to me. He gathers up the play books and places them in my outstretched hands. He places his hand on top of mine, giving them a gentle pat before releasing me and giving me a soft smile. I nod, taking the books to my chest and leaving the kitchen, heading straight to the library on the second floor.

During the fire, my father's book collection went up in flames. He cherished his collection and had a whole library where he kept first editions, collectibles, and every book he ever read to me, all safely nestled on his custom-built mahogany shelves. Since rebuilding, I've been trying to slowly build back up the collection we lost. Making my way down the long hall, I turn to the right where my favorite room in the whole house is.

Floor to ceiling bookshelves line all the walls, and a couple of comfortable reading chairs sit in front of the windows where I spend most of my nights getting lost in a book. My favorite part of this whole room is the secret room that is hidden behind one of the massive book-shelves. I tilt the Bible that is placed strategically on the shelf until it's at a perfect ninety degrees. The shelf then slides forward, revealing a smaller room that holds all my most precious books that are either super expensive or special editions I can no longer get. I keep the best in here, mainly because it's a fireproof room, and I know they'll be safe. I also store my easel and painting supplies here.

Looking at the painting I'm currently working on, I sigh to myself. I'm trying to recreate an image of my parents on their wedding day that I found in my father's room one day. He caught me looking through a box of photos in his closet and gave me the small polaroid. It was a candid shot of my parents smiling and laughing together. My mother looked absolutely stunning—her long blonde hair fanned around her shoulders as my father whispered something funny in her ear. However, the fire destroyed everything, including that one photo. I've been trying to recreate it by memory and have come to realize it's harder than I thought it would be. I chose this image as my final project for my art major, and I'm starting to think I won't be able to capture their intimate moment from memory. I close my eyes tightly before turning back to the shelves. Finding a free spot on the wooden shelves, I place all four playbooks together and step back to admire them once more. Who sent these to me? Whoever it was knew my love for books and spent what I can imagine would be a lot of money for these. For years now, I've been trying to determine the mystery gift giver, but have yet to find them. I've racked my brain for years, trying to pinpoint them. From members of the club, Mira, Frankie, but still no one has claimed to be my mystery person. I will find them one day, mark my words.

Closing my secret room behind me, I make my way back downstairs to the kitchen. I see Saxon is now on his cell phone, yelling at someone on the other line.

"It's an easy clean up—what's the problem?" he barks through the line. "It's the landfill beyond town. What's so difficult about that? You know what, never mind, stay put. Saint and I are on our way." Well, there goes our shopping trip. Hanging up the call, Saxon takes in a deep breath, frustration washing over his tired face. Turning to me, he gives me a sympathetic smile.

"Sorry, sis. I have a few things I need to take care of. Rain check?" Shrugging his shoulders, he puts his cell back in his pocket, looking at me through apologetic eyes.

"No worries, Sax. I have a few things I need to tweak on my bike at the garage today, anyway." I shoot him an understanding smile, the corner of his mouth turning up in a mediocre smile. Taking two long strides, he pulls me into his chest, giving me a hug before kissing the top of my head.

"Make sure you don't make your bike faster than mine; I don't think I can handle my sister beating me in a race."

"No promises." I smile at him as he and Saint make their way out of the kitchen and to the foyer. I follow them until I reach the front door. Leaning in, Saxon places a kiss on my cheek, reminding me to be careful. I assure him I always am. Sax exits the house first, and Saint comes up behind him and does the same, kissing my other cheek. As much as Saint and I bicker, he really is a part of my family, and we always make sure we give each other a kiss when one of us leaves. I punch his shoulder as he steps through the door for good measure.

I watch as the two of them mount their Harley Fat Boys, the roar of their engines echoing through the air. Revving their engines, Saxon pulls away first and Saint follows, but not before he flips me off first. I do the same, giving him my middle finger and whispering to myself, "Fucker," as a smile creeps across my face.

SAGE

# CHAPTER 3

## SAGE

I've been at the garage for three hours now, and I'm still nowhere near finished on the install of my new front tire and handlebars. What was supposed to be a quick and easy job turned out to be far more tedious than anticipated. The club owns, or rather my father owned, a small mechanic shop not far from town. It's a place where members can make an honest living outside of whatever they do privately. I love it here. It's small, dirty, never tidy, and smells of motor oil, but I feel safe and at home. Plus, I'm never alone. There's always a handful of club members either working or just hanging out on the old beat-up sofas in the corner.

My father always let me tag along with him when I was a kid. I was supposed to be his precious little girl, but growing up in this garage, I developed a love for motorcycles. I would watch club members working on their engines for hours, and learn anything I could from them. Of course, they always let me help them. I was what the club would call the "Garage Mascot." That is until I grew up and became one of them. I do my fair share of work here. Tuning, oil changes, installs, paint jobs—anything, really. I love it here; it's home. Ultimately, I want to add on to the shop and open my own custom paint shop that will allow me to showcase my work on other's bikes. Putting two of my passions, painting and motorcycles, together just made sense to me. This place is everything to me, and I never want to leave one of the places that raised me to be who I am today. This is where I see myself in the future, and I'm determined to make it happen.

"Come on, you piece of shit, loosen up," I say to myself, as I try twisting and turning to loosen the front axle on my motorcycle tire, but having no luck. After what feels like a good twenty minutes, I'm finally able to disassemble the front tire and remove it completely.

"Finally," I breathe out, standing up and stretching my now aching back as I shake out my arms.

"I'd ask you if you need help, dear, but I know the answer I'll get regardless," Sam says to me from the sofa he's been occupying for the better half of the morning. I smile at him, giving him a mock salute as I take a swig of water from my bottle. I know I'm stubborn, and he knows it as well. Sam is, or was, my father's best friend. He's in his mid-sixties and has been a loyal club member for most of his life. You could say Sam is like an uncle to me and knows me just as well as my father had.

"She's stubborn as shit, Sam, you know that," a voice chimes in from behind me, making my eyes roll.

"She's passionate, not stubborn, and to be fair, I'd probably just get in her way, anyway," Sam replies, shooting me a wink.

"Nah, she's stubborn. You're just too scared to say it,

Sam. That's okay, though. I'll let her know." Spinning around, I see Saint inspecting my work as he bends down, taking a closer look at my Electra Glide's new tire. "You sure you can handle this install alone, witch stick?" he calls to me over his shoulder, still hunched over, looking at my work. I just sigh at him as I continue chugging my water, not realizing how thirsty I actually was. When I finish the bottle, I recap it and make my way to the large garbage bin by the doors, but then decide against it. I turn back to my bike and chuck the empty bottle, nailing my target right in the back.

"Nice shot, sweetheart—nailed him!" Sam chuckles as he claps his hands together in approval. I turn my back to Saint, smiling to myself before a strong-arm twists me around, and I'm met with a hard chest to the face.

"Saint, you better let me go, so help you," I growl out, but he doesn't take my threat seriously. Instead, he hoists me over his shoulder and carries me to the office.

"I swear, Saint, if you don't put me down now—" I'm cut off as he tosses me to the couch in the office, nearly knocking the breath out of my lungs. "Damn it, Saint!" I bellow as I try to catch my breath. I'm only met with his deep chuckle as he leans against the door frame, folding his arms across his chest. I want to put up a fight. I want to beat his ass with my words, but as I see the clock on the wall, I begin to panic.

"Fuck, I'm late. Next time, I'm not letting you off this easily." I point my finger at him as I start towards the door. His broad frame blocks me in, his eyebrow furrowed across his forehead as he looks down at me.

"What's the rush, witch stick?" As I try to sidestep him, he continues to block me in, and I decide this is a fight I won't win. "What's got your panties in such a twist?"

I peer up at him, my eyes shooting daggers as he stands in my way. I sigh. "Sebastian is taking me out to dinner tonight for my birthday. There. Satisfied?" He remains unmoving, his large chest rising and falling with every deep breath he takes.

"I thought you two broke it off a few weeks ago? What's got you running back to that dipshit, anyway?"

"I don't have to explain myself to you, Saint. You're not my brother, remember?" I give him my biggest grin, thinking I've won this one, but a voice quickly has my smiling slipping.

"No, he's not, but I am." Saxon's voice trails in from behind Saint, the large office now seeming too small with the pair of them caging me in.

I rub my hand down my face, frustration causing a pinch in my head, and I feel a headache brewing.

"Listen, Sax, it's just dinner. I know you both don't get along, but I'm a full-grown adult who can make her own decisions." I cross my arms over my chest, trying to give off the impression that I'm a big girl and know what's best for me. Saxon peers down at me as he makes his way to the office desk and sits down in the large black roller chair.

"You're right, sis. You are smart and can make your own decisions. Just know if he does anything to disrespect you in any way, I know how to eliminate a person without leaving evidence."

"Ditto," Saint's deep voice chimes in, and I narrow my eyes at him, silently telling him to mind his business.

"My lord, you both are insufferable."

"Where is he taking you?" Saxon asks, as he moves the computer mouse, waking up the black screen. I hesitate a moment, not really wanting to tell them where I'll be because, let's be real, I know they've both spied on me while I was on dates before. Saxon stops fiddling with the computer and stares at me, awaiting a response.

"Ugh, fine. He's taking me to Raul's Seafood."

"Huh, did he make reservations? That place is impossible to get a table unless you make reservations," Saint says as Saxon nods his head in agreement.

"Of course, he did," I say to the pair of them, but honestly, I have no idea if he did or didn't. I send up a silent prayer that he did, but knowing Sebastian, I fear we'll be dining somewhere else tonight. Awesome.

I step up to Saxon and give him a kiss on the cheek before turning to the door and facing Saint.

"I'll let you know the plan, okay, Sax?" He only responds with a groan, his way of saying *you better*.

Saint then leans down towards my cheek but catches the corner of my lips with his as I try to give him access to the side of my face. I freeze. Heat blooms across my face as I stare into his eyes and see the shock of what had just happened burning through them. As quick as it happened, he recovers in record time, stepping aside to let me through. My chest suddenly feels a tightness that I've never felt before. I leave the office and head towards my bike. Swinging my leg over the seat, I settle in as I start up my bike, revving the engine a couple of times before putting on my helmet.

"What time is he picking you up?" Saint's dark voice fills my ears. Turning my head to the side, we are practically nose to nose, the sudden lack of space between us making my skin hot once again. What is he doing? Why do I suddenly feel so flustered? It's Saint, for God's sake. It was an accident—no big deal. Right? Then why do I feel like my lips have suddenly been struck by lightning? Did he feel that too?

"He's picking me up at seven. Is that good for you?" I say sarcastically. He just taps my helmet twice before backing away, letting me ride away from the shop and towards home. I give one last look behind me and see Saint is still standing where he was, staring at me as I ride away.

If one older protective brother wasn't enough, try

having two. Except the second brother is not actually your brother at all. Suddenly, I feel as though my world has tilted on its axis, all because of an accident. *That wasn't intentional; he didn't mean to kiss me.* I repeat this over and over in my head, but somehow, it doesn't make the tingles in my core subside. Great.

SAGE

# CHAPTER 4

## SAGE

What I hate most in this entire world is when my brother is right about a man I date. I know he's a man, and who better to know a man's behavior than a man? However, it's still the most infuriating thing ever. I should have known Sebastian wouldn't have made a reservation for dinner, but deep down, I wanted him to prove my brother and Saint wrong. Wishful thinking.

Instead of Raul's Seafood, we're at Olive Garden, of all places. Not that Olive Garden is bad, it's just not the most romantic of places. I hesitated to inform my brother of the change of plans. I was too embarrassed and didn't want to hear the "I told you so" that he and Saint would give me, but I reluctantly sent the text, letting him know where I would be. To my surprise, he just sent a text back with the thumbs-up emoji without the banter I was expecting. However, I know I will hear about this later, that's for sure. If not from Saxon, then definitely from Saint.

Sebastian and I have been dating off and on for the last

year. We have our high highs, but then we also have our low lows. Saxon tells me Sebastian doesn't respect me as a woman. If there is one thing about Saxon, it is that he's very big on respect. Give respect to receive respect. So, if you're not giving respect, you damn well don't deserve respect in return. Plus, I'm his little sister, and I will forever be his little sister, no matter how old we are. To be honest, he's never been approving of any guy I've dated. Big brother role, I suppose.

There are a couple of reasons why Sebastian and I have been off and on for a while. The first one being his blatant disregard for my own feelings. He is what some would call "self-absorbed." The second reason is he never has the time for me. We were spending more time apart than we were together. This last time, however, I caught him texting with another girl, and I swore to myself I was done with him, but here I am. Call me an idiot, but maybe it's just called being lonely, and being with someone and being miserable is better than being alone and being miserable. Right? To be honest, I think my boredom with my lack of sex life is what brings me back. I'm not someone who sleeps around; I only sleep with people I date. Meaning, I'm constantly running back to Seb. Am I using him? Maybe. But he's using me too, and, well, if we're both getting what we want, it can't be that bad. However, I am not okay with the idea of him sleeping with other women and me at the same time. That is a no go for me. I've told myself the next time he messes up, and he will mess up, I'm done for good. I have enough self-respect to know when I'm just being used to scratch an itch.

"So, what have you been up to today, Seb?" I ask from across the table. His face is buried deep in his phone as I wait for his response. He's quiet for a long moment, clicking away at a text message. Finally, he sets his phone face down and answers my question.

"Nothing really. Worked with Dad showing properties and that's really all." Sebastian and his father run a real estate company together where they make great money selling high-rise luxury apartments in the city. That's where he lives, Oakbury City, which is roughly thirty minutes from my home in Golden Heights. Since Saxon, and of course Saint, aren't too fond of Seb, that means I'm usually the one to drive to the city to hangout. Surprisingly, he came to me today for my birthday dinner. It wasn't the dinner I expected, but at least he's here.

His phone dings again, indicating he has a new text message, and I internally groan. He's quick to pick it up and begins typing away while smiling at his screen.

"Who's that?" I ask, keeping my tone calm so I don't imply that I suspect he's talking to another girl. Let's be honest though, once a cheater always a cheater. Shame on me for giving multiple chances. Seb ignores me, continuing to type away. My blood starts to boil, and I stand from my chair, grabbing my purse before turning my back to him. Before I can walk away, he grabs my hand, stopping me from leaving.

"I'm sorry, Sage. Here, phone is down. Let's just enjoy our dinner together." I give him a sarcastic laugh, but still, I give him another chance and sit back down. Without letting my hand go, we both take our seats again, and he pulls my hands closer to him. "If you must know, that is a new client looking to settle in the city, and I've been sending her new listings." I roll my eyes at the mention of "her" but don't want to continue fighting and sink deeper into my chair.

Rubbing my hands with his fingers, Seb looks down, examining my scars that cover the tops of my hands. I watch him as he traces his fingers over the thick, long ropes of the scar tissue and skin grafts they had to do at the hospital. I watch his eyes as he squints and tilts his head as if he's deep in thought. My insecurities take over, and I pull my hands from his palms.

"Have you ever thought about getting those covered up? Like tattoos or plastic surgery or something that could conceal them?" If I wasn't in a sour mood already, that comment alone sent me flying head first into a bit of fire, sparking my anger to its highest peak. My skin starts to feel hot as my anger stirs within my chest.

"Excuse me?" I say through gritted teeth, trying really hard not to let my voice crack. Out of all the insecurities I have, the scarring that covers both of my hands is by far the biggest. It's at this moment, I know I will never be good enough for this man. I will never be the picture-perfect girlfriend he so badly wants me to be. He can't just accept me for me. He constantly has to gaslight me into thinking everything he does wrong is because of something I did first. I know how he hates my scars; this isn't the first comment he's made about them. It's this comment that has all of Sebastian's red flags waving in my head at once.

"I just mean, maybe you'd be more confident if you got them covered. I know how much you hate them."

"Or is it because you hate them and can't stand being seen with me when they're visible?!" I don't hide my anger; I practically scream at him as I stand from my seat and lean over the table towards him. I should have just listened to Saxon and ditched this fucking pig a long time ago. Fuck, I hate when I'm wrong. I grab my purse and head towards the front of the restaurant. Sebastian's voice trails off behind me. I don't stop to hear what he has to say. I've known for a long time how much of an asshole Seb is; I just didn't like the idea of being alone or unwanted. That's on me. I will never lower my standards for someone else again.

"Wait, Sage. Wait, I didn't mean—" Seb is behind me as he grovels in an apology he can't get out. I turn my head over my shoulder to tell him to fuck off when I run into what feels like a wall, halting me in my tracks. A pair of strong hands grab my shoulders, steadying me before I turn to see Saint standing directly in front of me.

"Whoa, whoa, what are you doing here, witch stick? What's wrong?" Of all the people that could have shown up tonight, it had to be Saint—just my luck.

"Sage, listen, I—" Seb stops whatever he was about to say when he realizes who's now standing behind me. "What... what are you doing here?" Seb asks, his tone laced with disgust. I close my eyes as I take a deep breath.

"Looks to me like I showed up just in time. Sage, this date is over. Meet me in the car." He releases my shoulders, and I fix myself before answering him.

"Saint, I'm fine. I can—" He cuts me off. "I said, meet me in the car." I don't argue because, really, how was I going to get home anyway? Seb drove me here. I just sigh, giving Seb one last look of disgust before I turn on my heel and exit the restaurant.

SAINT

# CHAPTER 5

## SAINT

If we weren't in a public place, I would grab this piece of shit by the throat and watch as his oxygen supply slowly depletes while his life drains from his body. However, since we are at a restaurant, a very packed restaurant, at the moment, I will wait to teach him a proper lesson. I step up to Sebastian, his short stature making it easy for me to tower over him and invade his personal space.

"If you for one second think she will be calling you in the future, you are sadly mistaken. Don't call her, don't text her, forget she even exists. She is nothing to you. You don't deserve to breathe the air she breathes, you lowlife piece of shit," I whisper down at him. His eyes narrow into slits as his own anger starts to show.

"Or what? What are you going to do, Saint, huh? You think you're all high and mighty because you're a part of her family's club? Well, I'll have you know—" I cut him off by grabbing his throat, fear instantly flashing over his face.

The members of the restaurant are now becoming visibly frightened by the tension rising in the waiting area.

"Or I'll show you just how well I can make you disappear." Sebastian has always been jealous of the club and even went so far as to buy a motorcycle, which he can't even ride, in hopes of becoming part of the club. I push him away, releasing his throat so he can suck in a proper breath.

"For that little comment, I'd be counting my blessings if I were you. I'll be seeing you soon, Sebastian. You have my word." I leave him standing in the waiting area, looking like a lost puppy who's been scolded by its owner as I push through the doors and walk towards my Tahoe. Yes, I have a tracker on Sage's phone, which is the only reason I was able to hear Sebastian's comment about her scars. It's for her own safety. Saxon is busy ninety-nine percent of the time, and I'm sure he would appreciate me keeping an eye on his little sister. When I heard his comment, I saw red. The nerve of that man, or rather that fuck boy, for thinking that was an appropriate question to ask. I wanted his head on a plate.

Reaching my Tahoe, I look through the windshield and see Sage is already settled in the passenger seat, a scowl of anger etched across her face. Swinging the driver's side door open, I step into the vehicle, then slam the door behind me.

"I don't need to be saved, Saint. I can handle myself against that arrogant prick," she says to me, flipping down the visor to fix her mascara that's running down her cheek. She's been crying, but she'll never let her vulnerability slip like that in front of me. I buckle myself in and crank the ignition.

"I know you don't," I retort and pull out of the parking lot and onto the main road towards her house. She slams the visor shut, and I can feel her eyes burrowing into the side of my face.

"Then why are you here? Are you following me?" I let out a huff of amusement.

"Don't flatter yourself, witch stick. I was picking up my own food. Besides, you said he was taking you to Raul's. Why the hell were you at Olive Garden?" She turns her face away from me, shifting her body towards the door.

"Never mind," she practically whispers, her embarrassment too much to even try to explain. She doesn't speak for a long while. We drive in comfortable silence, but when I reach for the radio, she says something that stops me.

"Do you think my scars make me… undesirable?" My knuckles go white at how hard I squeeze the steering wheel, the leather squeaking beneath my grasp. She's letting that prick's comment get to her. I glance over at her profile; her head is down, and she's examining her hands. Scars cover every available inch of skin across her hands. The doctors tried their best to make the scars smoother and less noticeable, but when she was pulled from her house, she was in a bad state. Her hands aren't the only places she has scars. Her right shoulder blade, her right calf, and a smaller portion of her right oblique are scarred from the burns she endured.

I inhale a deep breath before I answer her. Looking ahead at the road, I reach over and grab one of her hands.

"Sage, no amount of scars, skin grafts, or burn marks could make you look anything but beautiful. Don't let the opinion of a lowlife piece of shit like Sebastian fill your head with such nonsense. You're gorgeous—don't ever forget that." I give her hand a small squeeze and turn my head to face her as her eyes begin filling with unshed tears. She doesn't respond, she just lets me hold her. Our hands intertwined the rest of the way home.

As we pull into her driveway, I notice the kitchen light is on and know Frankie must be preparing the last bit of details for an upcoming job we have. Putting the Tahoe in park, I jump out, circling the front and grabbing the passenger door, opening it up for her to step out.

"Don't act like you're some sort of gentleman now, Saint," she teases, stepping out of the passenger seat and grabbing her bag before tossing it over her shoulder. I shut the door behind her and follow her to the front door.

"You want me to come in? I could tuck you in, maybe give you a back rub to help you fall asleep?" I joke, leaning against the frame as she fishes through her bag for the keys.

"Ha ha, very funny. You forget we don't like each other, right?" She finds her keys and sticks them in the keyhole but stops before unlocking the door.

"All jokes aside, thanks for tonight. You keep saving me like this, and I'm going to think you have feelings for me." She twists the key, unlocking the door, and steps into the foyer. As she turns around, I flip her off, and a smile creeps across her face as she returns the gesture.

"Don't let it happen again, witch stick," I say. I turn to leave, but stop. "Hey." The door is almost closed, but she stops, peeking her head out to hear what I have to say. "Happy birthday." I don't wait for her to respond; I head to my Tahoe and drive off. I don't want to be late to my little rendezvous with Sebastian.

SAGE

# CHAPTER

# 6

## SAGE

*Men are truly exhausting,* I think to myself as my brother follows me up the stairs and towards the library. Saint's close on his heels as Saxon berates me about my boyfriend.

"Sage, are you even listening to me? I've had enough of that shitbag. You're not seeing him anymore. Have I made myself clear?" Saxon scolds me as I continue down the hall and into the library.

"Sage!" His tone is getting deeper, and I can tell he's about to blow his top. His anger is about to rear its ugly face, and I physically don't want to endure this fight with my brother anymore.

"I heard you, Sax. Loud and clear! You don't have to worry anyway—he dumped me. Are you happy? You got your way once again." I turn to face the bookshelf, searching for my favorite book, *Dr. Jekyll and Mr. Hyde* by Robert Louis Stevenson. Pulling the book off the shelf, I head for my chair that's facing the window overlooking the garden. I pull my legs underneath me and lean against the armrest as I flip open to the first page. The guys are silent for a moment, and I catch a glimpse of the two of them sharing a look before Saxon steps further into the library.

"He broke up with you?" Saxon asks me, his voice no longer sounding like he wants to strangle someone, but now sounding almost sympathetic. I sigh to myself, not wanting to explain why I was dumped but knowing my brother and Saint won't leave me alone until I give them an explanation.

"It's nothing, Sax. Please, just drop it," I say into my book, flipping the page, not having read a single word.

"Sage, why?" My brother is relentless, and I know he isn't going to let this go. I slam my book shut, my cheeks already heating with embarrassment as I blurt out, "Because I wouldn't have sex with him! Happy? Now, please, just leave me alone." I turn away from the two of them. The setting sun beams in through the window, warming my face. Loud footsteps exit the room and echo throughout the foyer as whoever left stomps down the stairs. I breathe a sigh of relief but know *he* is still in the library with me.

"Saint, you can go too. I'm fine. I don't need you giving me a lecture either," I say over my shoulder, knowing damn well Saint's still here. He doesn't speak; in fact, he's so quiet I turn to see if he didn't sneak out without me hearing him. Pulling my legs out from underneath me, I shift in my chair and see he's leaning against the door frame, his expression unreadable.

"What?" I say to him, sitting up straighter and turning my book in my lap. His eyebrows are pinched together, and he's giving me a hard look. Silver eyes are on me, and I'm about to tell him to leave me the hell alone when he finally clears his throat.

"Where does he live?"

"What?" I say, confused.

"I'm asking you, where does he live?" I scoff to myself, rolling my eyes but not answering him. Pushing off the door frame, he stalks over to me, his large frame filling the room and making me feel so small all of a sudden. Grabbing the arm rests of the chair, he leans his face close to mine. Our noses are practically touching.

"I'm not going to ask you again. Where does he live?" His scent invades my nose: warm notes of cedar and red sage. I discreetly inhale his scent, my eyes closing a moment longer than normal. When I open them again, he's still there. His eyebrow now lifted higher, waiting for me to respond. My eyes drift to his mouth, where he rolls a toothpick from one side of his mouth to the corner.

"He—uh—he lives in The Pines development with his mother," I stutter through my words. I'm suddenly feeling very nervous as he hovers over me.

"What house number, Sage?" Damn, I was hoping he wouldn't ask me that. My mouth falls open just slightly, my mind trying its hardest to find a way out of this, but I come up short. His silver eyes are still on mine, and I have to turn my head, the intensity of his stare becoming too much. Strong fingers grip my chin, forcing my head back towards his.

"One more time. What's his house number?" Saint whispers, his voice so low it almost sounds like a growl.

"219," I whisper. This man is insufferable. I wish he would just yell at me like Saxon and get it over with. This technique is far worse. I crumble beneath his gaze. He has a way of making me feel so flustered, so out of control, I give in almost immediately.

"Good girl." Releasing my chin, he kisses the top of my head before standing up and heading towards the door.

"What are you going to do?" I ask, standing from my

chair as fear begins to bubble in my chest. My brother is a scary man when it comes to intimidating the men I date, but Saint is terrifying. Last time a man, or rather, a boy, did me wrong when I was a freshman, he didn't show up to school for two weeks. When he finally did show up, he did everything in his power to avoid me. Never making eye contact and even going so far as to change his entire schedule, so we never shared a class together again. Saint and Saxon told me they didn't do anything to him, but I'm not stupid.

"Saint?" I call after him.

Stopping in the doorway, he turns toward me once again. He brushes his hair back with his hand, closing his eyes as he does so. As he reaches for his head, his white t-shirt rises just enough that I'm able to see just a bit of his lower abdomen. My eyes instantly focus on his tattooed skin, my face suddenly becoming hot.

When I look up at his face, his eyes are on me. The corner of his mouth tips up just slightly as his heavy gaze remains on me.

"Listen, Sage. Men like that need to be taught that a woman is more than just her pussy. If he keeps going through life thinking women are merely a gift to men, he will end up hurting someone, and I'll be damned if that woman is you. You're far more than just a trophy for him to win. You deserve more than anyone, Sage. Never let a man make you feel like you're not enough. You're more than enough." The room falls silent as the two of us stare at one another. Saint is a second brother to me, but when he talks like this, I envy the woman he ends up with.

I wrap my arms around myself, not sure how to respond. One minute, he's an overprotective brother, and the next, he's my defender from evil.

"Stop thinking too much on it, witch stick. I'm just going to pay him a quick visit. No need to start digging a grave just yet." He winks at me, then turns around, leaving me speechless. I let out a long sigh, before I send up a quick prayer for my brother and Saint not to kill this poor man who's about to get one of the hardest lessons of his life.

*Fucking hell.*

SAINT

# CHAPTER
# 7

## SAINT

He's been crying for so long. I've never actually witnessed a man cry as much as he has—it's pathetic, really. I suppose waking up and finding yourself tied to a chair with tape over your mouth may be frightening to some people. To be honest, though, I thought his man would have a little more balls than he's currently displaying. After dropping off Sage from her date, I came here to Seb's apartment to pay him a quick visit. It's become a hobby of mine to visit the men who do so much as look at Sage the wrong way. I've been doing this ever since high school, and I'll admit, I've come to enjoy it.

Seb is pleading with me underneath his duct tape as more tears pour from his eyes. Little bitch. I've only burned the top of his right hand, barely enough to blister, and he already can't take it. Sage didn't even cry when she was pulled from the house fire that left her with third- and fourth-degree burns. She's stronger than any man she's ever dated. Doesn't surprise me though. Growing up in her father's club has made her tougher than most people in this world.

"For fuck's sake, shut up," I moan, as I stand in front of him, flicking my lighter open and closed. The metallic clicks of the lighter ring in the air. It's a habit, and I find comfort in the noise it makes. Seb's attention is on the lighter, his eyes filled with fat tears as they dart from the lighter to my face. Well, not my face. I'm wearing my mask; it's a skull with three thick black lines that trail from the teeth portion to the bottom of the chin.

As much as I enjoy the torture aspect of my job within the club, this type of torment is my favorite. Torturing someone who's wronged Sage is my personal job that I take very, very seriously. Kneeling in front of Seb, his blood-shot eyes focus on me as I lift the lighter to his left hand. He moans louder, shaking and trying his best to free himself with no luck. I watch the flame dance in the air between us, the sight mesmerizing.

"I'm sure you know why I'm paying you a visit tonight, but let me reiterate it for you. Never call her again, never speak to her again, don't even think about her, or I'll know. She deserves better than you, and I'll make sure she finds it." Lowering the lighter to his hand, the smell of burning flesh invades my nostrils through my mask. Seb cries into the tape as I watch his skin bubble into bright red blisters. I hold the lighter in place, and only when one of the blisters bursts, do I flip the lighter closed. Satisfaction fills my chest. Seb's cries dissipate, but he continues to sob, his chest rapidly rising and falling as he tries to catch his breath. Pussy.

"Remember these consequences when you feel the need to disrespect a woman again." I rip the tape from his mouth, his apologies spewing from his mouth as he shakes his head back and forth.

"I swear, please, no more. She's forgotten, I promise. Never again." Seb has this annoying voice that makes me cringe. It's a cross between a high school boy who never reached puberty and a man who speaks through his nose. It's so fucking nasally it's hard to believe Sage found him even remotely attractive.

"Good man. Now, you may want to get your hands looked at. It's a shame you spilled that boiling pot of water on yourself. I think those burns may scar. Oh well. You can just get them covered up later, after they heal." With that, I place a small kitchen knife on his thigh, and head towards the door.

"Wait, wait! Aren't you going to untie me?" Seb babbles. Turning my head over my shoulder, I smile at him.

"That's what the knife is for, silly. Come on, now. I thought you were a smart man. Bye now." With that, I slam the door behind me, leaving Seb to find his way out of those ropes. A loud thud echoes from behind Seb's door, and I laugh to myself, knowing he's just flipped himself over in the chair. Fucking idiot.

———

Opening the front door, I take off my hoodie and hang it on the coat rack. It's been raining all fucking day, and the quick walk from my Tahoe to the door has left me soaked. Rubbing my hands through my hair, water droplets splatter across the marble floor when I hear laughter coming from the kitchen. It's Sage; I'd recognize her laugh anywhere. She has this low, wheezing laugh that comes from deep down in her belly, and I can't help but smile at the sound.

Before I make myself known, I lean against the wall,

concealing myself from whoever's in the kitchen, and listen.

"He hasn't called or texted you at all? Not even an apology?" Ophelia questions. Ophelia is Sage's oldest friend. They've been going to school together since they were in preschool. Ophelia's father has been a part of the club for all her life, so she is quite familiar with this lifestyle. I guess that's why she and Sage get along so well.

"Nothing, not a single word. To be honest, though, I didn't think I would hear from him again, not when Saint showed up at the restaurant." Hearing my name on her lips has my mouth curling into a wicked grin. That's right, baby. You know I don't take kindly to pieces of shit hurting you.

"Wait, Saint showed up at your date? Why? Did he know you were there?" Ophelia gasps as she lowers her voice, as if she knows I'm listening in on their private conversation.

"No, he didn't know. He just showed up to pick up his order, or so he says. I practically ran into him as I was leaving the restaurant. He told me to get in his Tahoe and wait for him. I don't know what he said to Seb, but knowing Saint, it wasn't good. I can probably guess he threatened him in some sort of way." Sage's voice is low, but she doesn't sound angry or mad; she just sounds indifferent.

There's a long pause in their conversation, and as I'm about to head into the kitchen myself, the front door bursts open, laughter filling the foyer as I turn to see who it is. Bristol and Frieda, Sage's other close friends, come running in the house, water dripping from their clothes as they try to shield their hair from the elements.

"Fuck this rain! It's messing up my outfit!" Bristol squeals. Bristol is tall and very thin; her long brown hair is tousled in loose beachy waves as she tries to fix herself. She's in a tight black dress that barely covers her ass, and the heels she's wearing make her legs look even longer than they already are.

Frieda is a fiery redhead, with bright blue eyes that make it hard to concentrate when she's talking to you. She, too, is in a dress, but hers is more of the flowy type. Longer in the back than in the front. She is a little shorter than Bristol, but her heels make them look the same height.

"Of course, today had to be the day it rained. Mother Nature loves to fuck up our outfits," Frieda says as she shakes her dress to get the water off the fabric. I lean against the wall, watching the two girls fiddle with their outfits. Thank God Sage doesn't like to dress like that—I wouldn't let her out of the house if she did. Just then, Sage comes running out from the kitchen right past me, and my heart stops. She's wearing tight leather pants, and what I consider to be a microscopic tank top that barely covers her chest. Her abdomen is on full display as well as her cleavage. Her long blonde hair is curled effortlessly, and the smell of fresh citrus fills my nostrils as her perfume invades me.

"Yay! You're both here! Now we can go," Sage says as she and Ophelia embrace both Bristol and Frieda. Ophelia is dressed almost the exact same as Sage, and from behind you'd think they were twins. The only difference is their hair length. Ophelia's is short, only reaching her shoulders, where Sage's is long, practically touching the top of her ass.

"And where are you all off to?" I say through gritted teeth. Pulling out my cell and sending a quick text to Saxon telling him to get the hell out here. Let's hope he doesn't let her out of the house like that. Sage whirls around, her eyes meeting mine in shock. She wasn't expecting to see me. None of them were. Ophelia practically screams when she turns around to stare at me.

"Jesus, Saint. You scared the lights out of me. I didn't even know you were here." Sage places her hand over her chest as if she's trying to catch her breath. My eyes dart to where her hand lies, right at the top of her cleavage, and my dick twitches in my jeans at the sight. I don't miss the nudge Ophelia gives Sage, as if silently talking among themselves while they both continue to stare at me, but it's Bristol who talks.

"We're going to Capital Vice."

"Shhh, Bristol," Ophelia says, giving me all the information I need. The girls didn't want me or the rest of the guys to know where they planned to be tonight.

"Shit, my bad. I didn't know we were keeping it a secret," she whispers to Ophelia, before looking over at Bristol, who gives her a shrug of her shoulders. My eyes land on Sage, her silvery eyes look towards the floor before she straightens up and gives me a look of defiance.

"Yes, the girls are taking me out for my birthday, and we all decided on dancing. Is that okay with you, *Dad*?" I love it when Sage talks to me in that sassy tone. I chuckle to myself, pushing my back off the wall and placing my hands in my jeans pockets before taking a step closer to them. I watch her swallow at not knowing what my next move is.

"No, he's not your dad, but I'm your brother, and what I say goes." I don't even need to turn around to know Saxon just entered the foyer behind me. He walks past me, coming to a stop right in front of Sage, making her crane her neck to look up at him.

"You know how dangerous it is to go out dressed the way all four of you are?" His tone is low and harsh. Sage doesn't answer right away; she just narrows her eyes on her brother before Ophelia speaks up from her side.

"We are just going dancing. No harm in that, right Sax?" I can't see Saxon's face from where I'm standing, but the way Ophelia just looked away from him has me thinking it wasn't the look she was expecting. Sage sighs, dropping her face to the floor in utter defeat, and it hurts my chest, watching her like that.

My phone chimes in my pocket, and I take it out, giving it a quick glance. It's Owen. The beer pitcher emoji is all he sent; I smile at my screen.

"Owen just texted; he wants to get a drink. How about we go to Vice too. They can dance, and we can unwind a bit."

"Ooo yeah, that sounds perfect!" Ophelia smiles back at Bristol and Frieda, but my eyes are still on Sage. Her eyes are pleading with her brother. His broad shoulders rise and fall with one big breath before finally agreeing.

"Fine." Saxon's tone is so low it's barely audible. Sage jumps up, wrapping her arms around her brother, giving him a tight hug before her eyes find mine once more. She gives me a wink, a silent thank you, before turning to her friends, and the four of them head towards the door.

"We'll be right behind you," Saxon says before the front door slams, echoing through the foyer.

"Text the boys. Tell them to meet us at Vice's in fifteen," Saxon says before making his way to the kitchen and cracking open a can of what I know is a beer.

"Say less, brother." I smile to myself. Pulling out my phone, I pull up the group chat with Owen and the twins.

*The Boys:*

*Me: Meet at Vice's in fifteen, boss's orders.*

I get three thumbs' ups before pocketing my phone, and I head to the kitchen for a beer. This should be a fun night.

SAGE

# CHAPTER 8

**SAGE**

The three of my closest friends and I pile into Ophelia's BMW X5—a gift her father gave her as a graduation present. Jumping in the passenger seat, I shake my hair to get the excess rain off.

"That was fucking close," Ophelia says, putting her key in the ignition and cranking her car. "I swear, Sage, Saint has it out for you. He's just as bad as your brother, if not worse."

"I keep telling her the same thing. I swear he's in love with you. Why else would he care so much about where you go or who you're with? I get it coming from Sax, but Saint? Why else would he care, other than he's madly in love with you?" Frieda says over my shoulder. The three of them laugh, agreeing with her comment.

"He is not in love with me. God, he hates me, if anything. He loves to give me a hard time. That's it," I say to them, pulling down the visor and checking my makeup to see if the rain ruined anything. The flash back of our "accidental kiss" comes soaring into my brain, and I hope the girls can't see the flush of my skin rapidly taking over my face.

"She's in denial. She'll see it one day." Ophelia smiles at me as she puts the car in drive and heads down my driveway.

The drive to the club is only fifteen minutes. The four of us chat about upcoming events at school or who each of us finds attractive. We all go to Golden Heights College in town. The four of us have been growing up together since elementary school. Ophelia and I have known each other since we were born. Our fathers were friends, and since they were at the club most of the time, so were Ophelia and I. Ophelia's mom passed away when she was in second grade, a drunk driver hit her car head on, killing her instantly. We both grew up without a mom, so the club has always been our home.

Bristol showed up in fifth grade, having moved here from the city. Her father is a big-time banker who wanted to raise his family away from the city. The moment her family moved to Golden Heights, her father, Anthony, found his way to the club. He's the official treasurer of the club. Anthony grew up in Golden Heights, so he was well aware of my father's club and took the opportunity to join the second he saw his chance.

Now Frieda, she came around in middle school; she was in and out of foster care most of her life. Her parents were big-time drug addicts and couldn't take care of her. She was living with her grandmother, but when she passed away from cancer, she found herself in foster care. One day, Ophelia and I saw her walking down the street outside of the club, and we called her over. She told us she was going to the corner store for bread for her foster mom. I told my dad about her that day and how she was practically on her own. My dad, being the man he is, found his way to Frieda's foster home, and a few weeks later she was adopted by none other than Sam himself and his late wife, Julie. Ever since then, she's been our fourth.

It's funny how the club brought us together. The four of us have been through it. From birthdays, heartbreaks, schools, and even deaths. I would do anything for these girls and I know they would do the same for me. We joke about it, but the club is what brought us together. The center of our friendship, a gravitational pull that links us together.

We pull up to the club, the rain still pounding on the windshield as we all look at one another. Ophelia gives us a countdown before all four of us take off towards the entrance to Capital Vice. There's a line at the door for entry, but the moment the bouncer sees the four of us, he steps aside, unlatching the velvet barricade and making way for us to enter.

"Thanks, Lance!" I say to the big man before I reach up and kiss his cheek. Lance is, could you guess, a member of the club as well. He makes extra money here at Vice every weekend because his girlfriend is expecting their first child any day now.

"Be careful in there, sweetheart," he says to me in my ear before letting me go inside. I give him a smile and a quick nod before I head through the tall black doors. The music is so loud it makes my chest vibrate with every drop of the bass. It's crowded tonight—college students and locals are flooding in over the final days of summer break, and it makes the atmosphere that much more fun. I follow the girls to the bar as we all place our order for a drink. The bartender hands me my whiskey sour, and I turn to scan the club.

The large square cages that are suspended in each of the corners are packed full, as girls dance and sway to the music. Some are so drunk they struggle to stay upright. The dance floor is equally crowded, so I turn to Ophelia and suggest we go to the second floor. She nods in agreement and turns to Bristol and Frieda to tell them the plan. I grab Ophelia's hand, and the four of us make our way to the spiral staircase in the corner of the dance floor. I prefer the upstairs level, if I'm being honest.

Once at the top, I scan the room and see my favorite table is open. Pulling Ophelia's hand, we make our way through the crowd and practically dive into the circular booth, laughing with one another.

"What fucking luck? This is the best table up here!" Bristol yells over the music.

"Yeah, and it's my favorite table at that!" I yell back, giving her a high five when the waitress approaches us.

"Hey, Skylar! How are you? I haven't seen you in a while," I say to my favorite waitress here at Vice. Sky is a tall brunette with the most captivating smile; it's no wonder Saxon has it bad for her. I stand, giving her a hug. She gives me a tight squeeze back.

"It's so good to see you, girl. I've missed you," she says in my ear before we pull away, but not before I notice the haunting smile she gives me. Grabbing her shoulders, I give her a look of concern before she gives me a nod of reassurance.

"So, girls, what are we drinking tonight?" She gives each of the girls a warm smile. I give myself a mental note to ask Saxon what's going on between them. The four of us all but finished our first round on our way up here and place an order for our second.

"Vodka soda, please!" Frieda says first.

"Ohh, same, please!" Bristol agrees.

"I'll have a rum and coke, please." Ophelia puts her hand up with my order.

"You got it ladies; I'll be right back." Sky leaves us, and I turn to my best friends, who have all started to sway to the music. It's EDM night at the club, my absolute favorite night.

"Come on, let's dance!" I yell at the girls. The four of us stand up and head to the floor. The music is so loud it helps drowns out the haunting memories that always find their way back in every year around my birthday. I close my eyes, letting the music seep into my core, moving and swaying with my four closest friends as we all let go and feel the energy of the night blanket over us. I needed this night. I needed this feeling of absolute freedom from everything around me. No stress from the upcoming semester, the club, or the emptiness I feel with every birthday since my father died. My heart and soul needed this escape, and I couldn't be more thankful to Ophelia for arranging this evening.

Opening my eyes, I grab hold of my best friend and hug her so tight she squeals in my ear.

"Thank you so much for this," I whisper in her ear. She pulls back, giving me a smile. Her mouth is moving, but I can't hear her from the sound of the music. We both laugh and embrace each other again before going back to dancing. A moment later, I see Sky delivering our drinks to the table, and I grab the girls as we all head back. Falling into the booth, we grab our drinks, each taking a sip before allowing the harsh liquor to burn its way down our throats. Sky is always a little heavy on the alcohol, but we never complain. We prefer it.

Taking another sip of my drink, I catch a glimpse of a man standing at the bar. His dark eyes meet mine for a split second before he turns toward the bar, grabbing his beer and continuing his conversation with the man beside him. My eyes roam over his body as he leans into the bar top. His broad shoulders stretch his black shirt across his back. I half expect him to bust out of the fabric at any moment. He's wearing dark blue jeans that accentuate his ass in the most delicious way. As my eyes roam up his legs, I stop at his forearms. The veins that rope around his arm and stretch across his hands have me staring at his fingers that are loosely holding the neck of his bottle.

I get a jab to the ribs. I wince and turn to Ophelia.

"Ouch, what was that for?" I yell over the music. But the moment I turn my head, I'm met with a pair of silver, animalistic eyes making their way towards me.

"Fuck, already?" I moan, just as Saint and Saxon breach the top of the stairs and make their way towards our table.

I steal another glance towards the bar, but the person I was hoping was still there is now gone. Just my luck.

SAINT

# CHAPTER 9

### SAINT

I follow Sage's line of sight as she looks over at the bar. The only person she knows at the bar is Skylar, and she is busy running up and down the bar serving drinks. Saxon claps his hand on my shoulder as he leans into the side of my face, telling me he is going to the bar to grab drinks. I snort, knowing exactly why he's going over there. I give him a nod as he brushes past me and heads to where Sky is serving a group of college guys at the end of the bar.

"No bullshit!" I call to him, not wanting to get into a fight tonight over whatever the fuck he and Sky are. He doesn't turn around, merely lifts a middle finger over his head at me. I shake my head, smiling to myself. The two of them have been playing hard to get for way too long; the sexual tension is about to spill over the dam.

"This place is packed tonight!" Owen yells from beside me. I give him what most call a bro handshake, pulling each other into a hug and slapping each other on the back.

"Where are the twins?" I ask, but before he answers, I hear the two arguing from behind me.

"I fucking beat you. What are you talking about? I was in the parking lot first!" Finn yells as Brooks shakes his head in denial.

"No, whoever passed the last streetlight won. Which was me!"

"When have those ever been the rules? You lost. Get over it! Now pay up, pussy!" Finn lifts his hand as Brooks slaps a twenty-dollar bill in his hand. The twins are always competing; the twin rivalry is strong between them. Owen starts laughing from beside me, and I turn to see the girl I'm here for. The table the girls once occupied is now vacant, and I scan the room in search of Sage, who is nowhere to be seen.

Fuck.

"Where are the girls at?" Owen yells over the music as the pair of us continue searching the dance floor.

"Who the fuck knows? I can already feel this night turning into a fucking game of hide and seek," I growl out, frustration growing inside me already, and I've only been here five minutes. The four of us head to the table the girls were at and pile into the cramped booth. Saxon comes over a second later, carrying five beers for the lot of us. The scowl on his face tells me his conversation with Sky didn't go smoothly.

"Hey, Sax, what's got you looking all pissy?" Brooks asks but gets no response, only a look that speaks volumes.

"Shit, never mind, man."

I continue scanning the room for Sage, and just when I'm about to stand up and go looking for her, I catch a glimpse of her long blonde hair spinning in the corner of the dance floor.

*There's my little witch stick. Thinking you can hide from me, huh? That's funny.*

Now, I know how I seem. It probably sounds like I have it out for Sage, and don't get me wrong, you'd be a fool for thinking I'm not attracted to her. She is gorgeous, insanely captivating, but I'm only being like this to make sure she's safe. I made a promise to Saxon a long time ago that I would protect her like my own sister. She has this thing with going after the wrong men, men that end up hurting her in the end, and I'm here to make sure that doesn't happen again. Plus, I see the way other men look at her. Her beauty isn't only noticed by me, but by every fucking guy that lays eyes on her. Men only want one thing, and Sage, well, she deserves more than that. She deserves the world, and no man will ever be good enough for her until they give her just that.

I watch her as she spins and moves to the heavy, thudding music that fills the club. Her smile spreads across her face. A genuine smile I haven't seen in a while that makes my insides heat up. She says something to Ophelia, but I can't make out the words. I just continue to watch as she allows the moment to bring her the happiness she needs. The happiness that was snuffed out after the fire. She's never been the same since, and I miss that smile every day. A part of Sage died that day, and I sometimes pray she finds that fragment of her soul again.

"Hey, look, there's the girls!" Brooks says, as if I hadn't already spotted them ten minutes ago. I look over at him and Finn, who've already stood up and started to make their way over to them. Owen, Saxon, and I follow as we walk through the crowd that parts as we make our presence known. It's no secret who we are or what power we hold over this town, so for things to go smoothly, people tend to stay out of our way.

Frieda rolls her eyes as Finn and Brooks pick her up and swing her around like a rag doll. I don't miss the look of jealousy from Bristol as she watches Brooks touch her friend.

"For fuck's sake, put me down! Both of you!" Frieda yells over the music, but it does little to stop Finn. Brooks has already made his way to Bristol's side, who looks at him as if he's poison and heads to the bar. Brooks shakes his head and follows behind her. Frieda was adopted by Sam, who is a longtime member of the club; however, Sam is also Finn and Brooks' father, making them stepsiblings of sorts. There is no denying the chemistry and connection between Frieda and Finn, but they both do a good job of hiding what we all know is true.

Turning my attention to Sage, I see she, Owen, and Ophelia stand close together in conversation due to the loud music.

"How long do you think it will be before Owen makes a move on her?" Saxon says to me over his shoulder.

"Sage would never be with Owen—he's not her type." My response came out a little harsher than I intended it too.

"No, you fool. I mean with Ophelia. He's been drooling over her since she was in high school." I shake off the heavy feeling building inside me and nod my head once in agreement. I hear Saxon laugh over the music and turn my head towards him.

"What, you think I'd let Owen go after my sister? Or any of them, for that matter?" He laughs and turns his head to the bar again. I stand there a moment longer, watching Sage and her best friend converse until her eyes meet mine. I narrow my eyes on her before following Saxon for another beer. I stay at the bar with Saxon, Brooks, and Owen for most of the night. Finn and Frieda disappeared early in the night, but I figured that would happen.

"Excuse me, bro." A man my height reaches in front of me to grab his beer before walking off towards the dance floor. I watch him for a moment; he has a large frame and walks with an air of confidence. But it's his face that brings some sort of familiarity to him. I can't for the life of me remember where, or if, I've seen him before, but something about him feels off.

"Sax, you know that guy?" I nudge my best friend as he turns to see who I'm talking about. We both stare for a moment before he responds.

"Nah, I don't think so." He turns back and continues talking to Sky, who is now on speaking terms with him again. Go figure. I watch the man make his way over to where Sage and Ophelia are still dancing. When I see him tap her on the shoulder, I straighten my spine. Who the fuck is he? Why is he going up to Sage?

Sage faces the man and gives him a bright smile before they both shake hands, introducing themselves. He leans closer to her when she speaks due to the music's volume being at max capacity. My skin starts vibrating as I watch his hand touch her waist as he speaks close to her ear. I take a sip of my beer, the bottle neck cracking from how hard I'm squeezing it. Their proximity is unnecessary, and frankly, it pisses me off how he thinks touching her like that is okay. Clearly, they don't know each other, and touching her like that is a good way to get his fingers sliced off.

"Sax, look!" I yell, slapping his shoulder a little harder than necessary, but honestly, I'm pissed at how he isn't keeping an eye on his sister in the first place. Wasn't that the reason for coming tonight? He turns and narrows his eyes on Sage as we both watch the interaction unfold in front of us. I wish I knew what they were saying, but the way she's smiling and laughing at whatever the fucker is saying has me burning up inside.

"Let's go," Sax says, as he downs his beer and slams in on the bar.

*Finally.*

We make our way through the crowd once again and

come to a stop right behind the mystery man. Sage notices us right away, and I don't miss the nervous glint in her eyes as she continues to talk to the guy.

"Who's your friend, sis?" Saxon interrupts the man mid-sentence as he turns around to see who's now hovering behind him. Sage doesn't respond right away. Her eyes dart from Sax to me before clearing her throat.

"Oh, uhm, this is Dante. Dante, this is my brother, Saxon, and his friend, Saint." She gives him a weak smile before glaring at the pair of us.

"Nice to meet you both," Dante says, reaching out his hand for Sax to shake. He obliges, but when he reaches for mine, I just continue to glare at him.

"Right," he responds when he realizes I'm not going to shake his hand. The tension between us is thick, and I can feel Sage's eye burning holes into my face, but I don't care if she's mad.

"How do you two know each other?" Sax asks. But before anyone can respond, Sage grabs the man by the arm and turns him away from us.

"Jesus Christ. Can you two please go away? We are just talking. Go and enjoy your night." She turns away from us, but Saxon reaches out his hand, grabbing her by the upper arm, halting her in her tracks.

"You're coming home with us, understood?" Sax whispers to her. She yanks her arm from his grasp without answering. She gives him a nod and continues following Dante to a vacant table across the room. The pair of us watch them as they slid into the booth, sitting closer than I'd like, and continue their conversation.

"Keep an eye on her, yeah?" Saxon says to me before turning his back to his sister and making his way back to the bar where Sky is held up. I don't need to respond, nor does he need me to answer. We both know I'll keep an eye on her, both eyes, to be exact. All fucking night.

SAGE

# CHAPTER 10

**SAGE**

Watching, he's always watching me. Never letting me get too far away or out of his line of sight. Saint is by far the biggest cock block I'd ever had the pleasure of knowing. Dante and I are sitting in our booth, chatting about his work as an artist and owner of his own gallery, while I speak about my studies, which happen to be art and a minor in classical literature. Apart from our love of the visual arts, literature, and music, we also share a passion for motorcycles. The similarities between us make talking easy and enjoyable. Dante is a breath of fresh air and the complete contrast to Seb. I was genuinely having the best time getting to know him, and he seemed like he was enjoying himself too.

However, the heat of *his* gaze is constantly burning my skin. I know he's watching; he's always watching me. No thanks to Saxon, telling him to babysit me while he took care of whatever fuck up he had going on with Sky.

"I have a show coming up this following week. You

should come." Dante's face is centimeters from mine as he extends his invitation, and his scent quickly invades my senses. He smells of fresh linen but also a musky cedar that has me inhaling deeply. He pulls away from me to get my response, and I give him a smile.

"Yeah, that sounds wonderful. I'd love to come," I say as I brush my hair behind my ear. Dante's eyes are on my face, his lips curling into a smile that has my stomach fluttering. I can't help myself; I look over at the bar, and Saint's eyes meet mine in a clash of fury as he sips his beer. Once done, he raises an eyebrow at me, as if challenging me to a stare off. This man is worse than my overprotective brother, if that's even possible.

"Dante, we're out. We need to go." A stocky man pulls my attention from Saint as he stands beside Dante. He is staring down at his phone, typing away. Once he's done, he pockets his phone and glares over at the bar. I follow his line of sight and notice Sky holding his gaze as well. A look of defiance, but also a hint of fear, is etched across her beautiful face. I suddenly feel uneasy and watch as Sky breaks eye contact and goes back to serving customers. I catch sight of my brother discreetly looking over his shoulder at the man, and I know whatever is going on, he will take care of it, especially if it involves Sky. Dante's friend then turns and walks away, leaving the pair of us alone once again. Dante clears his throat beside me.

"It was such a pleasure spending the evening with you, Sage. I look forward to seeing you on Thursday." With that, he lifts my hand, placing a soft kiss over my knuckles. I'm glad the club is dark because I swear, I blush before he releases me and follows his friend towards the exit. I watch him leave until he is no longer visible among the crowd. I smile, chuckling to myself as I raise my hand to my mouth.

Once I am sure he's left, I want to talk to Ophelia immediately and divulge all the details about him and our conversation. Turning in the booth, I let out a squeal when I practically fall over Saint, who is now sitting right beside me in the booth. How the fuck did he get here without me noticing? How long has he been here?

"Saint, what the fuck?!" I yell, clutching my chest to calm the shock of him magically appearing out of thin air. Lifting his beer to his lips, he peers at me over his bottle.

"Who was he?" His voice is low and gravelly, as if holding back what he truly wants to say. I scoff, turning away from him, not wanting to have this discussion now. I'm sliding my way out of the other side of the booth when a large hand clamps over my thigh, rendering me immobile.

"I asked you a question, witch stick." I go to push his hand off my leg, but he drags me closer to him so I'm now fully in the booth once again. I look down at where he is touching me—his large hand covers most of my thigh. Thick veins are visible over the top of his hand as he gives me a squeeze, awaiting my answer.

"Saint, I just met him. That's all. It's not like I let him jump in my pants or take me home with him."

"Like I would've let that happen." His tone is deep, the corner of his mouth lifting up as if he's disgusted with the thought of me leaving with someone.

"Saint, are you serious? I know you take your job of being my brother's bitch seriously, but don't forget I'm an adult and can handle myself." I was being brave. Liquid courage will do that to you. His eyes darken while his chest fills with a deep breath. As he leans closer to my face, I turn away. Warm breath hits my ear, giving me chills.

"Make no mistake, Sage, I'm no one's bitch. And if you think you can talk to me like I'm just another one of your punk flings, you don't know me at all." The scary thing was, I do know Saint. I know him enough to realize when I've pushed the wrong button, and right now, I've clearly pushed said buttons. I soften my face, giving him a desperate plea to stop being a caveman and just let me enjoy the night. Our eyes stay locked on one another, his expression holding firm with his scowl creating deep grooves between his brows. I'm about to give in and tell him about Dante, when a loud, high-pitched scream startles me out of our stare off.

"Sage! There you are! Here, I got you another drink—it's a double! Now come on, let's dance!" Thank you, Ophelia, for saving me from this standoff with Saint. He lets my leg go, and I quickly shimmy out of the booth, grabbing her hand as she leads me to the floor. I can't help glancing over my shoulder. He is still watching me as the corner of his mouth curls into a wicked grin. Fuck, that smile does things to me.

While dancing with Ophelia, I tell her all about Dante and our plans for the art show this Thursday. She squeals with excitement and orders another round of drinks to celebrate. It isn't until I've had two more drinks that I notice the warmth of the alcohol tingling all over my body. Yes, I am drunk. I don't care. This is the night to let loose and enjoy my friends. Bristol had joined in on the dance floor and told us Frieda had to go, but the three of us continue on as the music bumps through my body. I can't help the thoughts of Saint and his audacity to treat me like a child after Dante left. His possessive caveman behavior has gotten worse over the last year, and it is seriously becoming a problem for me. Not only do I have Saxon playing the big brother role, but it's almost like Saint has developed this constant watchful eye over me. I am going to have to talk to him about that, maybe even talk to Saxon about both of them laying off me and letting me live my life how I chose.

My thigh burns with the sensation of Saint's hand gripping me in the booth. The sheer electrical current that he created over my skin has me breaking out in a sweat. When had he been able to affect me so? If it isn't with his eyes, it is with a small touch here and there. Never inappropriate, but enough that I am becoming more and more aware of his presence.

I don't know how long we have been dancing for. My mind is swirling with thoughts of Dante, but Saint is always in the corners of my mind, lurking and drawing me in with his captivating eyes. I am spinning and dancing, but when I stop, the room continues spinning around me. Fuck, I am really drunk.

"Sage, you good, girl?" I can hear Ophelia laughing, but her body is swaying side to side.

"Stop moving, O," I giggle out, but Bristol's laugh comes from my side.

"She's not moving at all. Damn, girl, you're *drunk, drunk.*" The three of us laugh when a large hand presses against my lower back. I fall into their touch, appreciating the support so I don't fall on my ass, but when a deep voice fills my head, I know tonight is over.

"Sage, come on. You're done. Let's go home." Saint's voice is almost sobering, almost. I sigh, turning to face him and falling face first into his chest. Fuck, his chest is like a brick wall. Rubbing my nose, I look up at him. His hands grab my waist to steady me. and there it is. The electrical charge he always sends through my body whenever he touches me.

"Ophelia, Owen is driving you and Bristol home. I'm taking Sage home, and Saxon is driving your car back to your house." The girls don't argue because at this point, we are all pretty toasted and know arguing with the guys will get us nowhere.

The girls and I hug, agreeing we will call each other tomorrow, and I watch as my two friends follow Saxon and Owen towards the exit. I blow O a kiss before turning back to Saint, waving my hand towards the exit as well, in the most sarcastic way I can. He isn't impressed with my drunken behavior, and when his hand snakes around my waist and he starts leading us out, I can't help but look down at his hands again.

His beautiful hands.

SAINT

# CHAPTER 11

SAINT

After lifting Sage into my passenger seat, I close her door and make my way to the driver's seat. Settling in, I turn the ignition as the lights on the dash light up. Sage squints her eyes, as if the dash is too bright for her. Clearly, she is drunk. I hold in my laugh, pulling out of the parking lot and heading towards her house.

Sage is quiet. I keep looking over to make sure she hasn't passed out, but when her head snaps towards mine, I am met with an angry glare.

"Why do you do that?" She slurs her words, and her eyes are not able to focus on me properly.

"Do what, witch stick?"

"Always get in the way." Her voice is low and laced with an emotion I can't decipher.

"Get in your way?" I question.

"Yeah, you're always there. Whenever a guy talks to me, you're always distracting me." I was distracting her from giving her full attention to Dante. For some reason, that makes me smile.

"I'm distracting you?" I knew I had been. I just want her to explain more.

"Yes, I can feel you when you're looking at me. It makes me feel… warm." She pauses before saying the last word, as if she's trying to figure out for herself what I make her feel. "Why do you do that?" I look over at her. Her face is leaning against the headrest towards the window, the side of her neck on display. I want to touch it, to brush my fingers down her soft skin, but I don't. I squeeze the steering wheel instead, my knuckles going white. I'm quiet for a long moment, trying to think of how to respond to her. I want to tell her that no man will ever deserve her time. No man will ever be good enough for her. She's Aphrodite and all men are under her spell, but their intentions aren't pure. I can see it in their eyes. They give themselves away when they examine her body, as only predators do. No. Sage deserves someone who sees her for her inner beauty, for who she truly is on the inside, not just her obvious physical beauty. It isn't until she turns back towards me that I finally give her an answer.

"Sage, you look great tonight." I don't know why I say it, but it's the truth. Sage's eyes narrow on me, her eyebrows pinched together in confusion.

"Uh, thank you." She sounds stunned, as if I'm lying to her.

"You haven't smiled like that in a long time. You should do it more often." I don't look over at her; I keep my eyes on the road and watch her shift uncomfortably in her seat. The rest of the ride is quiet. Pulling up to her house, I put my Tahoe in park and shut off the engine. Looking at Sage, she has her eyes closed, and the softest snore is accompanying her breathing. I get out and make my way around to her side; I pop her door open and reach over to unbuckle her. She moans as I fit my arms underneath her to carry her inside.

"Saint?" she groans, her head curling into my chest. Kicking her door shut, I make my way to her front door, maneuvering my hand to the handle and pushing the door open. Frankie is in the living room, watching some tattoo reality show, talking to the screen as if they can hear him.

"Hey, Saint. Oh shit, long night?" He chuckles as he looks over at Sage curled up in my arms.

"Nothing some water and Advil can't cure." I make my way through the foyer and up the stairs straight to her room. I know this house; I grew up here with Saxon. When it burned down, a part of me died too. I was ecstatic when they decided to rebuild the exact house after the old remains were cleared. It made me feel like it never burned down at all. I know Sage was haunted by the thought of rebuilding the house she almost died in, but her stance on the matter changed when she saw the house come to life in little bits at a time. It reminds her of her father, and that's all she wanted.

I softly open her bedroom door with my boot, bringing her to her bed and gently laying her down. I pull off her boots and tuck her in beneath the covers. I'm about to leave when her voice fills the room.

"Can you help me take this top off, please? I can't reach the zipper." I don't move right away. The thought of helping her undress has my dick twitching. I know she is more than drunk because no way would she ask me to help her undress sober. I take two long strides towards her as she sits up and turns her back towards me. Grabbing her zipper, I slowly pulled it down, the small crop top falling to the sides as the zipper releases from the middle. Pulling her arms through the straps, she discards the top on the floor and stands up. She's perfect, the burn scars and all. She's facing away from me as she begins pulling down the tight leather pants, her black thong doing little to cover her.

I know I should turn around, but the sight of her being so free and comfortable in front of me has me mesmerized. Once her pants are off, she raises her arms over her head, stretching her shoulders and arching her back towards me before climbing back into bed. Once she pulls the covers over her naked body, she curls up on her side and brings the comforter underneath her chin. I wait for her to get comfortable and start towards her door once again. Turning off her lights, I grab the door handle, but what she says next has me freezing in my tracks.

"You look great tonight too. I like when you smile at me." Her eyes are closed as she speaks, and I can't pull myself out of her room. I watch as her breathing becomes shallower and her small snores fill her room. It isn't until I know she is fully asleep that I gently close her door and make my way back downstairs.

My chest feels tight as I enter the living room. Frankie is still watching his show, but it isn't until he asks me what's wrong that I pull myself out of the trance.

"Oh nothing. Just a long night playing babysitter with the girls." I rub my face with my hands, leaning back and sinking into the couch to wait for Saxon. My mind starts to race with Sage's comment. She was drunk. That's why she said it, right? She didn't mean it. She will probably forget everything she said and how she undressed in front of me by tomorrow. Sage undressed in front of me. Fuck, she is gorgeous. I know she hates her scars, but seeing them tonight had me thanking God that she made it out of the house before it claimed her.

I don't know when I drift off to sleep, but when I hear a familiar voice scream in the distance, I shoot off the couch. My feet move on their own accord, skipping three steps at a time until I reach her door.

"Sage!" I yell as I push her door open, my eyes finding her screaming into her sheets. She is dreaming, tossing and turning in her bed frantically as if she's trying to escape something.

"Sage, Sage! Wake up. I'm here!" I grab hold of her shoulders, shaking her to try to bring her from the nightmare she's having.

"Sage!" I yell again, and when her eyes shoot open, my stomach drops. The look of utter fear and panic that floods her eyes has me pulling her into a hug and squeezing her until she realizes it was all a dream. Her sobs follow as her arms wrap tightly around my neck; our bodies pressed against one another while she slowly comes back down from her panic. Soft sobs shake her body as I lift her from her bed and into my lap. I brush her hair with my hand, letting her cry into my chest, knowing the exact nightmare that put her in this state of panic.

Since the fire, Sage has had the same dream of being locked in her burning house over and over again. I've seen Saxon try to calm her down more than once, her sobs tearing the muscles around my heart with the sheer pain she endures each time she has this dream. I let her stay in my arms as long as she needs. We stay tucked into one another until her breathing evens out once more. Lifting her face from my chest, she looks up at me, gratitude now taking the place of her fear. Then it all shifts in a single moment.

"Shit! Saint, I'm so sorry. How did I get naked?" She jumps from my lap, grabbing her robe and wrapping the thin fabric around her body. She turns her bedside lamp on and faces me before crossing her arms over her chest. I stand from her bed, stepping up to her and invading her personal space.

"Don't apologize. I'll be downstairs if you need me." I brush a piece of her hair behind her ear and leave her room, closing the door softly behind me. Standing in the hallway, I see Saxon rush from the bathroom, his pistol tightly clutched in his hand. A towel is slung low on his waist while soap suds are still scattered across his body.

"Fuck, what's wrong?" He gets out, clearly out of breath from trying to get out of the shower quickly. I laugh as soap suds fall from his legs to the carpet.

"Nothing. Sage was having another nightmare. She's fine now." Rubbing his hand down his face, he curses under his breath before turning and heading back to the bathroom.

"Hey, Sax. You've got soap in your hair still." I call after him. He flips me off before disappearing into the bathroom. I make my way to the stairs, but the sound of a door opening has me turning around.

"Um, Saint?" Sage's small voice calls to me. I turn to face her. "Will you stay with me until I fall asleep? Please?" She isn't looking at me; she's looking down, as if embarrassed to ask. I don't need to be asked twice. Making my way back towards her room, I usher her to get back in bed while I remove my boots, discarding them to the side. She watches me as I take my wallet out of my back pocket and sit down on the edge of her bed. She is already lying down, still in her robe, and when I lie on my side, facing her, she instantly curls into my chest.

This is not like her. We don't do this type of thing. We bicker, fight, and torment each other. But this—this was a new side of Sage that she's never shown me. Her nightmare must have really been vivid this time. Her body is trembling against me, and when I wrap my arm around her waist, she instantly presses harder against me. I wonder what she had dreamed about to make her so desperate to not fall asleep alone? I know her terrors from the fire were constant and have never eased up since that horrific day, but I wonder what she sees when sleep takes hold of her? Will she ever tell me?

"I'm sorry if this is awkward for you," she whispers, but I don't feel the slightest bit awkward with her. Rather, I feel the complete opposite, like this is how we should always be. But I can't admit that to her.

"We can hate each other tomorrow. How's that sound?" I whisper back. Her small scoff is her response. We lie there together, embracing one another in a way I am not familiar with. Well, not familiar with her, at least. I wait until her breathing slows again, and I know sleep has finally taken her. Then I gently extract her from my arms and leave her alone. How the hell did the night turn into this? Is she going to regret this tomorrow? As much as I feed into the role of the annoying brother's best friend, I've always had this deep-seated emotional connection with Sage. I hoped one day she'll see or feel it too.

SAGE

# CHAPTER 12

**SAGE**

My fucking head is throbbing, and I look like I've been hit by a whole convoy of semitrucks. I haven't been this hungover in a long time. Don't get me wrong, last night was everything I needed. Dancing with my friends and just letting myself relax and enjoy the night had been something I didn't know I needed. Every year around my birthday, I fall into this deep dark corner of depression where the grieving process of losing my father begins all over again. I've been to counseling, but nothing will ever cure the pain of losing a parent—especially your only parent. It helped to talk with someone unrelated to our family, but the pain of reliving that day over and over while talking with a stranger quickly became too much for me. Being with the club helped me the most; they are my family and only they know and can sympathize with losing someone so special to me.

I'm on my second bottle of water when I hear arguing coming from the living room. It's Saxon, and by the way his conversation is going, I can assume he is arguing with Sky again. Poor girl. They go at each other's throats more often than not these days. I don't ask Saxon about it though, nor do I ask Sky. They have their own issues to hash out, and nothing I say or do will help their relationship. Finishing my water, I toss the bottle into the recycling bin and head to the coffeepot to start a fresh brew. Grabbing the coffee and filling the pot, I fall into the routine of making the coffee, a task I quite like to do every morning. It relaxes me. I can't explain it.

Hitting the on button, I lean against the counter and wait as the coffee machine starts up and begins slowly dripping the water over the fresh coffee grounds.

"Mind if I get a cup?" Saint's deep voice fills the kitchen as he yawns while walking to the table. I look over at him as he reaches his arms above his head, stretching out his tall frame and groaning in the process. I can't help but catch a glimpse of his abdomen as he raises his arms up, causing his shirt to lift as well. Looking at the hem of his pants, I see the ink that's painted across his skin and feel my face start to heat.

*What the fuck, Sage? Stop looking at your brother's best friend. You aren't supposed to be looking at him like that.*

I quickly snap my attention back to the coffee maker before he catches me checking him out. I mentally berate myself as I head to the cabinet to fetch another mug. Standing on my tiptoes, I try to reach the mug, but my fingers keep pushing it further and further towards the back of the cabinet.

"Shit," I mutter to myself as I continue to try to grab the mug. Just when I'm about to jump on the counter, I feel him behind me. His warm body presses against my back as a long arm reaches over mine to grab the mug I'd been struggling to reach.

"Here, let me," Saint says as he cages my body in with

his. My eyes close as I inhale his scent. He's so close, touching my back, and I instinctively lean back into his frame. He smells so good, so fresh, as if he just stepped out of the shower. Spearmint and aftershave fill my senses, making me take in another deep breath.

"Sage, you alright?" I hear him whisper in my ear as his hands rest on my hips, helping steady me as I've now completely leaned into his body, resting against his chest. Realizing what the fuck I'm doing; I quickly escape from his hold and head towards the now finished coffee.

"Um, yeah, sorry. I'm fine. Just a little hungover," I admit as I start pouring both cups and turn to hand him his. He's right behind me again. Our bodies are the opposite ends of a magnet, attracting one another in the worst way. Grabbing the mug from me, he narrows his eyes on mine and sips his coffee.

"You sleep, okay?" he asks, his voice low, with a look of concern etched across his face.

"Yeah, I did. Why wouldn't I?" He doesn't answer right away, taking another sip as he backs away and leans against the island.

"You woke up screaming again from another nightmare." I don't remember having a dream last night; all I remember is falling asleep and feeling safe in a way I hadn't in a long time. Looking in my mug, I take another sip before flashes of last night start becoming a whole lot clearer. Did Saint tuck me in last night? How did I get undressed and in my robe? *What the fuck, Sage?* He must have seen the horror of my unanswered questions because he sets his mug on the counter and comes to stand in front of me.

"I'm glad you slept well, and thanks for the coffee." Saint's large hands cup my arms, rubbing them up and down before placing a kiss to my forehead and leaving me utterly speechless in the kitchen. What the hell happened last night?

Topping off my mug, I take a seat on one of the barstools at the island and pull out my phone from my sweatpants. Pulling up Ophelia's number, I open the text chain.

*Sage: Thank you so much for last night. I needed it more than I realized.*

*O: Girl, we all did. But now as I sit, staring at the inside of my toilet, I think maybe we overdid it on the shots.*

*Sage: haha I feel pretty disgusting too this morning. But I have a question. Who brought me home last night? All I remember is falling asleep in my bed but don't remember how I got there.*

*O: Saint brought you home. Owen brought me and the girls home, and Sax drove my car back to my house. You don't remember? Girl you must have been way more drunk than me haha.*

I stared down at the message for a long while before responding. If Saint brought me home, did he help me into my pajamas? Fuck, I didn't even wake up in pajamas; I was only in my robe with nothing underneath. Had he seen me naked? Did he undress me and put me to bed? I have so many questions running through my mind, but my phone vibrating in my hand has me snapping out of my trance.

*O: I physically don't think I can throw up anymore. I have nothing left in my stomach. I'm going to grab water and Advil and sleep this off. Talk to you later. Love ya!*

*Sage: Love ya too.*

Rubbing my face in my hands, I groan to myself. *Why did you let yourself get that drunk, Sage? You're smarter than that.*

"I told you—we have to do it today. I'm over his shit, and he's starting to interfere with our own shit." Saxon sounds pissed; his tone is low, but I can still hear his conversation that I'm assuming he's having with Saint.

"You're right. Tonight then," Saint responds. When I hear Saxon walk to the study, curiosity has me standing and making my way over to the living room. Peering into the large room, I see Saint sitting on the sofa. His elbows are resting against his knees as he leans over, texting on his phone. He's still in his dark jeans and white T-shirt, and his hair is now messy from his hands constantly brushing back the thick strands.

"Everything okay?" I ask quietly, not wanting Saxon to hear me. Saint's head snaps up, and his silver eyes meet mine.

"Yeah, witch stick. Everything's good. Just a little mishap that needs to be handled. That's all." I can't help myself. The question comes out faster than I could think.

"What has to be done today?" He stands then, making his way over to me so he's towering over me once again. Looking down at my face, he brushes his thumb along my jawline.

"Nothing you need to worry about." His fingers barely dance across my skin, making me shiver as he pushes my hair over my shoulder. Just then, a loud bang echoes through the house. Saxon storms in after slamming the study door and enters the living room once again. I jump back from Saint; my eyes widen into saucers as I look to my brother who's buried in his phone. Saint doesn't move from me; his hand falls to the side, but his eyes remain on mine as if he's not concerned about his best friend seeing him touch his sister.

"Right, everything's good. We'll pick him up outside of Mack's tonight. That's where he'll be." Saxon then looks up from his phone, eyes landing on me before a scowl breaks out across his face. "Fuck."

"What are you talking about?" I ask, worry now settling into my skin.

"Nothing, sis. You didn't need to hear that. Just take it

easy today and relax, yeah?" he says to me. Rolling my eyes, I look back to Saint, who has stopped staring at me since Saxon entered the room.

"Right, I see I'll be getting no answers. With that, I'll go then." I turn to head out and when I reach the stairs, I hear whispering coming from the living room.

"Fuck, man. You could have said she was in here. Now she's going to wonder what the fuck is up!" Saxon whisper yells to Saint.

"Why you keep things from her about the club, I'll never know. Now, let's get our shit together for later." I hurry up the stairs when I hear footsteps heading towards the foyer. I stand against the banister as I watch Saxon head out the front door with Saint following close behind. Before he shuts the door behind him, Saint turns around. Silver eyes land on mine before he shoots me a wink, giving me his back once again and closing the door behind him.

*What the hell is going on?*

SAGE

# CHAPTER 13

## SAGE

The warm water sprays my back as I stand in my shower, allowing the water to wash away this intense hangover. Leaning my head towards the tiled floor, I watch as the water swirls around as the remnants of my hangover disappear down the drain. I start to wonder when mine and Saint's behavior towards one another changed. Was it the accidental kiss the other day? We've always had this tumultuous relationship that's worked for us. We pick on each other; he calls me witch stick, while I call him a big over possessive caveman. We love to bicker with each other—simple as that. However, standing in the shower now, I slowly begin to recollect what happened last night.

Saint brought me home; I know that. He followed me upstairs—no—he carried me upstairs, maybe? Fuck, I can't remember. Once I was in my room, I vaguely remember feeling like my clothes were suffocating me. I took off my clothes one piece at a time, but don't remember Saint leaving at that point. I stripped in front of my brother's best friend.

*Sage, are you serious?!*

After giving Saint a free show, I remember falling into my bed. Saint then covered me up and left. I think. That's it, right? Saint said I had a nightmare though, so when was that? The water starts to fall across my face, causing me to close my eyes and breath against the stream of water. The heat of the water is soothing my headache, and I take a break from racking my brain to allow the warmth to heal me from the inside out. As the water puts my soul back together, I can't help seeing a pair of silver eyes in my head. Thinking of his warm body pressed against my back this morning has my stomach flipping in Olympic style back-flips, but why now?

Brushing my hair back with my hands, I freeze with my hands tangled in my hair. He slept in my bed last night! I remember now. I woke up from my nightmare, and like after most of my nightmares, I couldn't fall back asleep. I got out of my bed, swaying on my feet from the liquid courage that was still flowing through my blood, and asked him to stay with me until I fell asleep! I asked him. Me, the sister of his best friend. Fuck, what have I done?

As I stand in the shower, buzzing with nervous energy, I start washing my hair. He didn't question it though; he came to me in my room and held me while I fell asleep. There wasn't any hesitation from him. Saint came to me and cuddled in my bed. He could have said something sly and picked on me for being a little bitch from a silly bad dream, but he didn't. Tyler Saint Bones had lain with me. His arms wrapped around me as his presence helped me fall asleep. As much as I want that encounter to feel weird, it honestly doesn't feel weird at all. It feels… right.

Why didn't he say anything this morning? He acted like

nothing happened. Was he waiting for me to say something? Is that why he asked me if I slept well? *Jesus, Sage, why are you so worked up? It's Saint, your friend, your closest frenemy, if you will. He was just being nice, helping you fight off the demons of the night that haunts you.*

Saint is no stranger to my nightmares. He practically lives here too and has heard me have a fit once or twice over a nightmare, but it was always Saxon who came in to investigate. It's never been Saint. Last night it was him. He came to soothe me, calm me, and bring me back down from the terrors my mind likes to torture me with. *Fuck, why am I thinking too hard about this?*

Finishing my shower, I step out and grab my towel, wrapping it around my body. Grabbing another towel, I twist my hair and place it on top of my head to help my hair dry. I look myself over in the mirror, the look of confusion evident on my face. Rubbing my hands down my arms, I become hyperaware of the places Saint touched me this morning. The electric energy his fingers created against my skin has my nerve endings on high alert. Rolling my eyes, I brush any more thoughts of Saint out of my head and storm back into my room. Grabbing a pair of jeans and a long-sleeve black top, I decide I need to get out and go for a ride. That will surely help clear my head. I dress quickly; lacing up my boots and heading back into the bathroom, I quickly dry my hair. The task isn't as quick as I was hoping for, though. My long blonde hair is not the easiest to dry.

Once done, I head downstairs and wolf down half a bagel and head to the garage to grab my helmet and keys to my bike. As I enter the garage, I smile to myself when I see my all-black Ducati sitting so perfectly in the garage bay. I haven't ridden her in a long time, and why not break that streak with a long ride through the back roads? As much as I love my Harley, there's something about my Ducati that makes me feel like I'm lightning—fast and free, able to zigzag through traffic and reach speeds I know I shouldn't.

I smash the button that opens the garage and pull my full-face helmet over my head as I swing my leg over my bike. I quickly pull out my phone and send a quick text to Saxon, informing him I'm going for a ride to clear my head. I always like for him or Frankie to know when I'm out riding alone; just in case something happens, they'll know where I am. I get a quick thumbs up emoji from him and turn on my bike. The loud engine fills the garage, and I flip the kickstand in as I back out of the garage.

Looking at my phone one last time, I note the time. It's close to six in the evening, so nightfall will be soon. It still being summer, I know the sun doesn't set until a little after eight, so I have some time. I decide to take one of my favorite routes that heads out over the hills and towards a quarry I used to swim at as a teenager. My father always forbade me from going there, but Ophelia and I were never really the teens that followed our fathers' orders. It's no wonder she and I are still alive after the stupid shit we got ourselves into.

The quarry is closed to the public due to the dangers within. The high rocks and steep ledges that lead to the water below have claimed many lives over the years. However, Ophelia and I were never reckless; we usually went out there to sunbathe on the rocks and talk about our latest crushes.

I head out of the driveway and speed towards the winding road to the hills. I ride for about an hour, not caring where I'm going, simply enjoying the road ahead of me. The air is warm, and since it's a Sunday night, there is little traffic for me to worry about. Once I hit the road that forks off, I turn right. This road leads to a very small pull-off that is gated off with a *No Entry* sign on the front.

Parking my bike behind a set of thick bushes so no one sees, I take off my helmet and hook it on my handlebars. My hair blows in the subtle wind, the smell of the woods hitting me as I make my way over to the gate.

The gate is just that, one gated door that doesn't allow vehicles to pass through. However, the gate does nothing to hinder people's ability to jump over it. I jump over with ease and quickly disappear beyond the trees. It's dark beneath the trees' coverage. It is now a little after seven thirty, and I know I don't have much time left before the sky grows dark. Walking a little further through the woods, I know the rocks are just up ahead. Once I reach the rocks, I smile to myself as a flood of memories hits me from my teenage years. So many Saturdays were spent here on these perfectly flat rocks, allowing for the best sunbathing. I smile to myself as memories with Ophelia fill my mind. So many long, deep conversations were had on these rocks, so many tears were shed over boys, hardships, and, of course, the loss of our mothers.

I make my way over to the spot Ophelia and I always chose, due to it being the flattest spot, and I sit down, leaning my hands behind me and looking up to the sky. It's beautiful—oranges and pinks coat the clouds as the sun rapidly starts to descend. I lay back against the rocks and watch as the sun dips below the trees, and soon I'm lying in darkness. It's so soothing out here. The sound of the birds in the woods, the absence of sounds from the city, and just being in the fresh air is everything I want at this moment.

As I sit there, I can't help but think of Saint again. His presence this morning was so different from usual. Yes, he always gives me a kiss goodbye like my brother, and all the other club members for that matter, but his touch this morning had felt so… different. Different in a way that was more sensual. I scoff to myself, standing up and brushing off my jeans as I decide it's getting late, and I need to head back. Looking at my watch, I see I've been here for well over an hour, and it's now close to nine o'clock. Saxon is going to kill me. As I look at my phone, though, I see no missed calls or texts from him, which is weird because he usually always checks in on me. I pocket my phone and head back through the woods.

The sound of distant voices has me freezing. Spinning around, I can't see anything right away, but I can still hear someone, or maybe more than one person, talking in muffled tones. I stand behind a thicker tree, peering out across the quarry's ledge, trying to spot whoever is here with me. Squinting my eyes, I start to think it's too dark, and I won't be able to see anyone, when a shadow of something, or someone, comes into view at the edge of the quarry. I step out from behind the tree, squinting harder as the shadows become clearer. Two large—what look to be— men are carrying someone who appears to be unconscious. One man is holding onto the person's arms, while the other is holding the legs. Both men are wearing all black with masks covering their faces, but they are so far away, I can't see what the masks resemble.

I step a little further out into the open to try to see better. The men set the unconscious man down for a moment as they stand to their full heights—they are both huge, towering men. They start conversing about something in voices so low, I can't hear. A moment later, the mystery men pick up the guy and toss him over the ledge into the quarry. It takes a moment for the body to hit the water due to the height of the cliff, but the moment it does, a gasp leaves my throat, shock bubbling in my core. My eyes lift from the water back to the mystery men who are now staring directly at me. I run. I don't hesitate—I have to get back to my bike and leave right fucking now.

I waste no time. Turning on my heels and racing through the woods, it takes me no time at all to reach the gate as I hurdle over it. Finding my bike, I don't even bother with my helmet and swing my leg over my bike. As I try to get my keys from my pocket, a strong-arm wraps around my mouth, muffling a scream I can no longer get out. I've been caught. Fuck my life.

SAINT

# CHAPTER 14

### SAINT

What the fuck is she doing here? She's thrashing in my arms as I try to get her to calm the fuck down. I don't know if she saw Saxon and me, or what she is even doing out here in the first place, but I spin her around so she can see it's just me.

"Why the fuck do you look like you've just seen a ghost?" She freezes, her eyes wide as saucers, and she continues to breathe like she just ran a marathon.

"Sage? What's wrong?" I ask, trying to play everything off as if this is totally normal. The both of us in the middle of an abandoned quarry late at night is completely normal, right? I shake her shoulders when she doesn't respond, the panic in her eyes starting to make me worry.

"Sage, speak. What the fuck is wrong?" Just then, she throws her arms around my neck, squeezing as if I might disappear. I wrap my arms around her small frame as I watch the taillights of Saxon's truck pull out from where we hid it and give him a quick wave to hurry the fuck up before Sage sees him. I brush my hand down her long hair, trying to comfort her as I watch Saxon's lights slowly disappear down the road. As soon as I know he's gone, I pull Sage from my chest and peer down at her face. She's still shaken up, no doubt from what she just saw, but I can't give myself away.

"Saint, I've never been so happy to see you in my life," she whispers to me while looking over her shoulder. I don't respond; I just let her speak, not sure what she truly saw.

"Saint, I was by the quarry, and, yes, I know I'm not supposed to be out there, but when I was by the ledge, I saw something," she says so fast she starts fumbling over her words. Trying to catch her breath, she continues, "I saw what looked like two men, and they threw another person over the ledge into the water." Another glance over her shoulder before she grabs ahold of my shirt. "We have to get out of here. I'm sure one of them saw me, and it won't be too long before they find us here. Please, we have to go now." I lower myself to her level and cup her chin in my hand.

"I got you; no one is going to hurt you. Now get your helmet on and slide on the back. I'll drive us home." Sage quickly does what I say, throwing her helmet on without buckling the straps and situating herself on the back of her Ducati. I throw my leg over the bike as well, careful to not hit her, and settle myself in. Just as I reach for the keys, Sage squeezes my shoulder.

"Hang on—how did you know I was here? What are you doing out here?" I don't answer. I just turn the key, kick up the stand, and rev the engine as we peel out of the small dirt area. Her arms wrap tightly around my waist as I pick up speed down the windy roads. It doesn't take long for us to get back to her house. I clearly hadn't been following the speed limit requirements through the back roads, nor did I care when we hit the city limits.

Pulling into her driveway, I see Saxon is already here and breathing a sigh of relief. If Sage asks me why I was out there in the first place again, I don't know what I'm going to say. Do I flat out lie, or just pretend like I go there often? You know, to clear my head and shit? That sounds like something I would do, right? Fuck, I'm screwed.

Parking the bike back in the garage, I flip down the kickstand and wait for Sage to climb off first. As soon as she does, she rips her helmet off and gives me a concerned look.

"Please, no word to Saxon about where I was. He'll be pissed if he knew I was up there." She's worried about being scolded by her brother… I may be able to get around this after all. I swing my leg off the bike and stare down at her.

"Listen, Sage, you don't think I need to tell Saxon? Especially after what you saw? He needs to know that." I cross my arms over my chest, pretending like I care if her brother knows she was up there. She looks to the side door as if Saxon will appear there any moment.

"Please, Saint. We don't need to say anything. Plus, it was dark. I may have just been seeing things. You know how I let my imagination get away from me sometimes." She shrugs her shoulders, gaslighting herself into thinking what she saw was just a figment of her imagination. But I know the truth. I run my hand down my face, letting out a sigh.

"Fine, I won't say anything, but I don't want you going up there anymore by yourself, understood? Especially at night." I shake my head back and forth as if I can't believe she would do something so irresponsible and turn to head towards the house. I quickly pull out my phone and send Saxon a quick text, telling him not to mention a thing. Heading in through the garage door, Sage and I make our way to the kitchen where Saxon is sitting at the island drinking a beer.

"What up, man?" I say, giving him a nod before opening the fridge and grabbing a beer for myself.

"Sup," Saxon replies, then looks to Sage, who hasn't looked up from the floor since entering the house. If she is trying to make herself look innocent, she's doing the opposite. Sage looks like she did something she knew she wasn't supposed to.

"Sis, how was your ride? Took a long one, huh?" he says to her, looking down at his watch. She pulls out a chair at the small dining room table in front of the bay window and sits down before she answers him. Looking at her brother, she gives him a sweet smile before nodding.

"Yeah, it was such a nice day I lost track of time, and before I knew it, it was dark." Her eyes shift to me quickly, as if to remind me not to say anything about where she really was.

"Yeah, I saw her enter the city and followed her back up here." My bike is already in the garage, Saxon knows that, but I want Sage to think I am explaining why we both came in at the same time, rather than me driving her here on her bike.

"Cool. Glad you had a good ride." Saxon downs the rest of his beer before standing from the bar stool and cracking his back. "I'm going to take a quick shower. You staying here tonight, man?" he asks me before giving me a bro handshake. He knows I am, but for the sake of this ruse the three of us are playing at, I nod, taking a swig of my own beer. I stay here a lot since my work, a.k.a. the club, needs me close to Saxon at the drop of a hat. The spare room had practically become mine. It was once Frankie's, but since he moved out, it sort of turned into mine. It is on the opposite side of the house and has its own en suite bathroom. I enjoy staying here, more so than my own apartment. I grew up with Saxon and Sage, and knowing the three of us are under the same roof makes me feel like I can protect them, mainly Sage. Saxon can protect himself—he's a ruthless fucker.

Sage and I stare at each other as Saxon leaves the kitchen, and neither of us says a word until we hear his bathroom door shut behind him. She finally lets out a long breath of relief and lowers her head to the table. I chuckle to myself. It's cute how nervous she got with her brother, as if he was her actual father, and he just caught her breaking curfew or something.

"You know, he's not that scary," I say to her, making her head snap up as she gives me her usual scowl.

"Not to you, but I don't want any more lectures from him about how I'm reckless and need to be more careful." I shrug my shoulders; I mean, he was right. She does need to be more careful. Her family is the head of a pretty well-known motorcycle club; that automatically puts her at risk of danger. She narrows her eyes at me, knowing I agree with Saxon, but she doesn't say anything. Standing from the table, she brushes her hair back over her shoulders and freezes mid-brush.

"Hang on—you still haven't told me what you were doing out there either." Fuck, I was hoping she would drop that question. I finish my beer, trying to buy myself some time to think of an answer. She just stands there, staring at me and waiting for my response.

"Listen, Sage. I sometimes like to go out there, beneath the stars, and allow my inner self to reflect back on the times when life was, you know, simpler." If the look she gives me could kill, I'd be six feet under right about now.

"Saint, I'm serious," she scoffs.

"I am serious! What, men can't have a deep connection with their astrological moon phase like women?" I leave her with that, turning on my heels and heading towards my room. I hadn't even left the kitchen when she calls after me.

"Saint." Her voice is small and no longer sounds like she wants to kill me. I turn to face her.

"Thanks for covering for me. I owe you one." I give her a wink in response and head to my room, closing the door behind me. I give myself a pat on the back for narrowly dodging her questions and head for the bathroom. Knowing Saxon, he'll want to discuss what she knows, just the two of us.

SAGE

# CHAPTER 15

## SAGE

I watch his back as he disappeared into his room, or the room he calls his, since he stays here often enough. He never answered my question about why he was really out at the quarry, but I'll find a way to get it out of him. I head to the fridge to grab a bottle of water, and it finally sinks in: I saw two men throw a body in the quarry. What the actual fuck? I saw what I saw. I just didn't want Saint ratting on me to Saxon. I saw two shadowy figures grab hold of what looked to be an unconscious body and toss it over the ledge, right? I swear that's what I saw. I know it was dark, but how could my mind make up something that sinister? I'm hungover, yes, but I've never been so hungover where I start hallucinating things. Especially something like murder.

My phone dings in my pocket, temporarily bringing me back to Earth from the panic I'm conjuring up in my head. Pulling it out of my pocket, I see Saint's texted me.

SAINT:

Could you grab me a towel and lay it in
front of my bathroom door? I forgot again.

ME:

You're hopeless. Sure.

I stay in the kitchen for a long moment, finishing my water before I head to the linen closet. Retrieving a towel, I head back to his bedroom. Opening his door, I go to the bathroom and drop the towel at the door. A faint groan has my feet stopping and turning to investigate where it's coming from. The bathroom door is slightly open, allowing the smallest bit of light to filter into his room. Another moan hits my ears, and I turn back towards the bathroom. It's Saint. *What is he doing?* I know I shouldn't be snooping in his room, especially since he's taking a fucking shower, but curiosity takes hold of me.

Staying light on my toes, I press my ear against the gap in the door and the frame and listen. Besides the water splashing against the tile, I hear nothing else. I shouldn't, I really fucking shouldn't, but I can't help myself. I turn to peek through the opening, and I'm not prepared for what I see.

Saint has his hand against the tile wall, his head is lowered while his other hand is... stroking himself. Now, I know I should turn back around and leave. I'm severely invading his privacy. However, my feet don't move. I continue watching him. His tattooed, muscular back is flexing with each stroke of his cock, the water cascading down his body, making his tanned skin glisten in the dim vanity lights. Then there's his ass, his perfectly perky ass that should be illegal for a man to have.

I watch his forearm as his strokes become more rapid. Another groan escapes his mouth as his obliques flex harder. He's close. The way his body is tensing with each stroke shows just how close he really is. Another groan leaves his parted lips, his head leaning back as the water pellets over his face. Faster and faster, he strokes himself, and when he turns his body just enough, I see what his fist is holding. He's big, and I mean very, *very* big. I swallow, not realizing the amount of saliva that's pooled in my own mouth. Thick veins become visible along his cock as his hand grips his thickness, stroking back and forth.

I lick my lips and wonder how soft his skin would feel inside my mouth. Just then, a deep moan filters up through his chest and out of his mouth as ropes of his arousal spray across the tiled walls. I watch as he slowly comes down from his high, his body releasing the tension each muscle was holding. I should leave. I shouldn't have stayed.

"My Sage." I'm frozen to the spot. Did Saint just say my name? Am I hearing things? Pulling back from the door, I straighten myself, and I quickly realize that Saint was just masturbating to the thought of me. Am I going insane? I can't be seeing and hearing things, can I? The sound of the shower turning off has me sprinting to leave his room—like hell am I sticking around to be caught being a peeping Tom.

I make my way to his bedroom door but fall over my own feet as I kick the corner of his bed, trying to make my getaway. Toppling to the ground, I crawl as fast as I can to the door, knowing he would have heard me face-plant. I successfully make it to the door and quietly close it behind me. Once I'm in the clear, I sprint to the stairs and to my room. Breathing heavily, I rest my head against my bedroom door and curse myself for being so fucking nosy.

I can't shake the feeling that I've been caught, so instead of just standing in my room, I head to my bathroom and flip on my shower. Plus, I need to cool off from the show I just witnessed that's left me feeling needy myself. I don't wait for the water to warm up; I strip out of my clothes, piling them in the corner and step underneath the cold water. He was thinking of me while he was touching himself. Saint, my brother's best friend, someone I believed to only see me as a little sister, was masturbating to the thought of me. I was wrong for staying and watching, but is he wrong for thinking of me in such a way? Does he think of me as someone more than his friend's sister? Do I think of him differently?

*Sage, no, that's impossible.* There's no freaking way that would ever work in the first place due to his friendship with my brother. Saxon would never allow that. Plus, it could have just been an accident. He said my name, right? He might have meant to say someone else's, or maybe it's a different Sage he knows. Fuck, I need a drink after today. I can't stop my mind from racing in all different directions, and quite frankly, I'm giving myself a headache. I'm stepping from foot to foot in the shower, realizing I'm now shivering from the freezing water. I quickly decide to turn the water to a warmer temperature and let out a sigh as the warm water sprays against my skin. I to try to halt the sensations building between my legs at the sight of Saint. I need to reel it in and stop this before it turns into anything further. I push away anymore thoughts of Saint and start washing my hair and then my body.

When I'm sure all thoughts of the impossible have left my mind, I finish my shower. Stepping out, I wrap my towel around myself and fetch the second towel to dry my hair. It hasn't dawned on me that I've already washed my hair today until now. Rolling my eyes at myself for letting Saint fluster me so, I leave my bathroom and step into my room.

"Thanks for bringing me my towel." I about jump out of my skin when I'm met with a half-naked Saint sitting on the end of my bed, wearing nothing but his dark gray sweatpants. His hair is still wet from his shower, and the way he's leaning forward with his forearms resting on his thighs has his back muscles on full display.

"Saint, what the hell are you doing in here? Leave, I'm naked! Can't you see?" I clutch the towel around my chest as I curl in on myself from his gaze on me. Giving me his devious smirk, he stands and takes two long strides towards me until he's standing right in front of me. I have to crane my neck to look up at his face. Fuck men who use their height as an advantage.

"I was just coming to say thanks. How was I supposed to know you were in the shower? Unless I was spying on you or something, right? That would be an invasion of your privacy though. I would never do such a thing." He then glides his thumb across my jaw, making me shiver. What is he insinuating? Did he catch me spying on him? Fuck, I've been found out.

"Your brother's ordering pizza, if you want any." Dropping his hand, he turns on his heels and heads towards my door, but not before turning back around and giving me a crooked smile. "Next time you can join me, if you'd like." Closing the door softly, he leaves me utterly speechless as the embarrassment of being caught heats my cheeks.

# SAINT

# CHAPTER 16

## SAINT

Saxon is going on about something, but I've stopped listening as the thought of Sage catching me in the shower fills my head with so many unanswered questions. How much did she see? Was she watching on purpose, or did she accidentally catch a glimpse while bringing me my towel? What was I thinking, seeking her out in her room? What was my plan? Was I going to flat out ask her if she was spying on me? Then she comes out in a towel, and it's like all my thoughts evaporated from my brain. Her toned legs were a sight to see as the bottom of her towel just barely covered her. All I wanted to do was follow the droplet of water that trailed down her neck and slid beneath her towel. What the fuck was I thinking?

"Saint, are you even fucking listening? This is serious, man. Tell me what she knows. Did she see anything?" Saxon's voice draws me out of the mental fog involving his sister in a way I definitely shouldn't be thinking about. I brush my hair back with my hands and over my face before looking up to respond.

"She said she saw two shadows toss what she thought was a body over the ledge into the water. When I asked her if she was sure, she fumbled over her words and thought maybe she was seeing things. We're okay, man. Stop stressing." He rolls his eyes at me, not convinced we're in the clear.

"She can't find out—she's not to know about the inner workings of the club. I can't imagine what she would think if she truly knew the depths of what we do to eliminate the threats against the club. We're not good people, Saint. Murder, torture, gun running—I can see her face now if she found out. Luther was her hero, and she never knew how truly brutal that man could be to his enemies. I never want her to think anything less of him."

"What exactly does she think we do with the club?" I ask, never actually knowing what he's divulged to her about what her family's created with the club.

"I've told her we provide people with the resources they need to accomplish the tasks they've been handed." I let out a scoff of a laugh.

"Cryptic," I respond. He nods, a menacing smile pulling the corner of his mouth before it disappears just as quickly as it came. Letting out a long sigh, he continues. "She's been through enough in her life. She doesn't need to be constantly worried about us."

"Us?" I question him, giving him a sly smile, knowing damn well he knows the love, hate relationship between me and his sister. Letting out a chuckle, he eyes me.

"Yes, dumbass. She cares about you too. As much as the pair of you pretend to hate one another, I know she sees you as a brother figure too." The doorbell rings, alerting us the pizza has arrived. Thank fuck cause I'm starving. Saxon leaves the kitchen and heads to the door to retrieve our dinner. I mull over his words. Sage does care about me, it's obvious. She and I go way back, and he's right, we do have a close bond, but does she see me as a brother or something more? Would she ever admit it to herself if she does have stronger feelings for me? Would I?

Before my brain explodes from the constant inner turmoil I'm creating for myself, Saxon returns with pizza in hand. I stand from my barstool and grab three plates for us. Footsteps filter in through the kitchen as I hear Sage making her way down the stairs. This ought to be an interesting dinner.

"Hey, sis. Pizza's here. Grab a plate." Sage does so without saying a word. The smile she gives her brother is warm and inviting, and I can't help watching her as she grabs her plate and dishes out a slice of extra cheesy pizza for herself. Her long blond hair is still wet, dampening her oversized sweatshirt that's swallowing her completely. She looks so small right now. She licks her bottom lip as she drops the pizza on her plate. This small gesture makes the bulge in my pants grow. I can't remember when my feelings for her went from being innocent to this, whatever this is. This isn't good. I can't be the one who falls for my best friend's little sister. It's so wrong.

Just then, a pair of bright silver eyes meet mine. I hold her gaze, a silent conversation being spoken between us. A light shade of red dusts her cheeks. Her mouth opens and closes as if she can't say what she truly wants to. She's so cute when she's flustered.

"Come on, let's finish watching that *Saw* movie." Saxon leaves us in the kitchen, assuming I'm going to follow behind him. But instead of immediately following him, I make my way over to her. I lean my back on the island while she's still facing her plate. She doesn't look at me. She continues peering down at her food as if she's too nervous to turn towards me. She smells so delicious, like vanilla and strawberries. The perfect dessert flavors. I lean into her, my lips right at her ear, and whisper, "I won't tell your brother you watched me in the shower." Her whole body stiffens before she turns toward me, fire now burning in her eyes.

"And I won't tell him you came into my room while I was in my towel." I give her a chuckle before pushing her hair back from her shoulder. "Do I make you nervous?" My voice is still a whisper. Her eyes narrow on me. The feisty and sassy Sage is out to play tonight, and it does something to me. She's about to say something hateful by the expression she's wearing, but suddenly her demeanor changes.

She shifts closer to me, her body now completely pressed against my side. I can feel her warmth even beneath her obnoxiously large hoodie. With a delicate hand, she threads her fingers through my slightly damp hair, scratching my scalp just enough to give me goosebumps. Standing on her tiptoes, she presses the side of her face to mine, her lips brushing my ear.

"No more nervous than I'm making you right now. We're playing with fire, Saint. If we're not careful, we'll both get burned." She gives me a kiss on my cheek before grabbing her plate and leaving me utterly speechless in the kitchen. She's right. Fuck, is she right. This "thing" we're creating between us is more than dangerous, it's straight up inappropriate. Again, I can't help thinking, what would Saxon say?

Letting out an exasperated breath, I head to the living room where Saxon has already started watching *Saw VI*.

"These movies are so crazy. Ugh, seriously, whoever made them needs to see a therapist. They can't be right in the head." Sage is wincing as she looks away from the screen. I take a seat beside Saxon, who loves horror movies so much it might be concerning to some. I've never seen the guy watch anything besides a horror film. I can't say I hate them either. I personally like watching horror films over any other genre. We all sit and watch the film as Sage adds her commentary throughout.

Having finished eating, I lean back further into the couch, but my eyes keep betraying me by wandering over to where Sage is sitting. She's on the opposite couch, her knees drawn into herself while she clutches a throw pillow. Her eyes are locked onto the screen as the torture device called The Shotgun Carousel begins spinning around with its victims tied to the metal poles. I have to say the creativity in these movies is top tier.

I watch Sage as her eyes look like they're going to bug out of her head. Her reactions to all these torture devices are how most people react to such horrors. Then it dawns on me: Sage is so innocent. So innocent in the sense that if she knew the true inner workings of the club, she would be horrified. The lives we've taken, the families we've destroyed, the people we've tortured, and so, so much more. This is what Saxon was talking about; she can't know the truth about us. About me. What would she do? How would she feel? My stomach churns at the thought of her hating me, or even Saxon, for doing what's necessary to keep us all safe. What we do can be considered over the top and illegal, obviously, but the pair of us have been doing fucked up shit for so long we've become desensitized to it. I think back to all the guys I've hurt and tortured simply because they said the wrong thing to Sage, or broke her heart, or dumped her for not having sex with them. My latest victim, Seb, wasn't even a full month ago.

My eyes lower to the shag carpet in front of me. Do I regret the things I've done? No. Would I do them again? Yes. Why? Because no one, and I mean *no one*, hurts Sage and gets away with it. She is the light that this world needs, that I need. I will prevent anyone from trying to snuff her out, even if that means eliminating every one of them. Saxon is right. She can't know what we've been up to these past few years. Can't say we're going to stop either, not until the mission is complete. Not until everyone that was involved is dead.

Saxon's phone vibrates in his pocket. When he pulls it out, I see the expression on his face go from neutral to pissed in 0.4 seconds flat—a new record. He lets out a deep sigh before pocketing his cell and standing from the couch.

"I'll be back later. Don't wait up." He extends his arm for mine and gives me a slap on my hand before side stepping between me and the coffee table to give Sage a kiss on the cheek.

"Need me to tag along?" I ask, but deep down, I'm not wanting to leave.

"Nah, man. It's just that bullshit, ya know." He means Sky. The two of them have what some call a toxic relationship, constantly bickering or arguing over stupid shit. I see why Saxon gets so annoyed, but then I wonder why he stays.

"You mind staying here tonight? Keep an eye on things just in case I get held up?" A scoff from the couch draws my attention to Sage; her eyes are narrowed on Sax.

"I don't need a babysitter, Sax. Jesus, I'm twenty-one. When are you going to realize I'm an adult?" Shaking his head, he turns back to her.

"It's more for my peace of mind, knowing you're safe, sis. That's all." Exiting the living room, his boots echo across the tile floor before opening the front door and closing it softly behind him. Sage and I look at each other at the same moment the lock clicks on the door, and I can't help the smirk that spreads across my face.

"Just you and me, witch stick. Just you and me," I practically purr out, only getting me an eye roll from her before she turns back to the movie.

"Fantastic," she says on an exhale.

SAGE

# CHAPTER 17

## SAGE

Why am I being tested? What have I done in my life to continuously be put in these situations with Saint? Situations that have become increasingly tense, and, dare I say, sexually frustrating. I love Saint, yes. He has been a part of my family for as long as I can remember. He's been here for me and Saxon after the fire and has always been another brother figure for me. He's someone who would protect me without any hesitation. We've always just... been. I don't know how to explain it further. But recently, the bond between us has become blurred and has started to morph into something... dangerous. When I saw Saint in the shower, a burning sensation exploded in my core, climbing up my spine and leaving my head feeling dizzy. I have never, and I mean never, felt anything greater for Saint in a lust filled way, however, my body is suddenly betraying me.

As we sit here in silence, watching the remainder of this insanely disturbing movie, the tension between us becomes palpable. Whether he feels it too, I don't know. I'm constantly stealing glimpses of him from the corner of my eye, and I can't help but feel the heat of his gaze on me as well. Saint has this presence about him, an electrical charge that has my senses on high alert. He dominates a room just by being in it. I can't help but feel this pull towards him recently, and I don't know if I will be able to stop it. Especially if he keeps acting the way he's been acting towards me. It's clear he's noticed a shift between us as well, if his constant hovering and need to invade my personal space is anything to go by. I can't say that I hate it. He's intoxicating —his scent, his stature, his animalistic eye color. I become hypnotized when he looks at me like I'm his prey.

Suddenly, a loud crash has me jumping out of my skin and whipping my head towards the window where it came from. It all happens so fast. One minute, I'm daydreaming about Saint, and the next, he's wrapped his arms around my waist and tosses me over his shoulder like a sack of potatoes.

"Saint, what are you doing? Put me down!" I say as I try to crane my neck to get a better look at the window where the noise came from.

"Get to the secret room in the office. Shut the painting door behind you and stay quiet," he whispers to me as he places me back on my feet.

"But wha—"

"Now, Sage. Don't argue, just listen." Giving me one last stern look, he retrieves his pistol from the back of his waistband and pulls the receiver back, racking a bullet in the chamber. Another sound has my attention shooting to the front door. Saint places his finger over his lips to tell me to be quiet and then points to the office door. I waste no more time; I turn and hurry down the hallway. Heading for the large painting called *The Execution of Lady Jane Gray*, I grab the corner of the artwork and hit the concealed latch that allows me to swing the frame open, revealing a secret room. I look over my shoulder towards the hallway, wondering if I should do as he says or help him. What was that noise? I can't just leave Saint alone to fend for himself. What if there's more than one person? He'll be outnumbered.

I close the painting and grab the small pistol I know is attached underneath Saxon's desk. Saint is going to be livid, but I'd rather do something than cower behind one of the most haunting paintings I know. Lady Jane was only seventeen when she was executed, surrounded by her ladies-in-waiting. The executioner, before performing his duties, asked for forgiveness from Lady Jane, which she gladly bestowed. Once blindfolded, she was then unable to find the chopping block displayed in the painting. She was searching for the block on which her head would be decapitated. It's eerie to look at and heartbreaking that she was so strong and young.

I tiptoe to the hallway and peer around the doorframe—it's empty. I continue down the hall until I reach the foyer and press my body against the wall to try to conceal myself. Still, I hear nothing.

"Saint?" I whisper but get no response. I stay in the shadows, not allowing my body to be exposed by the lights we have on while I creep to the kitchen. It's eerily quiet; I can hear my heart beating. Just as I'm about to head to the living room, a faint groan comes from the sliding back door. I freeze. Another grunt, then it dawns on me: it sounds like people fighting—a struggle of some sort. I squint my eyes, trying to see out of the glass, but can only see the reflection of the kitchen. I head for the lights and flip them off. To my horror, I see Saint wrestling with not one, but two men at the back of the house.

Without thinking, I run for the door, sliding the glass open and pointing my gun at the chaos in front of me.

"Stop, or I'll shoot!" My hands are trembling, because

not only am I pointing the gun at the intruders, but Saint is in the mix-up too. I watch as Saint lands blow after blow to both men, as if he's enjoying a leisurely workout sparing with his buddies. The moment the men see me standing, they notice my gun and run. Both men make a dash for the wood line, Saint chasing behind.

"Saint!" I call to him, not wanting him to go in there alone. He freezes at the sound of my voice. We watch as the two men disappear from view and seemingly vanish beyond the trees. I watch Saint's back rise and fall as he begins to steady his breathing. With his back towards me still, he pulls out his phone and shoots off a text before pocketing it again. He then turns towards me with a look of pure rage and disbelief plastered across his face. It's then I realize just how much trouble I'm really in. Fuck.

SAINT

# CHAPTER 18

## SAINT

What the fuck is she doing? I gave her strict orders to go to the secret room and wait for me there. Did she listen? Of course not. That would be too easy. Instead, she's standing on the back patio with a gun in hand, looking at me like a deer in the headlights.

"What the fuck did I tell you to do, Sage?" My tone is murderous, and all I want to do is strangle her for not listening to me. I slowly make my way up the patio to stand in front of her.

"You're bleeding," she whispers, her eyes wide and still in shock at seeing me fight two fucking thugs who thought they could rob the house. Wrong fucking house. I lift my hand, wipe at my nose, and peer down at my hand.

"It's nothing. Just a moment of weakness where one of them got a punch in. I'll survive." Rolling her eyes at me, she grabs my hand and pulls me back into the house, closing the sliding door and locking it behind us. She pulls me to the island and tells me to stay put while she fishes out the first aid kit that's in one of the cabinets. I head for the alarm system that's on the side wall and check to see if everything is still armed—it's not. When I ran outside, it sent a silent alarm to the security company.

"This is Home Security Protection. What's your emergency?" a calm woman says over the intercom.

"My mistake, I didn't turn off the alarm before taking out the trash," I say back to her.

"Can I get your security passphrase please?"

"Witch stick," I respond again, looking at Sage, who is shaking her head and trying to conceal the smile that's threatening to show. It was my idea when Saxon got this new security system for the passphrase. In the middle of setting it up, Frankie asked us, "Where is witch stick?" and that's what we landed on. It's easy to remember and honestly hilarious when you know the concept behind it.

"Thank you, Mr. Wilder. Have a great night." The woman from the security system says before ending our brief conversation. I don't correct her when she calls me Mr. Wilder; she probably assumed it was Saxon talking, anyway.

I turn the system back on and head back over to the island.

"I thought you guys were going to change that stupid passphrase." She scowls at me while rummaging through the first aid kit and grabbing gauze and antiseptic ointment.

"Yeah, well, why change something that works?" I say, pulling out one of the barstools and taking a seat. Fuck, I haven't fought like that in a while, and the ache in my ribs tells me I will be feeling every punch they landed tomorrow.

"Who the hell were those guys?" she asks me, gently wiping away at my blood, one gauze piece at a time. I shake my head at her.

"Probably two thugs who thought they could rob us but

didn't know who actually lives here. Bad move on their part." I close my eyes as she starts putting a wet gauze over my nose, stinging my skin. "Which reminds me, why didn't you listen to me? You could have gotten hurt." I say to her in my stern tone.

"I couldn't just let you get hurt without helping." Her voice is small. "But by the looks of how scared those two were, you handled yourself okay." I laugh at her last comment.

"I handled it just, okay? If I would have had more time, I could have ended both of them with my hands. You don't give me enough credit, witch stick." She swats at my thigh before closing the first aid kit and leveling me with one of her looks. That intoxicating fucking look that goes straight to my soul and makes my cock want to escape from my sweats.

"I'm saying that I couldn't just let you do that alone. I wouldn't forgive myself if something were to happen to you while I was hiding in the closet." Her face softens and her eyes remain fixed on mine.

"So, you're saying you love me now?" I tease, winning me another slap to my thigh as she turns to put away the kit. With her back towards me, she stands on her tiptoes to put the kit away.

"I'm saying that you're important, Saint, and I don't want anything happening to you." She doesn't turn around right away, her back to me as she lowers her head slightly. A small sigh escapes her throat. I stand from my chair and step up behind her. Again, her smell of vanilla and strawberries fills my nose, and I inhale deeply. She takes a deep breath, aware of my proximity.

"You're important, Sage, and I will never let anything happen to you," I say on a breath, noticing the sharp inhale she takes before finally turning around to face me. We stare at one another, the color of her eyes, so similar to mine, drawing me closer to her. She doesn't step away; instead, she raises her hands, placing them on my chest.

"Saint, I don't know what's changed between us, and I don't think Saxon would be very happy."

I brush a loose strand of her now dry hair behind her ear, resting my fingers on her jaw.

"I don't know, but I'm not going to pretend to hate this feeling either." Her eyes close for a long moment. A frenzy of mixed emotions swirling through her mind. I rub my thumb down her cheek a few times, and with a slight adjustment of her face, she presses into my touch.

*Don't do this, Saint. This isn't right. This is your best friend's sister.*

My brain is screaming at me to walk away, to forget these feelings and pull back. But my heart is pulling me towards her. I'm drawn to her. Ever since watching her dance with the punk in the club, all I've wanted to do was tell her I'm the only one allowed to touch her from now on. I want her—body, mind, and soul. I've been confused about these emotions building in my chest ever since she was in high school, and I realize now what my body is trying to tell me. It wants her, all of her, and only her.

"Tell me to stop if you don't want this," I whisper to her, our lips so close I can feel her warmth radiating off her face. Opening her eyes, she sees how close I am.

"Saint." Just one word, my name. A whisper on her tongue, and I can't stop myself. I crash my lips onto hers in a frenzy of desire, and I can't stop. My hands reach around, grabbing her thighs and hoisting her up towards me. She wraps her legs around my waist as I turn to sit her on the counter. Her soft lips open to mine, and the taste of her on my tongue has me feeling out of control. An animal that's finally been set loose. I grab her face in my hands, deepening our kiss even more as I grind my now rapidly growing cock against her. The clothes between us suddenly feel like a prison, restricting me from getting what I want. A barrier I will demolish.

She pulls at my waistband, her fingers dipping below the fabric. My abdomen tenses, my skin igniting from her touch. She pulls away from our kiss, her forehead resting on mine as we both try to catch our breath.

"This is crazy," she says breathlessly.

"I happen to like crazy." I step back and pull my shirt over my head in one quick motion. I don't miss the sudden jump in her eyes as she stares at my chest, every inch covered in elaborate ink. Soft fingers touch my collarbone and slide down my skin to my abs. My body reacts to her touch, flexing every muscle she caresses. Her fingers leave a trail of embers, burning and marking me as she explores my body.

Silver eyes reach mine.

"Why now, after all these years?" she asks. I give her a small smile as my hands run up the outside of her thighs and wrap around her small waist.

"It's always been you." I pick her up again and carry her to my room. I'm tired of acting like this is nothing more than a brother-sister bond. We've been harboring our feelings from one another, and now that I know where she stands, I won't hold back. We'll figure this shit out with Saxon later, but for now, Sage is mine.

# SAGE

# CHAPTER 19

**SAGE**

*What the fuck are you doing, Sage?*

You know that little voice in your head you're told to listen to and always trust? Well, my little voice is currently berating me, yet I continue to ignore it. Saint tastes too good, like cinnamon toothpaste. I can't stop devouring his mouth as his hands squeeze my waist like a man capturing his prey. He carries me to his room, kicking open the door and then kicking it shut behind him. His lips haven't left mine, as our tongues continue exploring each other. Setting me gently on the bed, he turns around to hit the lock on his door, just in case, before looking at me with heat in his eyes.

"Take your sweatshirt off," he demands, his voice gruff as he stalks back towards me. I do as he says, grabbing the hem and pulling it over my head. To his surprise, I'm bare underneath. I sit on his bed with nothing but my sleep shorts on, staring up at a man I've known all my life yet feels as though I'm just now seeing.

"Fuck, you're perfect." Our lips find each other again as

the bed dips around me. His warm chest covers mine as he directs us further on the bed. His large hands wrap around my wrists, and he holds them above my head. Saint's ability to kiss is indescribable. It's rough but gentle, fast but also slow, controlling yet submissive. He pulls away from me, his mouth making its way down my neck and across my collarbone. I arch into his touch, needing more, needing so much more.

"Greedy little thing, aren't we?" he growls out, his mouth now reaching my breast as he covers my nipple with his soft mouth. A moan slips past my lips as he sucks and pulls at my nipple, making the pulsing between my legs grow stronger. I rub my thighs together, desperate to create more friction. I'm so focused on his mouth on my breast that when one of his hands cups my pussy, I flinch into his touch.

"Do you want me to touch here?"

"Yes, oh God, yes." I sound so pathetic, but he's worked me into a frenzy. My body is dying for a release. Lifting his head, he watches me with a sly smile on his face as he directs his hand beneath my sleep shorts. When his fingers dip between my wet folds, he growls a deep moan that vibrates through his chest.

"Look how your body responds to me. Already so wet for me." He sinks a finger inside me, and I can't help but grind against his hand, needing him desperately. He watches me as I melt into his touch, my mouth parting as he inserts a second finger.

"Like that?" he asks, but I can't speak. I nod my head, my core aching for more, needing to reach a release. Three fingers slip inside me, and I let out a moan of pleasure as he works his hand in and out of me, but when his thumb presses on my clit, I see stars.

"Fuck, Saint. Please, please," I whine, needing to be filled, needing his warmth against me, inside me.

"Tell me what you need, Sage."

"I need you, please." I'm begging at this point. My body is wound so tight I feel like I'm going to erupt and not in a good way.

"As you wish." His hand leaves my most sensitive spot, leaving me cold and shocked by the sudden absence of his touch. Sitting up on his knees, he makes quick work of his sweats and then his boxers. Freeing himself as his cock stands at attention. I can't help but gape at his size. He must have been hurting from the strain of his boxers holding him prisoner.

He grabs my sleep shorts and rips them down my legs. Spreading my legs for him, he then grabs his cock with his hand, giving himself a few long strokes. I watch him as he works himself up like he did in the shower.

"I admit it—I was watching you in the shower," I say to him, his eyes darkening with mischief as he leans over me, lining himself up with my entrance.

"Such a bad girl you are." The sultriness of his voice is unlike anything I've ever heard. So smooth, yet dark at the same time. He makes it hard to breathe, my breath getting caught in my throat as my body forgets how to function.

"I've wanted to do this for the longest time. I'm going to enjoy every fucking minute of seeing you fall apart for me." Just then, he swipes his cock between my folds a few times, coating himself in my arousal. As if he sees how much he's teasing me, he finally pushes himself inside. My walls stretch and adjust to his size, shooting a sharp pain through my core that quickly morphs into the most delicious pleasure I've ever felt. As he continues pushing himself deeper and deeper, he lets out a groan followed by curses I can't understand. Just when I think he's going to be too much for me, he thrusts himself in fully so he's completely seated inside me. Our hips press together like two puzzle pieces clicking in place. A squeal leaves my lips at the over-whelming pleasure.

"You okay, baby?" His voice is breathy.

"Yes, please don't stop." His chuckle fills the room at my plea.

"Wasn't going to." He pulls out just a bit before thrusting in once again, this time a little harder. Again and again, he does this, increasing his intensity with each bruising thrust. I look up at him, his eyes still on mine as he watches me chase my orgasm that's slowly building.

"Don't come yet," he demands. He grabs my throat and squeezes his fingers around my delicate skin. I almost lose it right then. I wrap my hand around his wrist, desperate to hold on to something as his thrusts get faster and harder, the sound of our skin slapping together fills the room.

"Saint, I'm about to—" He cuts me off.

"Not yet. Look at me." I do as he says, trying to hold off, but I know I won't be able to for long. His fingers squeeze a little harder around my neck, not cutting off my airway but making it harder to inhale a proper breath. Just when I'm about to lose it, his hands squeeze even tighter, my eyes closing on their own.

"Come for me, baby. Come for me now—" He doesn't even finish his sentence. I completely fall apart. His hand releases my throat, and I'm free-falling into a euphoric paradise that fills my entire being from my feet to my neck. Pleasure explodes in every crevice of my soul. I never want this feeling to stop; I never want to leave this world of ecstasy we've created. This pleasure is unlike any I've ever experienced with another person, almost magical in how perfectly we fit against each other. It's powerful enough to become addictive and make you do anything to feel even just a second of this bliss.

It's at this moment I know I've fucked up. I've given myself to the one man that's forbidden to me, and I want to do it again and again and again. What have we done? A few thrusts more and Saint finds his release as well. A deep, gruff moan leaves his throat as he empties himself inside me. I have an IUD, so I'm not worried, but I'm sure he doesn't know about my form of birth control. What if I didn't have one, or the pills, would he still have come inside me?

"Fuck, Sage. Your pussy was made for me." Collapsing on the bed beside me, he folds an arm behind his head while his other hand finds my thigh. As he rubs his long fingers up and down my sensitive skin, I turn my face towards his. His eyes are closed, and his face is neutral as he comes down from his own high. I don't know why, but I roll towards him, wrapping my arm around his chest and lay my thigh across his waist. His arm wraps around my body, holding me close to his. We stay like this, just him and me, soaking in this moment I thought would never happen in a million years. The moment that never should have happened, but here we are. The soft touch of his fingers gliding across my back has my eyes closing and lulling me into the place between asleep and awake. I'm content, safe, and at peace in this moment, and I wonder if he feels the same.

Just as I'm about to open my mouth and ask, the sound of the front door opening has the both of us sitting straight up and staring at the bedroom door.

"Saint? You awake, man?" Fuck, it's Saxon. I jump out of Saint's bed, grabbing my clothes and darting to his bathroom. Saint fumbles with his boxers and sweats, pulling them over his hips.

"Yeah, I'm up. Once sec." I scramble to get my clothes on but stay put in the bathroom. How am I going to get out of here? Saint peers at me around the door, putting his finger over his lips, telling me to be quiet.

"I'll handle this. You stay here and don't come out." I

nod a few times, panic enveloping my chest, where a tight-ness builds with anxiety.

I hear Saint make his way to his door, unlocking and pulling it open. I peer through the crack in the door and watch as Saxon walks right in, sitting on the corner of Saint's bed as he leans over, resting his elbows on his knees.

"I'm sorry it took so long. Shit got complicated. Now tell me everything that happened. Could she see who the guys were?" I was momentarily confused by his question. Then it dawned on me, the incident with the two guys who tried to break in. Shit, how could I have forgotten?

I waited in the bathroom as Saint walked Saxon through the incident, informing him he couldn't see who they were due to the masks they were wearing.

"Where's Sage? Is she shaken up about the whole thing?" Oh, I was shaken up alright, but not about the almost robbers.

He didn't answer. I caught Saint through the crack, looking at me, a look of guilt passing across his face at having to lie to his best friend. Saxon let out a long sigh.

"Fuck, man. You don't think this has to do with the guy we tossed in the quarry, do you?" What the hell did he just say? Did he just admit he and Saint were the ones I saw that night? No, this is a joke; they wouldn't do something like that. Would they? My blood starts running hot, anger coursing through my veins. And without thinking, I step into the room, leveling my brother and Saint with a look of pure rage.

"What the fuck did you just say?"

SAGE

# CHAPTER 20

## SAGE

The look of shock and guilt of being caught floods Saxon's system. He looks from me to Saint, his brain working overtime, trying to decipher what the hell is going on. It takes him a few seconds, but when he shoots up from where he sits and turns to face me. I know I've just fucked up.

"Sage, what the hell are you doing in Saint's bathroom?" His tone is laced with death—my skin prickles at the coldness of his tone. But I don't falter.

"No, Sax. I asked you what the hell did you just say? It was the two of you at the quarry, wasn't it?" He doesn't move. Hell, he doesn't even look like he's breathing, but his eyes give him away.

"I'm going to ask you one more time. Why are you in that bathroom?" I'm trying to think quickly without giving away the slightest bit of fear, when an idea hits me.

"Jesus, Sax. I was using his toothpaste. I ran out in my bathroom, and he said I could come use his. Fuck, what did you think I was doing?" *Keep cool, Sage. Hold your ground and don't lose eye contact. Diverting your eyes is the first sign of lying.* We both stay like that, holding each other's stare before the crease between Saxon's eyebrows begins to smooth out.

"Right," he says, turning his head to Saint to give him a weary look. "Could have warned me she was in here," he whispers to him, obviously not wanting me to hear, but I do anyway.

"Now, what the fuck did you two do?" I finally look at Saint, whose face is unreadable. Saxon lets out a long, exasperated sigh before brushing his hands through his hair.

"Let's go into the kitchen. You might want to sit down for this, sis." He leaves the room without giving me another look. Saint and I stare at one another for a long moment, the realization of what we just did hitting me like a fucking sixteen-wheeler as guilt fills me up. I can't decipher his expression, so I head for his door, but a hand grabs my arm, stopping me.

"I'm not sorry—I don't regret what we did tonight. And I'll do it again." He drops my arm and steps in front of me, heading to the kitchen and leaving me so confused yet so turned on all at once.

*What have I gotten myself into?*

I gather my composure before exiting Saint's room and head into the kitchen, finding Saint already sitting at the island while Saxon has grabbed a Corona from the fridge, already having downed half of the contents. Clearly, he wasn't expecting to have this conversation tonight. I make my way to the island and sit at the barstool beside Saint. I can't help wanting to be close to him, his pull on me suddenly so strong I can't ignore it.

"Right, tell me everything. Don't leave anything out. What were you doing at the quarry, and who was that guy?" I ask flat out, needing answers to whatever mess they've found themselves in. The pair give each other a look before Saxon settles his gaze on me.

"Before we tell you, sis, you need to promise you'll stay out of it and let us handle what needs to be handled."

"What the hell do you mean, Sax? Just tell me what's going on!" My tone is louder than I intended it to be, but I'm getting frustrated by the stalling.

"For the past couple of years, Saint and I have been doing some digging on the fire." Well, that's not what I expected him to say, yet I don't know what I was expecting at all. I don't say a word, just let him continue to explain.

"We received a tip a while back that suggested the fire was not an accident but was intentional." My hand covers my mouth. All this time, I had never believed the fire to be an accident. I've had a feeling in my gut ever since the day I got out of the hospital that something, or *someone*, started it.

"What was the tip?" My voice is low as I try to keep the sting of threatening tears at bay.

"We were told, by a very reliable source, that a member of the Hellstorms was paid to set the fire and make it look like an accident."

"Wait, the Hellstorms? As in Skylar's family's motor-cycle club?" I look from Saxon to Saint, but it's Saxon who nods once to my question.

"So, Sky told you that her family's club killed our father and almost killed me?!" I was yelling at this point. "Your girlfriend, or whatever you call her, ratted on her own family to you? I don't believe it. What does she have to gain by doing that? If her family knew she ratted, they would kill her! Does she realize that?" I am so confused I want to scream; no way is this true—it can't be.

"Her father had planned to marry her off to a disgusting excuse of a man. His goal was to expand their club by combining with another northern club. Sky wanted nothing to do with the guy. Apparently, he's an abusive piece of shit and has already been married twice. However, both of his previous wives have died under mysterious circumstances. That's why she fled here two years ago, seemingly out of nowhere."

That's right; it has been two years since Sky showed up in Golden Heights. One day she had just started working at the club, and I never asked where she came from or what brought her here. She was so nice, and we connected immediately. So did the other girls—Ophelia, Bristol, and Frieda. It never crossed my mind that she was running from anyone. She's so confident and social, and not once has she ever seemed scared. As if Saxon can see the wheels turning in my head, he continues, "After she'd been here for about a year, we ran into each other at the club. We talked, and I got to know her more. Then she started receiving threatening texts whenever I was with her. She always said it was nothing until the threats turned into someone physically stalking her. I pressed her about what the hell was going on, and she finally admitted who she was. It wasn't until she realized I was Saxon *Wilder* that she started asking me about the fire. I thought it was suspicious that she even knew about the fire, since I'd never told her. I was wary of trusting her and distanced myself, but she was insistent that she was no longer affiliated with her family and admitted that she ran away. To prove she wasn't a part of the Hellstorms anymore, she told me it was a couple of thugs from her father's club that were hired to set the fire." He paused for a long moment, finishing his beer and grabbing another one.

Saxon looked rough—he has dark rings under his eyes like he hasn't slept in days, and his whole demeanor is off. The calm and stoic Saxon currently looks like he is battling a war within himself and his opponent is winning.

"Listen, Sage, the next bit I'm about to tell you, you

have to realize I did it all for our father and for you. Christ, you almost died from smoke inhalation, not to mention the physical scars you have." I give him a small nod, telling him to go on.

"Remember when Saint and I left for those few days last month for business?" I nod, looking from Saxon to Saint and back to Saxon.

"We were up north, interrogating the two guys from the Hellstorms who supposedly set the fire. We were informed that they were only hired to set the fire, they had no other affiliation at all. Hell, they said they didn't even know who was inside the house. So, someone else must have wanted Dad dead. We did what we had to do to get answers, but in the end, we had to eliminate them. Besides, they were the ones to physically kill Dad." I lean back into the barstool, allowing everything to sink in. My brother and Saint were the ones I saw throwing a man into the quarry.

How has it all come to this? Lies, secrets, murder. This is not what Father had in store for his club. He wouldn't want his son becoming a ruthless, murderous heathen without any remorse for human life, or so I thought. A sharp twinge of pain starts growing behind my eyes, and I rub my temple with my fingers to try and ease the pain.

"What was his name?" I don't know why I ask; it just comes out before I can think.

"What?" Saxon responds, confusion etched across his face at my question.

"The guy at the quarry—what was his name?" I repeat. Saxon and Saint exchange a look of confusion, likely wondering why his name matters. To be quite honest, I'm not sure why I want to know either.

"Damien Devonte. He gave the other two thugs the address of the house. He was the messenger of sorts. Another member in the long line of rats who were paid to set the fire." Saxon's voice is cold and emotionless as he speaks the name of the man he murdered. I don't respond. I don't know how to; I simply nod a few times, pushing his name to the back of my brain. The three of us remain quiet, not a sound but the hum of the refrigerator fills the kitchen. It is all so much. So much information in such a short amount of time, not to mention the tension vibrating between Saint and me. If it were possible for your brain to intake too much information at once and crash, mine was doing so at this moment.

"So, what do we do now?" I finally ask, not sure how all this information would lead us to discovering my father's murderer. Saxon tosses his bottle in the recycling before turning back towards the pair of us.

"*We* aren't doing anything. You are not to get involved in any of this. Do you understand me? Shit, I shouldn't have told you this much." My jaw hits the countertop. Is he for real right now?

"Excuse me? After everything you just said, you expect me to not be involved? News flash, big brother, it was *our* father who died, not just yours. I'm involved whether you like it or not. You can't—" Saxon slams his hands on the countertop. The slap of his skin against granite is so loud I can't help the jump of my shoulders from the sudden noise.

"Damn it, Sage, you're not to be involved! You're to focus on school, friends, and your plans to open up the custom paint shop, but from here on out, you are to act as if this conversation never happened. You hear me?" My skin prickles at the scolding my brother is giving me. There is nothing I hate more than my brother yelling at me like I'm a child, especially in front of others. I can feel the heat radiating off Saint beside me, as my own heat floods my face from embarrassment. There is nothing left for me to say; when Saxon is in his mood, his word is final. I nod a few quick times before he lets out a sigh and leaves me and Saint in the kitchen.

I can't look at Saint—the sting of unshed tears fills my eyes, and I can't bear him seeing me cry. I'm not one to cry, but whenever Saxon yells at me like that, I feel like a burden. His problem that I was never supposed to be. I know big brothers are supposed to protect their little sisters, but since Dad died, I feel like Saxon has been more of a fatherly figure towards me, and I can see the stress it causes him. I never want to disappoint him or be the cause of his worry.

The slam of Saxon's bedroom door has me flinching another time as the loud slam filters down the stairs. I let my eyes close, trapping the tears from escaping at all.

"He loves you, Sage. That's why he doesn't want you involved. He can't bear losing you too." Saint's voice is full of empathy, soft, smooth, and caring, as his hand slides over my thigh and gives it a little squeeze. This gentle touch shouldn't feel so good. The heat of his palm and the tender squeeze of his hand tells me he's here with me and has my stomach twisting in a way that it shouldn't. Especially towards Saint.

I jump off the bar stool, averting my eyes from him as I make my way to the foyer and stairs.

"Um, I'm going to bed. Good night, Saint." I reach the foyer before I hear the scraping of a barstool against the tile floor. His footsteps come up behind me before a deep voice has me stopping with my hand on the railing.

"Sage." My name on his tongue has shivers traveling up my spine, his sultry voice making me hold my breath. I don't look back towards him. I just wait for whatever he has to say next.

"I had fun tonight." His voice is low, careful to not let it echo through the foyer. My lips part just slightly, unsure of what to say back.

*I had fun too, in so many ways we shouldn't have. I don't regret what we did, and I'm craving more,* is what I want to say, but we're already on thin ice, and I don't want to fall under and drown.

"Good night, Saint," I whisper back. I take the stairs two at a time before I reach the safety of my room and gently shut the door behind me. What have I done?

SAINT

# CHAPTER 21

### SAINT

It's been three days since the quarry, three days since the break in, and three days since Sage and I allowed ourselves to cross the invisible line of our lust. We haven't seen each other since that night, and I can only assume she's trying to avoid me. I can't say I blame her though; I've been doing the same. However, as much as I'm avoiding her, I can't escape the images of her beneath me as I pound into her over and over again. The sweet sounds of her moans, the softness of her skin, and the taste of her lips have my mind in a frenzy. I need more, so much more. She's the strongest drug there is, and one taste wasn't enough. I want to taste every inch of her skin. I want to be inside her, relishing in her warmth. Fuck, I need more of Sage Wilder.

I've been at the garage all morning, working with Owen and Brooks on a rebuild, but my mind has been anywhere but here.

"You're holding it crooked. Lift your end up a bit more,"

Owen grunts to Brooks as the pair of them try to align a front tire correctly for the axle to fit through.

"I'm holding my end up!" Brooks grunts back, frustration laced between each word. As the pair of them continued bickering, I'm finally able to thread the axle through, securing the tire properly in place.

"Are you two girls done yet?" I ask, standing from where I was crouched down and grabbing a hand towel to wipe away the grease coating my fingers.

"Yeah, yeah," Owen grumbles, wiping his hands on his jeans while giving Brooks a side-eyed glance.

"Hey, we don't claim them as girls. I know a girl or two that can change a motorcycle tire all by herself." A familiar voice filters into the garage, and I turn to see Sage and Ophelia strolling in, looking like they're off to a five-star restaurant.

"I'm pretty sure Sage did her own rebuild by herself. Isn't that right, Sage?" Ophelia elbows Sage, who hasn't looked at me since walking in.

"I mean, she's not wrong," Sage drawls, the pair of them giving Owen and Brooks a hard time. Sage is wearing black dress pants and a small white tank top that's exposing just a sliver of her abdomen and doing little to hide her breasts. A black blazer and heels give her an extra three inches. Her hair is down with loose waves that cascade down her back. Her makeup is subtle, but her mascara is dark, allowing her eyes to pop even more so than normal. Fuck, she is stunning. My cock starts painfully straining against my jeans. Where does she think she's going dressed like that?

"What's up, girls? Why are you two all dressed up?" Brooks asks. I look at Owen, but he is too taken aback by Ophelia—he hasn't picked his jaw up off the garage floor since they walked in. Unlike Sage, Ophelia is wearing a long white dress that reaches her ankles and has spaghetti straps that are holding on by a thread to support her breasts. Her dress has a slit that goes up her leg, exposing her thigh and black heels that lace up around her calf. Ophelia's hair is in a low messy bun, allowing several strands to frame her face. She's a beautiful girl, don't get me wrong, but to me, she's got nothing on Sage.

"An art exhibit. Sage got invited by a guy she met at the club; he gave her a plus one. Lucky me, right?" Ophelia claps her hands in quick succession in excitement, but my eyes stay on Sage. When she finally decides to look my way, her face wears an apologetic expression. Her red lips lift into a half smile before slightly parting.

"I needed to come by and grab the tickets I left in the office." She gestures to the garage office and begins walking towards the door. I don't hesitate. I follow close behind her. She smells of vanilla and strawberries, and I inhale a deep breath as we step through the doors. I close the office door behind me, harder than I should have, but I'm not too sure about this so-called art exhibit, or the man who invited her, for that matter.

"What's his name?" I ask her, my tone low and murderous at the thought of her dressing up for this man. Like hell am I letting her go out with a man I know nothing about. I'd seen Sage go on dates before, ever since we were kids. It never phased me. Well, okay, it did phase me, but not like it does now. Having had a taste of her has made my feelings for her more possessive by tenfold. There is a weird sensation in my chest that I'm unfamiliar with. Almost like a tightening squeeze that's bringing on the feeling of nausea, and I don't like it, not one bit.

"Whose name?" She's rummaging through the desk, looking for said tickets, but they're already burning a hole in my pocket. I found the tickets earlier today, and when I saw they were for tonight, I felt the need to hang on to them —for safekeeping, you know?

"Don't play dumb with me," I practically growl out. As

she continues searching through every drawer, I decide to grab her attention.

"Are you looking for these?" I pull the tickets from my pocket and hold them between us as I watch Sage's spine stiffen as she turns to face me. Extending her hand towards me, she cocks her head to the side and gives me a lazy look.

"Can I please have my tickets, Saint?"

"What's. His. Name?" I ask again, not handing over the tickets until I get my answer. She lets out a long sigh, dropping her hand to her side and admitting defeat.

"His name is Dante."

"Dante, what?"

"Dante Macari." I study her facial expression for a long moment. Her lips and cheeks are soft, but her eyes are shifty, as if she can't hold my stare for too long. Almost like a child when they know they've done something wrong and they can't look you in the eyes. I have so many more questions to ask her but don't want to sound crazier than I already feel. I need to know more about this Dante character. Where the exhibit is, how long it is going to be, are they doing anything after the show? I need to ask her all of this, but I don't.

I lift the tickets for her to grab, our fingers touching for a brief moment, but the shock that I feel the moment our skin touches, traveling from my fingers straight to my core, is unexplainable. Did she feel that too? Why, after all these years? Why has this invisible string between us suddenly appeared, pulling me closer and closer to her? She looks so different now. So grown up, so independent and capable, so painfully stunning, she could bring the King of England to his knees with just one look. I've been enamored with her since the first time I laid eyes on her but always kept my distance out of respect for Saxon. Now, I'm having the hardest time reining in my desire to claim her fully as my own.

"Be careful. If you need anything…" I don't finish my sentence; I just look down at the beautiful woman before me and pull open the door to let her out. She doesn't leave right away. She stares at me as if I'd just grown three extra heads.

"That's it? Just be careful? No 'Where's the exhibit at?' 'What's his social security number?' or 'When will you be back?'" Crossing her arms over her chest, she cocks her hip to the side, suspicion written all over her face.

"I don't need to ask you those questions to get my answers. I have his name. Now go and have fun." I give her a mischievous wink. All I need is his name, and I can find out who his third-grade teacher was, what his favorite color is, or what he ate for breakfast on January 21, 2003. I know my way around a computer, and she knows just as well as I do that I will know exactly who Dante Macari is before the end of the night.

Rolling her eyes at me, she steps up to me as I lean down, allowing her to give me a kiss on the check before exiting the office.

"Don't wait up for me." She throws me a wave over her shoulder before grabbing Ophelia's hand and practically dragging her away from Owen to her Audi. I chuckle to myself, watching as the girls get themselves situated in the car and zoom out of the parking lot. I hadn't noticed Owen and Brooks approaching my sides.

"What's the plan, big man?" Owen breaks my trance, and I turn to head back into the office and retrieve my laptop from my bag. I don't like using the office computer for these things; I need access to programs only the software on my laptop can give me.

"We're going to figure out just who this Dante Macari really is." Both Brooks and Owen give me devilish grins before Owen closes the office door behind him, flipping the lock on the top. Let's get to work.

SAGE

# CHAPTER 22

## SAGE

Leaving the garage, a sick sensation in my gut twists its way to my chest.

*I don't need to ask you those questions to get my answers. I have his name. Now go and have fun.*

I've known Saint for a long, long time, and this statement alone should mean nothing to the average person, but for Saint, this was a cryptic message. Driving down the road, I squeeze the steering wheel so hard my knuckles start turning white. The feeling of unease tenses my shoulders. I wouldn't put it past Saint to show up at the exhibit just to "check on me" as Saxon would say.

Saxon is out of town for the next three days doing God knows what. After learning about his and Saint's secret activities over the past couple of years, I'm nervous about what he is doing out of town. Plus, he took Finn with him, and everyone knows Finn is the silent friend, but he's the one you call when you need some sketchy shit done. Frankly, he scares me a bit, and I can't imagine what it must have been like for Frieda to grow up in the same house with him. With Saxon being gone, Saint is my unofficial, official babysitter, and it's left me on edge, especially because of what happened three days ago.

"What was up with Saint? I know he's always been protective of you, but he seemed different just then, don't you think?" Ophelia asks me as she adds another layer of her lipstick in the mirror. I haven't told a soul about Saint and me. She's my best friend, yes, but I can't take the chance of Saxon finding out through the grapevine.

"Ugh, Sax is out of town, and of course, he assigns Saint to babysit me. You know he takes his bromance with my brother seriously." She chuckles at my response, nodding a few times in agreement.

"You could say that again. He's almost worse than Sax at times, with how protective he is. Seems odd, doesn't it?" She doesn't let me respond before she continues on. "God, I can't imagine having Sax as my older brother, then having Saint as well. I would lose my damn mind." I let out a soft chuckle. If she only knew the truth.

I love my brother—hell, I love Saint too—and I can't express enough how grateful I am to have both of them care for me in the way they do. Always keeping me safe and watching out for me is everything my father would want, and for that, I thank them. On the other hand, I can't help feeling like I'm smothered or weighed down by their constant hovering. They're like two helicopter moms, not willing to let the wheel go enough for me to experience my own life. Being protective of someone you love is normal. Being protective to the point you hinder their ability to live their life to the fullest? Now, that's not normal.

I'm pulled from my thoughts when Ophelia cranks up her newest favorite band through the Bluetooth speakers. "Chokehold" by Sleep Token blares, and I can't help the smile she puts on my face as she sings along, gripping and waving her arms as if she's front row at their concert. Looking at my friend, I envy her carefree personality. She's always smiling and rarely does she ever show any emotion other than pure happiness. I want to bottle up her energy and carry it with me to use on my worst of days.

"Damn, his voice is like a squeeze to my heart! He sings with so much emotion it gives me chills! Am I right?!" she screams over the song to me, and I give her an agreeing smile. She's right. The lead singer has the most unique voice I've heard in a while, and I can't help but love their music as much as Ophelia.

We sing along as we continue to our destination, and we arrive more quickly than I expected. I guess having a mini concert on the way helped pass the time. I pull into an open parking spot across the street from where the art studio sits. We both do a quick makeup check before exiting the car and crossing the road to the entrance of the art exhibit. There's a small line at the door, but after a quick five minutes, we show our tickets to the gentleman and make our way inside.

Immediately, we are greeted by a server who offers us flutes of sparkling white wine that we take without hesitation. The room is full of attendees of all ages. The massive showroom is clean, with white walls displaying numerous pieces of art. The room is dimly lit, but each piece of art has a small light hanging above it, illuminating the piece beautifully. Soft piano music plays off in the distance, setting the mood, and I can't help but feel so at peace in this moment. Art, like books, is beautiful in the way that it shares emotions we are sometimes too scared to share with our voices. Authors, painters, and photographers experience their pain or happiness through their work, leaving it up to the viewer to interpret the true meaning behind each piece.

"Oh my gosh, this place is—" Ophelia's cut off by a familiar deep voice that flows like silk from behind us. We turn to see Dante in an all-black suit with a black button up beneath his jacket, but it's his eyes I can't help but stare at. I hadn't noticed in the club the other night, maybe because it was so dark, but his eyes are a deep shade of emerald. They are stunning. My father always said the eyes are the windows to the soul, and at this moment, I can't help but feel a sense of unease, but I quickly push down the unwanted feelings.

"A bit ostentatious." He finishes whatever Ophelia was about to say, but I don't think ostentatious was the word she was looking for.

"No, not at all! I was going to say alluring," Ophelia says quickly before she takes a sip of her wine.

"Sage, I'm so happy you made it. I've been looking forward to seeing you again." Dante leans in, giving me the smallest kiss on my cheek that makes my cheeks flush. He smells of dark spice and a hint of whiskey—it's delicious.

"Thank you so much for inviting me. This place is truly stunning. This is my friend, Ophelia. Ophelia, this is Dante Macari." I turn to Ophelia, who's staring at Dante like she's just seen her celebrity crush. Dante reaches for her hand, giving her knuckles a soft kiss before saying, "It's a pleasure to meet you, Ophelia. A beautiful name for a beautiful woman." The shade of red that spreads across her face is definitely not a shade that is in the sixty-four-count box of Crayola crayons. I try to hide my amusement at her sudden stunned state and nudge her arm to get her to come back to Earth.

"Oh, yes. It's nice to meet you too. Thank you." Ophelia practically stumbles over her words, making Dante grin as his eyes find mine once again.

"I have to make my rounds, of course, but please, enjoy yourselves. There's wine, champagne, and food on the back tables. Please, help yourselves. I will come find you in a bit." Dante brushes his hand down my arm, and he leans closer to me.

"You look absolutely breathtaking, Sage." His warm breath fans over my earlobe, giving me goosebumps as his cologne, once again, fills my senses. His proximity is all-consuming. He has a presence that envelops you, making you feel as though there's nobody else around. Like a cloud that's swooped in and encased me in a shell. It's unnerving but also comforting in a way. I briefly close my eyes, but the moment my eyelids touch, the image of another face fills my mind. Saint.

As quickly as he appears, he's gone. When I open my eyes, Dante has already disappeared, leaving me, and an equally stunned Ophelia, left to wipe the drool off our chins.

"Holy. Moly. Cannoli. What the hell was that?" Ophelia whispers. Her choice of words has a squeak of a laugh slipping through my lips.

"What did you just say?" I turn to face my best friend, who is still looking in the direction Dante went.

"Did you not feel that energy he was emanating? And what did he whisper to you?" I pull my lips into my mouth before responding, heat rushing to my face.

"He said I look breathtaking." The noticeable sigh she responds with is that of a love-struck teenager, fawning over the new attractive, yet mysterious, student in class.

"He's gorgeous, Sage. Like seriously gorgeous. Like he just stepped out of a Calvin Klein underwear photoshoot gorgeous. Damn, girl. He's got me all hot and bothered." She tips back the rest of her wine before she starts fanning herself with her hand as if her core temperature suddenly spiked ten degrees.

I whisper laugh at my friend's not so discrete reaction to, dare I say, the most attractive man in this building. I interlock our arms before dragging her further into the showroom.

"Come on, let's go decipher some art, shall we?" We spend the next half hour roaming from piece to piece. Each of us gives our opinions on the paintings and photographs one by one. Ophelia and I share a love for the arts, and there was no doubt she was the one I was bringing to this event.

"I'm going to get some food. Want to come?" Ophelia asks, but I'm drawn to a specific painting displayed further in the corner of the room that has my curiosity heightened.

"You go ahead. I'll catch up; I want to see something first." Ophelia nudges my arm before disappearing to the food table that's been calling her name since entering the building. I have to say, the spread looks delicious. My stomach growls at the thought, but there's something about this painting that's drawing me in.

As I approach the painting, I study the model depicted. There's no color, just black paint showcasing a beautiful female's profile. She's shirtless, but she's turned in a way that nothing is visible but her back. Her long hair cascades down her back while her arms are stretched above her head. Her head is tilted back and is halfway blocked from view by her arm, but there's something oddly familiar about her. She's a thin woman. Her skin is dusted lightly with a few freckles here and there, but it's not until I see her hands that I freeze.

If I could see myself in a mirror right now, I would see all the color drained from my face. Small beads of sweat develop across my forehead, and there's a slight tremor in my hands as I lift them up in front of me to examine them. The tops of my hands house thick, uneven skin, bumpy and raised, angry and aggressive as they stretch across my fingers one at a time. On my right hand, the scars twist up my arm just a bit higher than my left before they disappear beneath my blazer.

I drop my hands to my sides as I peer up at the painting. It's me. The girl in the painting before me, who has the same ugly scars, looks as though she's dancing, her arms up and head back, so carefree as her body bows with her movements. It's me. The night at the club.

"I see you've found my painting?" That same sultry, smooth voice invades my ears as a warm presence emanates from behind me. He's close. I don't turn to face him.

"You painted this?" My voice comes out shakier than I wanted it to, shock and disbelief still pulsing through my body.

"I couldn't get the image of you dancing out of my head, so I put it on paper." Dante painted me, scars and all. I hadn't thought he noticed my biggest insecurity in the darkness of the club. It's beautiful, everything about it. So why am I suddenly angry? No, not angry, self-conscious, as if everyone can see my hands and the ugly scars, I try so hard to hide. The most insecure part of my body is up on the wall in full display for others to see. I quickly scan from my left to my right, seeing if anyone is near me and can put two and two together that the girl in the painting is me. But there's no one, just Dante standing painfully close to me as I start having the beginnings of a panic attack.

"You painted me? Even my... scars?" My breathing starts picking up, becoming shorter and choppier.

*Calm down, Sage. No one knows that's you. You're just over-thinking. Not everyone in the world thinks scars are hideous. Relax.*

"I know I probably should have asked you first, but like I said, I couldn't stop thinking of you after that night." I finally turn to look at him. Even the way Dante stands radiates confidence and poise: his hands in his slacks' pockets as he looks over my head at his painting with his brow furrowed just a bit, as if he's in deep thought.

"Your beauty is hard to forget, Sage." Slowly his eyes meet mine, his hand coming up to the side of my face. His touch is gentle, his thumb gently sliding across my cheek as he steps in closer to me.

"But my scars?" I didn't know what I was asking him, or what to say. All I wanted to know was why he painted my scars as well. Most people wouldn't think that was a detail that would make their work beautiful, but his response didn't falter.

"Our scars tell our story—the good, the bad, and the ones we'd rather not show. Whether we have physical scars or mental scars, they play a significant role in who we are or who we're destined to become. It's important not to hide from them but to show the struggles we've faced even when we'd rather forget." His words wrap around me and squeeze so tight I start to feel the undeniable sting of tears I'm determined not to shed.

I swallow hard and wipe my hands on my pants before taking a step back. I need fresh air; I need a moment alone. I want to run to the bathroom and wash away the scars that have plagued my hands since the fire, but I can't move. I'm suddenly too hot, my skin feeling like I'm back in the house. The wall of heat becomes too much, and I'm struggling to breathe through the smoke all over again.

"It's a beautiful painting… really, it is. But could you—" Before I could finish talking, a familiar voice interrupts me.

"As moving as your speech was, some people's stories are best left to be told by them. Not forced upon them in a room full of strangers. Sage, let's go."

SAGE

# CHAPTER 23

### SAGE

I have never been happier to see Saint in my life, but even as I try my hardest to reel in the panic attack that's growing within me, I can't control it any longer. I excuse myself from Dante and practically run towards Saint as my lungs begin restricting right there in the middle of the showroom floor. I can't get a big enough breath in; my chest is caving in against my lungs. The room is narrowing in, black dots appear in front of me, and I don't think I could have made it to the door if not for Saint's guiding hand on my lower back.

As I step into the fresh air, I run straight into Ophelia and Owen. They're standing close to one another as they speak, but the moment Ophelia sees me, she grabs my arms in a panic, holding me up in front of her.

"Shit, Sage, breath. Slow down your breathing. Slow, slow, steady breaths. Copy me. Inhale big. Exhale big." I copy Ophelia, but I still can't slow down. The world is spinning around me, and the fear of the lingering flames creeps into my mind.

"What the fuck happened?" Owen yells to Saint, but I tune them out. All I need right now is to breathe. I need to get out of the house, away from the flames. My hands are burning.

"She's having a panic attack; she thinks she's back in the house fire." Saint's voice is right beside me. A pair of strong arms scoop me up and carry me across the street. Still trying to breathe, I can't catch my breath fast enough. The dark is closing in on me again, and the last thing I hear before fading into the dark is Saint's voice.

"Sage, stay awake. Stay with me. I got you." Then everything fades away.

*Sage, stay awake. Stay with me. I got you.*

It's funny how one can go months or even years without having a panic attack, and then out of nowhere, the intense fear comes barreling in so fast there's nothing you can do but succumb to the attack. It's exhausting and slightly painful due to the tension held in every muscle of your body.

"She hasn't had one in a while. What happened in there that caused it?" Ophelia sounds like she's a million miles away, her voice so small, but I can hear the concern in her tone.

"That fucker painted a picture of her from the club, her hands and scars on display for all to see. Her biggest inse-curity. I wish she could see how her scars represent just how strong she truly is." Saint sounds far away too, but with each word he speaks, his words become louder and louder.

"She imagines she's back in her old house the day it caught on fire. It's horrible." A soft hand threads through my hair, relieving the pressure that's squeezing my brain. "I shouldn't have left her side to go get food. I didn't know about the painting." Ophelia's words are full of guilt.

"Please don't think that way," I whisper to my best friend. The harsh lights of the evening sky make it hard for me to open my eyes. "Where are we?" I ask.

"In the back of Saint's Tahoe. You passed out while he was carrying you out here." I finally manage to crack open my eyes and see a worried Ophelia cradling my head as she peers down at me. I go to sit up, but another arm holds me down.

"Wait, wait, wait. Just stay there for a minute until you fully wake." Saint's arm is resting over my waist, preventing me from sitting up. When my eyes finally adjust to the light, I see Saint sitting beside me, my legs draped over his thighs while my head and shoulders rest on Ophelia's lap. Her fingers are still brushing through my hair in the most soothing way.

"You alright, witch stick? You scared the shit out of me." Owen's voice has me smiling.

"Yeah, I'm okay. Thanks." I go to sit up again and dangle my legs out of the back of the Tahoe while I brush my hands through my hair.

"What an embarrassing way to end the evening, am I right?" I try to laugh it off, but the embarrassment is there in my tone.

"Don't be embarrassed, hun. If anything, I should be. Look at my dress." She gestures to her gorgeous dress that now has a huge wine stain, starting at her breast and extending down to her abdomen. "I tripped over my damn heels coming to find you and spilled red wine like a fool. I was ready to disappear at that moment." She laughs it off, and I join in laughing at how pathetic the pair of us are. Two peas in a pod.

"Are you sure you're okay?" Saint's tone is full of worry.

Putting my hand on his thigh, I reassure him I will survive and jump out of his Tahoe.

"Right, where did we park again, O?" I ask, looking around to see where the hell we are.

"Nah, I think you need to ride with me. I don't want you passing out behind the wheel. Owen will drive your car back behind us." Saint steps out of the back, adjusting his club vest before straightening to his full height in front of me.

"Ophelia, can drive my car back." He gives her a once over, his eyebrow raising in doubt.

"Yeah, I don't think she should drive either. Her dress clearly gives her away." Saint says to me as Owen lets out a soft chuckle behind me.

"Hey, I am right here, you know." I smile at my best friend. She really does look adorably ridiculous with her huge, and I mean huge, wine stain. Her dress is surely ruined. Too bad it's a gorgeous dress. We share a small laugh before agreeing with the guys.

"Fine, whatever. I'll go with Owen and meet you back home." Before she follows Owen back to my car, she steps up close to me, giving me a hug and whispering in my ear, "Are you sure you're okay?"

"I'm okay, I promise. I probably should apologize to Dante," I whisper to her, not wanting the others to hear me.

"No need. I talked to him and explained the bare minimum. He said he'll contact you later." I give her a slight nod. Ophelia gives me a kiss on the cheek before stepping back and following close behind Owen. I watch as the pair makes their way to my car before turning back to Saint.

"Thank you. You didn't need to do that."

"Do what? Not let you pass out in the middle of the showroom floor so strangers could hover over you, not knowing what to do?" I don't know how to respond; I just shrug my shoulders before making my way to the passenger side of his Tahoe. Reaching for the handle, I go to pull the door open, but a hand slams it shut over my head. Turning, I'm met with silvery eyes, pinning my back to the Tahoe. Anger or fear—something —plays across his face as he cages me in with his large arms. Our noses practically touch as he steps into me. We're so close.

"He's not allowed to touch you like that ever again, Sage. Do you understand me?" Who was he talking about? What was he talking about? As if he can read my internal thoughts. he continues, "Dante, or any man, for that matter, is not allowed to touch you." I inhale a deep breath, his clean citrus bodywash filling my nose.

"You can't dictate who I'm allowed to be with, Saint. What, am I not allowed to date now?" I am playing with fire. I know that. His jaw ticks at my defiance, but what does he expect? Am I supposed to be celibate for the rest of my life just because we had sex once? We aren't together, so what is it to him who I date?

"I can do whatever the hell I want, especially when it comes to keeping you safe. Dante is not safe. Now, get in the car." Dropping his hands from beside me, he opens the car door for me and gestures for me to get in. I'm momentarily stunned, but I get in and grab the door handle, slamming it shut. A second later, Saint gets in the driver's seat, turning the key and starting up the Tahoe before he rips out of the parking lot with so many unspoken words rippling between us.

We sit in uncomfortable silence all the way home. We had sex, yes. Does that change anything between us? No. It can't. It was a mistake that felt amazing in the moment, but it can't be any more than just that: a momentary lapse in judgment. What did he think it would turn into? Friends with benefits? A full-blown relationship? We both know that is off the table. Saxon would kill us.

It's not until we pull into the driveway that I finally break the silence.

"Saint, I don't know what you think has changed between us, but we need to go back to how we were." Staring at the side of his profile, I watch as his jaw tenses, the muscles protruding from his sharp jawline, and I can't help the pulse between my legs.

"You're right," is all he says. Nothing more, just "You're right." Good, that was easy. Then he continues on, "Let's forget about how well my cock fits in your pussy and just go about our lives hating one another. Sound good?" His hard eyes freeze me to the spot. My jaw drops and the heat of my core increases from his vulgar words. "Because right now, you and I both know the wet spot forming in your sweet little panties isn't from spending the evening looking at paintings." He unbuckles and leans into my personal space, making me hold my breath. "No, I think it's there from the thought of me on top of you while I thrust my cock so deep inside you, you forget your own name. Am I right, baby?" He pauses for a moment, but my brain can't form words, let alone a full sentence. "Don't act like you haven't touched yourself reliving what we did that night. Because every night since, my cock has been painfully aware that it's not inside you, and soon enough, it's going to need relief. I don't know how to move forward as if everything's the same. Maybe I just need to fuck you over and over again to get you out of my system, but know this, I'm hungry. No, I'm starving, and eventually, I'm going to need to eat, baby. And there's only one person whole will curb my appetite."

A knock on my window has me jumping so high I practically headbutt Saint due to how close he is to me. Fuck.

"Sage, I'm going to head home. I need to shower this wine off my skin. I feel gross," Ophelia says through the glass. I unbuckle hastily and jump out of the car, needing to get away from Saint before I do something I'll regret.

"Yeah, yes, of course. Thank you for going with me today. I'm sorry about how it turned out. Maybe one day we can both act normal and get through an evening without making fools of ourselves." She laughs her contagious laugh as she walks to her BMW.

"Yeah, I don't think you and I will ever be normal, babes. Call me tomorrow!" She climbs in her car before giving me a wave, and I notice at the last-minute Owen is in her passenger seat. What the hell? Why is he going with her?

A hand grabs mine, gently leading me to the front door of the house. I don't protest. I follow him up the stairs and through the door before he drops my hand and closes the door behind me, locking the locks one by one.

"You hungry?"

"What?" I ask, thrown off by his question.

"Hungry. Are you hungry?" Oh, yeah. I hadn't eaten at the show since everything happened so fast. The sound of my stomach growling answers his question for me. He laughs before he heads into the kitchen.

"I'll make something to eat. Why don't you go clean up? I'll be down here." I watch him disappear into the kitchen before making my way up to my bathroom and starting a steaming hot shower. I need to wash this night off my body. How the hell was I going to explain myself to Dante? And why was I so wet from what Saint said in the car? Fuck. Me.

SAINT

# CHAPTER 24

## SAINT

As I squeeze the lemon juice over the salmon filets, I imagine squeezing the life out of Dante for touching what is mine. *Fuck, Saint. She's not yours. You had sex once. That doesn't make her yours.* I was being too protective of Sage, more so than would be normal for our friendship. Everyone knows I am protective of her because she's Saxon's little sister, but my protectiveness is fast becoming an obsession at this point. Even Owen has started asking questions about my intentions towards her. I shut that shit down immediately. I can't have rumors starting, especially rumors that could easily make their way to Saxon.

When I saw Dante's hand brush against her face, I swear the devil himself entered my body and sparked a rage that only demons could possess. The moment she backed away from him, and I saw her breathing pick up, I knew she was cresting on the start of a panic attack. I know her like the back of my hand, and I've been there with her when she's had these episodes. They're terrifying and incapacitating for her, but mostly she's consumed by an overwhelming sadness that's been forced upon her due to the trauma of the fire. She would never have to experience those attacks if it weren't for the bastard who planned the fire. That's why Saxon and I will stop at nothing to figure out who caused the death of her father, and almost Sage herself. Because not only did her father die, a piece of Sage died as well. She will never cope with the loss of her father or the fear that strangles her whenever she sees a fire, a candle lit, or even a match being stuck. The painting of her scars sparked the start of her attack today, and all I wanted to do was eliminate the person who caused it.

Dante.

During my research on his background, it was hard to find any flaws with the guy, which made me despise him even more. He graduated with honors from Berkeley in business with a minor in the arts. He has two siblings, Amelia and Josephine, from their parents, Luis and Marina Macari. Growing up in Miami, his family moved to California when his father took a position in the Silicon Valley, where he became a very well-known entrepreneur dealing with massive public relations companies. His mother, Marina, was a stay-at-home mom due to Josephine having disabilities that kept her from attending public school. Bound to a wheelchair, Marina was her caregiver 24/7. All and all, a pretty normal American family living the dream and working hard, right?

However, when I reached further into his family history, I couldn't find anything about his grandparents, paternal or maternal. It was as if Luis and Marina magically appeared one day and had kids. Nothing, and I mean nothing, was found about any family member outside his immediate family. Which struck me as odd. It felt odd enough that I decided to go to the exhibit myself. Owen insisted he come with me, and I was so focused on getting to her I didn't care who the fuck came with me. I just needed to get to wherever Sage was.

As I stand in her kitchen now, I couldn't be happier that I trusted my gut. Her panic attack happened moments after I let myself into the exhibit against the door man's wishes. I told Owen to get Ophelia and wait for me outside while I took care of Sage and Dante.

I put the salmon in the oven and grab the tossed salad out of the fridge, along with the vegetables I need to chop up. Before I can even lift the knife to start prepping the rest of our dinner, a deep feeling of anxiety pools in my stomach. I slap my hand down on the counter and drop my head for a long moment, counting my breaths to try and stop the war that's raging inside.

*One. Two. Three. Four. Five.*

Why, why now? I can't pinpoint the exact moment my feelings for Sage changed, but they have, obviously. I've always loved her, but always been able to keep myself from going too far with her. I can't control that aspect of myself anymore. It's becoming harder and harder not to touch her. The feeling of helplessness as she struggled to breathe, the fear that was clear as day on her face, and the thoughts of her house engulfed in flames as she struggled to escape has my stomach twisting in a way it's never done before.

I know I started off being friends with Saxon, but I've been with Sage for so long I can't remember a life where she wasn't a part of it. I can't fathom a world where she's not in it. A world without Sage Wilder is no world I want to live in. She's got my head all fucked up. I want her and need her, but I also don't want to deal with the emotions she brings out of me. I just want things to go back to what they were. The bickering and constant insults we slung at each other seems like a lifetime ago, but in reality, it was all of two weeks ago. I want things to rewind. At least, I think that's what I want, right?

"I know you don't like vegetables, but damn, you don't need to cry over them." Her voice floods my brain, and I turn to see Sage; she's fresh out of the shower, wearing her pajamas. Her tiny night shorts expose her long, lean legs while her tank top does little to cover her stomach and breasts. She also has her fluffy white robe lazily draped off one of her shoulders. Fuck, I'm really screwed. I give her a weak smile at her comment, but go back to chopping some carrots and tomatoes, tossing them in the lettuce bowl as I go.

The room is quiet for a long moment, only the sound of my Spotify playlist on in the background fills the kitchen. She sits at the island in front of me, wrapping herself in her robe as she watches my hands at work. I can't help but steal a glimpse of her every now and then, but her face remains lowered, her eyes transfixed on my hands.

"Saint?" Her voice is so low I almost don't hear her.

"Yeah?"

"Why did you come to the exhibit?" I stop mid-cut into a carrot and put the knife down. Planting my hands on the island, I look into her eyes; silver meets silver as I try to think of an answer.

"Sage, I... I had a weird feeling about this Dante character and felt like I needed to—I don't know—investigate, I guess." I sound utterly ridiculous, stumbling over my words, trying not to sound like a total stalker. I hold her gaze, waiting for her counter, but she stays still, not giving any indication she is going to talk.

"That's it then? You had a weird feeling?" She is fishing for something other than the answer I gave her, and I'm torn between giving her more or staying locked up tight like I always do.

"Yeah, it's called listening to your gut, and the moment I saw you leave the garage, something didn't feel right. It's my job to take care of you while Saxon is away, and I wasn't going to ignore my gut—it's usually right." I went back to chopping the vegetables. The heat of her eyes remain on my skin.

"I see."

"Lucky, I did come," I add.

"About that." She pauses for a moment, and I looked back up to see her examining her hands, the angry thick scars that haunt her daily, still present now and forever. I put down the knife again and walk over to her, taking her hands in mine. She doesn't look up at me. Her gorgeous face lowers to the ground, unable to look me in the eye.

"Look at me Sage." She doesn't.

"Look. At. Me." I grab her chin with my thumb and tilted her face towards mine.

"Stop that right now. Don't let your fears win. You give too much power to the demons that haunt you, and it hinders the way you live. You're beautiful, and nothing, and I mean *fucking nothing*, will take away from the light that you are. I wish for only a second you could see yourself the way I see you. You're beautiful, painfully so, but you're also so fucking smart, funny, interesting, and sometimes a pain in my ass, but these scars right here do not control you. I know you hate them, but every time I see them, I'm thankful." Her eyebrows furrow just enough to be noticeable, but I continue.

"Why am I thankful? Because these scars mean you survived. You escaped that house and chose to live. And I thank God every fucking day he left you on this earth because I wouldn't want to be here if you weren't here too." I lift her hands and kiss her knuckles one by one.

When I'm done, I cup her face with my hand in time to wipe away a single tear from beneath her eye.

"Saint." Just one word, my name on her lips, and I can't stop myself. My lips collide with hers, soft, pliable, and painfully delicious. I crave more. No, I need more. I lean against her, her legs opening for me as I step closer. My hands thread through her still wet hair, while her hands drift beneath my shirt. Nails scratch gently up my back, causing my muscles to tense from the sensation. Need quickly turns into desire, and before I know it, my hands grab her ass, lifting her from her stool so I can carry her into my room.

Our lips never part; our tongues are fighting for dominance neither of us want to relinquish. Her hands pull my hair just enough to spark pain, but I love it. Pain means I'm alive, and alive means I'm with her. Walking over to my bed, I set her down gently, pushing her back towards the top. She discards her robe as I remove my shirt in one swift movement. I had changed into sweatpants when she took a shower, thank God. My cock is already pushing against the fabric, and it would have been more painful if I was still in my jeans.

I kneel on the bed between her legs, finding her lips and kissing her again, unable to satiate my hunger for her.

"Saint, are we doing this? Again?" She speaks in a breathy whisper, our lips brushing against each other as she does.

"There's nothing in the world that could stop me from getting what I want." I grab the hem of her shorts and pull them down her legs, her panties along with them. As soon as she is free of her shorts, I place my hand on her chest and gently push her down so she's lying flat.

"Just relax, baby. I'm going to make you feel so fucking good." I don't give her time to respond. I grab her thighs and drape them over my shoulders, her arousal already glistening for me.

"So eager for me already, aren't you, baby?" I can't wait any longer. I start off with long, lazy licks, finding her clit and circling her most sensitive spot, making her moan in satisfaction. The sweet, sweet sound of her pleasure edges me on, and I dive deeper. I lick and suck up her arousal. The taste of her on my tongue has me in a frenzy. Like a kid in a candy store, I want more. I want it all. I press my thumb against her clit while my tongue continues its fierce assault, dipping in and out of her, making her buck against my face.

"Saint, ugh, fuck. Don't stop—please." Her voice is needy as she chases her orgasm with each lash of my tongue. I suck her clit into my mouth before letting it go and repeat this over and over. Her thighs tense around my head, and I know she's getting close.

"You taste so fucking good." I don't even recognize my own voice—a man possessed with need and lust. I never want to stop. Her fingers thread through my hair, pushing my face further into her as I enter my finger, curving it inside her to find her sweet spot. Pumping in and out, her breathing becomes more and more rapid. Two fingers and then three. Her thighs begin trembling against my face.

"Fuck, Saint. Yes, right there!" I continue thrusting my fingers in and out as my tongue flicks over her clit. She holds her breath for a moment, right before she explodes beneath me. Her pussy clenching around my fingers as her arousal coats my lips. Every muscle in her body tenses as she rides out her high. Breath after choppy breath fills the room as she moans her pleasure. It is everything and more.

"That's my good girl," I groan out, removing my fingers when her body finally relaxes against me, but I am far from done. This is just the beginning, and by the end of the night, I am going to make sure Sage Wilder knows exactly who she belongs to.

SAGE

# CHAPTER 25

## SAGE

If you could die from orgasmic bliss, I swear I see the pearly gates before crashing back down to Saint's bed. I have never, and I quote, never, climaxed so hard in my life. If I was hesitant to do this again from fear of the repercussions, Saint's tongue quite literally erased any thoughts of doubt I had. I am hooked on Tyler Saint Bones, and I need another fix. Like a crackhead on the streets, my body aches for more. More of him, his tongue, and his delicious cock that is now straining so hard against his sweats I need to free it. So, I do just that.

After I crash back down from heaven, I slide myself to the edge of his bed, grabbing Saint by his waistband and freeing his erect and throbbing dick. Wrapping my hand around his base, I spit on his velvety smooth skin and start pumping my hand up and down his length as I stare up at him with post-orgasmic eyes. He tilts his head back, his Adam's apple bobbing up and down. But when I wrap my lips over him, the moan that escapes his throat has my pussy dripping all over again. Looking up at his bare chest, his abs are on full display for me as his chest rises and falls in quick successions. Raising his arm, he twists his fingers through my hair and pushes me forward against his pelvis so his dick invades the back of my throat, eliciting a gag with every thrust. Drool drips down my chin as wet, guttural sounds come from my mouth. It sounds so dirty, so filthy, but I love every disgusting slurp of my tongue. Even when he hits the back of my throat, he's still not completely inside. He's too big, too thick, but I take him as best as I can.

"Fuck, Sage, you're taking me so well." I hum around him, the vibration making him moan again.

"Fuuuck." I continue sucking and swallowing him as best I can, needing to hear more of his satisfied moans. I've never been someone that needs to please others, but with Saint, all I want is his praise, his encouraging words. Like a desperate whore needing the approval of her master. Who the hell am I?

"Come here, baby. I need to feel your sweet pussy right fucking now." Saint picks me up and pushes me back against his bed, his hands finding the hem of my tank top and pulling me free of the restrictive fabric. Removing his sweats completely, he gets on the bed and straddles my waist.

"You're so fucking perfect, Sage, and you're all mine." He leans over me, grabbing both my wrists and pinning them above my head. Warm, hungry lips find my neck as he kisses his way to the sensitive spot behind my ear. The gentle sensation of his lips dusting my skin gives me goose-bumps. I groan as his body presses into mine, heating my already burning skin. I rub my thighs together, desperate for more friction, and feel the wetness pooling against my inner thighs.

"Saint, please, I need you now." Yes, I'm begging, but I

can't go another minute feeling like I am going to burst with no relief in sight. I need something—him, his cock, his mouth, his fingers—fuck, I just need him.

"Whatever you want, I'll give you." Saint thrusts fully inside of me. The sudden invasion and feeling of being painfully full makes me gasp. The pain slowly morphs into a delicious pleasure that has my core screaming for more. I push against him, needing him to move again. Pulling all the way out, he pushes inside again, but only halfway before pulling out. He does this over and over, and I want to scream. My climax gets so close, but then slips away like a whisper in the wind. I'm chasing my orgasm, but it never comes. He's playing with me, purposefully keeping me from reaching the top, and I groan in frustration.

"Tell me what you need, baby. Tell daddy what you want." Oh, fuck. I could come just from his words alone. The sultry way he whispers in my ear has my eyes rolling back to my skull.

"I need you, all of you. Please—" I'm unable to finish my sentence because the force at which Saint pushes inside me has me seeing stars. Hard, fast, punishing thrusts over and over again are hitting that spot that causes me to explode all over again. Stars dance across my vision, little black dots threaten to obscure my eyesight, and my name fills my ears as Saint chases his release right behind me. I never want this feeling to subside; I never want this to end.

Our heavy breathing is the only sound I can hear besides the pounding of my heart. Saint rests his forehead against mine, our noses touching and our breaths mingling as we slowly come down from our highs.

"I'm never letting you go." Saint kisses me with so much force, with so many unspoken words, I fear we've both found ourselves in a situation we can no longer come back from. I, too, never want to let him go. He's who I crave. And for the last few nights, he's who I see in my dreams. He's everywhere, his scent, his voice, the sound of his motorcycle when he pulls up to the house, the way he dominates a room just by being present. There is no escaping Tyler Saint Bones, and if I'm being honest, I don't want to.

With him, I feel different, more than just wanted or needed. He makes me feel beautiful. I never feel like I need to hide myself when I'm around him. I've always been hyperaware of my scars, but when I'm with him, I've noticed I couldn't care less if he sees them or not. Saint has never made me feel like my scars make me undesirable. If anything, I feel more like myself than I have in a very long time.

As much as we bicker, it's hard to see past our relationship as being more than just friends, but then he says things that make my heart constrict and beat faster than it ever has. Saint knows me, all of me: the good, the bad, and the scars that haunt me daily. Even with all my insecurities, he's never treated me differently. Rather, he's celebrated me in a way I never thought a man would. Slowly, I've come to realize, he's right. He's right when he says my scars should be the reminder to live my life as a blessing from God, who gave me a second chance. He's right.

———

That night, I sleep beside Saint, his arm wrapped around my waist as I slip into the deepest sleep I've had since the fire. I feel safe, secure, and, above all else, I feel happy. Truly happy, and I can't remember the last time this feeling filled my body. Yes, I love my life, and I'm happy in the sense that I'm healthy, Saxon is healthy. We have food, this house, and the club that loves us all fiercely. However, this deep, soul-warming joy has been absent in my life after losing my father. Waking up next to Saint, hearing his gentle, deep breathing and knowing he would do just about anything to protect me, awakens butterflies inside me that had been dormant for so long.

"Sage, sweetheart, are you home?!" Mira's voice echoes throughout the house. Saint tenses behind me as we scramble out of the bed once again.

"Fuck, is this going to happen every time?" Saint laughs as he grabs my clothes, putting them on the bed and dressing himself as quickly as he can.

"I'll distract her. Get dressed and make a grand escape." I laugh at his choice of words; he shoots me a wink before reaching his door and slipping out without opening it fully. I dress as quickly as I can, wrapping my robe around me before I wait at his door and listen for a moment to escape.

"Mira, gorgeous, good morning!" Saint coos to Mira, and I stifle a laugh, covering my mouth with my hand as I continue to listen.

"Oh, Mio, you're too much. When are you going to find a girl you can spew your compliments to, huh?" I wait for his response.

"Oh, Mira, how do you know I don't already have one?" My back stiffens. What the hell is he doing? We're supposed to be lying low, not shouting from the rooftops we had sex. Twice!

I wait a moment longer until their muffled voices drift off into the distance before I quietly exit Saint's bedroom and head straight for the coffee machine. I get busy, making it look like I'd just woken up, which I did, and came downstairs to make coffee. Which is what I would normally do. As I grab a filter, I hear the faint ping of my cell phone, indicating I have a text message. Looking around the kitchen, I don't see my phone until I realize I'd left it in his room. Shit.

I quickly run back to his room and grab my phone off his nightstand before quickly running back out. As I turned the corner to enter the kitchen, I run straight into Saint. His hands fly to my face, holding me still, and he kisses me stupid. Fuck this man and his magician powers of jumbling my brain and making me melt into his embrace. His kiss is deep but quick as he holds me close and pushes me back against the wall.

"Saint, she's going to catch us," I whisper as his hard body molds into mine, where I can feel the unmistakable bulge beneath his sweats, pushing into my abdomen.

"It's invigorating, huh? The thought of being caught at any moment." His lips brush against mine as he continues to grind into me, my strawberry bodywash emanating off his skin from last night. Damn, it smells good on him.

"Sage? Where are you, Mia?" I stiffen, and try to push him away, but he holds me firm.

"Respond to her. Tell her you're busy." His face is at my ear, his perfectly maintained beard tickling my cheek. I suck in a jagged breath.

"I'll be right there, Mira." My voice quivers.

"That's not what I told you to say. I said tell her you're busy." Another hard grind of his body against mine, and there it is again, the wetness settling in my panties.

"I'm a little busy," I choke out. This man is going to be the death of me.

"Now, go and get rid of her, I'm not done with you yet." Letting me go, I instantly feel cold and empty, with his body no longer pressed against mine, and I instantly want more. I'm in trouble.

I find Mira in the laundry room, fiddling with my clothes, as well as Saxon's and Saint's, before she sees me at the entrance.

"Ahh, there you are, lovely. How was your night? How was the exhibit?" I had mentioned the show to Mira a couple of days ago and had shared how excited I'd been. I'd half expected her to forget, but that's not Mira.

"It was nice, yeah. Lovely pieces and good vibes." I can't look her in the eye; I feel like I am lying, but it had been a nice night, except for the unexpected panic attack.

"Wonderful, and the gentleman? How was he?" Fuck, I knew that was her next question. I shift my eyes again; I am horrible at lying. I guess that's not a bad thing, though.

"Uh, he was nice, pleasant. Yeah." Mira stops messing with the clothes, giving me a knowing glance.

"Just nice?" The pressure of her gaze is too much. I give her a hug to distract myself.

"Yeah, Mama. He was nice, that's all." I roll my eyes at her, playing the usual daughter role. She chuckles at my response before I head out of the laundry room, but then stop in my tracks. Saint is waiting for me, leaning his body against the wall and giving me a stare that does things to the now awakened butterflies in my stomach. He raises an eyebrow at me, but I turn back around to Mira.

"Why don't you let me do that today? I don't have class, and it's supposed to rain all day today anyway." The semester just started, and I am lucky enough to have Wednesdays off. "It will give me something to do. You go enjoy a day for yourself." I step close beside her, grabbing the garment in her hand and sorting it into the colored pile of clothes.

"No, dear. This is what I do."

"Please, Mira, I insist. You work too hard. You need to take time for yourself. Why don't you use that gift card I got you for your birthday months ago and go to the salon for a mani-pedi day?" She sighs, tilting her head back a bit.

"That does sound nice, doesn't it? Why don't you come with me then?" Fuck, I hadn't expected that answer. But before I can think of another response, or lie, Saint saves me.

"Hey, Sage, are you going to help me today with that install at the garage?" Mira and I turn to the laundry room door to see Saint leaning in with his hands resting on the door frame. After practically drooling at the bit of skin that shows from his shirt rising up, I turn to Mira.

"Oh, yeah. I promised I would help the guys finish an install on a bike they're building. You know the guys don't have a clue what they're doing." I nudge Mira, who laughs her deep belly laugh that always makes me smile.

"What would you boys do without my girl, huh?" Mira pats Saint's chest before leaving the laundry room.

"If you need me to come back, sweetheart, please call me. I love you. Have fun showing those boys how it's done!" I respond with a "love you" back, and Saint and I wait for the sound of the door closing as we hold each other's stare. Then, when the door finally clicks closed, Saint pounces on me like an animal attacking his prey.

SAGE

# CHAPTER 26

SAGE

The rest of the day, and well into the next day, Saint and I fuck on every surface of the house. His room, my room, the shower, the hot tub, the kitchen counter, he even had me bent over his bike before we made our way to the garage where the club members were waiting for us. Saxon had returned that morning and told us we need to be at the garage for a club meeting. Well, Saint had to be present at the meeting. I was told to man the office. Yay me.

As the boys, or men, rather, handle their meeting, I choose this time to finally respond to Dante, who had texted me now almost twenty-four hours ago. I pull up his text and reread his message.

DANTE:

I'm so sorry for springing that painting on you. Your friend briefly explained your concerns. I can't apologize enough. I hope I can make it up to you.

ME:

> I'm sorry I'm just now responding. Please don't apologize. You didn't know. Your painting is beautiful, and I'm happy about how your event turned out.

It doesn't take long for the three bubbles to pop up, indicating he is typing a response.

DANTE:

> How about a redo, and I make it up to you? Tomorrow night for dinner at the Pink Flamingo. Let's say 7?

Fuck. What am I supposed to do? Do I want to go on a date with Dante? It's not like Saint and I are exclusive, we never could be.

*You're so fucking perfect, Sage, and you're all mine.*

Clearly, Saint has already staked his claim, and his words replay on a loop in my brain. But how would he and I ever work? Our situation is far from normal. We have to sneak around, plus I am lying to Mira now, and it makes me feel insanely guilty. We wouldn't be able to go on dates, be seen in public. Fuck, we can't even hold hands without the fear of being caught. I want so badly to have the chance to go on a date with Saint and explore whatever this is between us without having to hide.

I set my phone on the desk, not responding right away, when another text pops up on my screen. Rubbing my hands down my face, I pick up my phone and see another text from Dante.

DANTE:

> I'm so sorry to do this so quickly, but could we move that date to two days from now?

That's weird. I wonder why he'd change it so quickly? I decide to agree to the date just so I have the opportunity to let him down gently. He deserves that much, rather than a text saying I'm not interested.

ME:

Yes, that sounds great. Tuesday night it is. I hope everything is, ok?

I don't want to flat out ask him, but I can't help the curiosity that grows in my stomach. Call me nosy, but, well, yeah, I guess I am nosy. The three dots display on my screen again before his message pops up, and I am not prepared to read what he sends.

DANTE:

I don't want to lie to you, Sage. My friend has been missing since Sunday, and I'm afraid they just found his body on the outskirts of town. You met him at the club the night we met. His name was Damien Devonte. We are having his service Monday.

My legs start moving before I can even comprehend what Dante had just texted me. Damien, his friend from the club. Damien, the man that was once at the bottom of a quarry. Damien, the man Saxon and Saint admitted to killing. What the fuck is going on? I make it to the room in the back of the garage where the meeting is still proceeding, but I can't wait. Pushing through the doors, all eyes instantly turn towards me.

"I need to talk to you and Saint immediately. It's an emergency." I train my eyes on Saxon, who now glares at me with so much anger, but also a hint of concern. His curiosity wins because he then dismisses everyone, leaving only him, Saint, and myself.

"This had better be good." Saxon gestures his hand to a chair beside him, but I have so much energy swirling in my gut, I can't sit down. Matter of fact, I can't even be still.

Pacing back and forth, I go through the text messages between Dante and me in quick succession. When I finally drop the last bombshell of a text message, I don't miss the tick in Saxon's jaw as he processes this information. While he battles the silent war in his head, his eyes narrow on me. His silvery irises look as if they've grown three shades darker. He doesn't say anything, but the anger bubbling in his chest, or at least it looks like anger, is on the precipice of exploding.

I shift my attention from him to Saxon, who now has his head lowered while he brushes his hands over his head. Looking back at Saint, I startle. When I turn, I almost bump right into his chest. I hadn't heard him get up.

"Mine." One word is all he says. His tone is a low whisper, laced with so much promise. I am his, and he is reminding me. Fuck, I had been so worried I hadn't thought about how Saint would react to Dante asking for another date. Saint's hands are by his sides, curled into tight fists, as if he needs to release the pressure coursing through his blood.

"There was no mention of this guy, Dante, when we went up north. Who is he to Damien and how the fuck did they, whoever they are, find his body? It's the quarry, for fuck's sake." Saxon slams his hands on the table, rising from his chair and turning to look at the club's insignia hanging on the wall: a large gold crown sitting crooked on top of the large *A* that represents The Kings' Aces. Saxon walks over to the wall, hands in his pockets as he looks up at the mural.

"Did you forget already, witch stick? Or do I need to remind you? You belong to me now. No one else." Saint's lips are dangerously close to my ear as he whispers so low I almost can't hear him. My body is tingling all over; I'd been worried about the consequences of their actions, but now my body can't help the desire to have Saint's lips all over my most sensitive spots. I put my hand on his chest to put some distance between us before Saxon turns around, but the rumble that vibrates against my hand tells me all I need to know. He doesn't move, not an inch, as I press into him. We are going to get caught. I can feel it.

As if he knows Saxon's body language, Saint takes one step back seconds before Saxon turns around to peer at the pair of us.

"This is what we're going to do. Sage, you're going to go on this date like you were initially going to before he mentioned Damien. You stick to your plan, but instead of breaking it off with him, I need you to get close to him." The audible growl that comes from Saint is so loud, but Saxon doesn't flinch, so I assume he doesn't hear it. "We need to find out his connection to Damien, and how he's flown under our own fucking radar."

"You think that's wise? Sending your sister in when we don't even know how he's connected? It's too dangerous." Saint is worried, and I can't blame him. Now that I know Dante was friends with Damien, it's started to make me worried about his own intentions. However, concerned or not, this date could lead us to the person who killed my father.

"I'm fine. I can do this." What the hell am I thinking? Dante seems like a genuinely nice guy; however, I hung out with him once at the club and for like five minutes at the exhibit before everything went to shit. He is still a stranger to me, and now meeting up with him makes me nervous, anxious even, at the thought of his connection to the fire.

"One of us will be there with you the whole time. You won't be alone. One of us will be watching the whole time."

"Me." Saint speaks in a tone I've never heard before. Dark and thunderous, dominant and possessed. Heat rolls off his large frame, making my skin feel insanely hot all of a sudden, even with the air conditioner at its usual sixty-eight degrees.

"Perfect. I would myself, sis, but I got some shit I need to do that evening with Finn. Saint won't let anything happen to you." Coming up to stand in front of me, Saxon puts his hands on my shoulders and leans in to kiss my forehead. "You okay with this, sis?" A question to which I'm not entirely sure of the correct answer. But I give him a confident nod and a small smile.

"Like I said, Saint's got you. He'll protect you." He gives Saint a fist bump and a manly pat on the back before leaving the two of us alone in the meeting room. The room suddenly begins to close in on me. His presence is smothering. I can feel him all over me as he turns to face me, his now dark silvery eyes boring into me with so much lust, so much anger, I can't hold his gaze.

"So, you agreed to meet up with Dante?" I'm not sure if it is a question or a statement. "Have you forgotten already, or do you need to be reminded of whose cock you've been riding the past couple of days?" He takes a step closer to me. "Whose name you've been screaming." Another step. "Or whose bed you've been sleeping in?" Our chests are practically touching at this point as my back hits the wall. Raising his hand, he brushes a loose strand of my hair behind my ear.

"Because I haven't forgotten, baby. I can't stop picturing your sweet pussy dripping for me every time I close my eyes." My breath hitches at his confession, the room finally caging me in and making me feel so claustrophobic I want to run. "Since it seems like you've forgotten who I am already, the next time we're alone—which will be very, very soon, by the way—I'm going to remind you just who your tight little pussy belongs to." Any woman would be terrified at those words, so why do I suddenly feel an unmistakable wetness building between my thighs? He's right. I do belong to him. My body's response to his words makes it very clear.

"Saint." I don't know what to say. I'm not agreeing to date Dante. Hell, I want to break it to him gently that I don't want to continue whatever this is, but Saxon has different plans. I don't want anyone else; I've never craved a single soul as much as I crave Saint. No one else elicits the emotions, the feelings, like he does.

"That's right, baby. You belong to Saint. I'll see you at home. Be good." He leans in and kisses my forehead. Heat and warmth instantly spread throughout my body from my head to my toes. When I open my eyes, he's already at the door, his back disappearing as the door closes behind him.

He is right—I am his. And I love every bit of it.

SAINT

# CHAPTER 27

## SAINT

What in the actual fuck is Saxon thinking? Sending his little sister, my girl, into a situation with someone who could very well be the cause of, or at the very least, involved in, their father's death? I love my best friend, but he must be losing his damn mind if he thinks sending Sage into this situation is a good idea. I've looked into Dante's background again, trying to scan through everything possible and find anything that could be considered suspicious.

"Fuck!" I scream out in frustration. I've been sitting at the island for well over an hour now, but I can't find anything.

"What's got your panties in a twist, huh, big guy?" Frankie's voice filters into the kitchen as he walks in and pulls out a water bottle.

"Nothing, just can't figure out this background check," I mumble, brushing my hands through my hair and leaning back in the barstool to ease the tension that's been building in my back and shoulders. Footsteps come up beside me and bring my attention back.

"Who are you looking into?" I sigh and briefly give Frankie a condensed version of Sage's upcoming date. I didn't let slip about the body we discarded in the quarry. As much as I trust Frankie, Saxon and I have been adamant not to tell anyone about our secret plans to find out the real person who started the fire. All I divulge to him is Sage has a date with a man I don't trust, and I've been looking into him. When I look up to meet Frankie's eyes, he furrows his eyebrows just briefly before fixing his face and turning his back to me. Like I said, I trust Frankie, but what was that?

"Do you know the guy?" I ask, getting straight to the point. With his back still towards me, he responds, "Nah, I don't think so. Thought I did, but it's not the same guy." He pulls his phone out and starts typing away. When he finally finishes, he turns back to me, a smile now spread across his face.

"Maybe you're just being paranoid. Trust that Sage can handle herself. She's a big girl." He looks back down at his phone, sending off another quick text. "Listen, I got to go. Let Sax and Sage know I'll be home if they need me." With that, he leaves.

I can't shake the feeling of unease Frankie gave me with our brief interaction earlier. I put that to the back of my mind the moment I hear Sage make her way down the stairs. Closing my laptop, I stand from my chair and meet her halfway. As I reached the foyer, I can't help but stare at her as she descends the last few steps. My chest does this weird thing I've never felt before: it's a similar sensation as someone knocking the wind out of me and that inability to catch a proper breath.

"Well, how do I look?" She spins around, her long, sleek black dress not even fanning out with her movement. No, her dress is plastered to her body, hugging every curve. I so desperately want to be the fabric against her skin. Her spaghetti straps sit delicately atop her shoulders, and the dip of her dress allows just enough cleavage to show, but not enough to be distracting. Hell, what am I saying? Her beauty is always distracting. Shit, what is Sage Wilder doing to me? I love it.

I don't say anything, I just grab her by the waist mid-spin and pull her tight against my chest. Inhaling her sweet strawberry vanilla scent, I bury my face in the crook of her neck.

"There is not a word strong enough for how absolutely divine you look. However, I have to ask, why so dressed up for this punk? He doesn't deserve to see you like this. Fuck, nobody does." I can't let her go; my arms remain around her waist, holding her steady as she stands on her tiptoes to reach my neck with her arms.

"Are you jealous, Saint?" Her tone is playful, but I am anything but playful at this moment. I'm not a jealous man; I'm simply protective, slightly obsessed, and utterly allured by all that is Sage. Okay, that sounds like it could be jealousy, but fuck it, whatever.

"Not jealous, just concerned. We don't know this guy, and I'm not comfortable sending you in like an undercover agent or some shit." I pull back to get a good look at her face. My chest does that weird thing again the moment her eyes meet mine, and I am starting to realize the hold this woman has over me. I would do anything, kill anyone, be anything she wants me to be just so she will smile at me the way she is now.

"I need to figure out who he is and what his connection is with the fire. If I can help in any way, I will. Plus, I'll have you right outside waiting for me. I'm never really alone, am I?" She raises her eyebrow at me as if she's known all along I've been watching her. If only she really knew.

"I'll be right outside in my Tahoe." I reach into my

pocket and pull out a mic that she will wear during the date. "Here's your newest accessory." I lift it up to show her —a tiny circular pin that will fit on the inside of her dress, invisible to the naked eye.

"Gee, thanks. Can't wait," she says with every ounce of sarcasm she can muster. I help put the mic on her dress, and I can't stop my knuckles from grazing over her smooth skin. My dick instantly begins to harden, but I need to remain focused.

"There, now I'll be able to hear everything going on." Fitting my earpiece in my ear, worry starts to bubble in my gut for her safety.

"Let's go, or we'll be late," she says, turning around towards the door. Before she can even take a step away from me, I grab her arm and spin her back around. I crash my lips to hers in a searing kiss that instantly sparks heat in my core. She tastes so fucking good; all I want to do is carry her to my room and fuck the thought of any other man right out of her pretty little head.

Our kiss speaks volumes. We are desperate, like we both know this will have to end eventually. Deep and needy, our mouths consume one another, as if kissing isn't enough. It isn't. I always need more of her. I'm always wanting to feel the heat of her pussy wrapped around my cock. The sweetest moan slips past her lips, and I begin to crumble. She pulls away, her face flush, and her lip gloss completely absent from her now swollen lips.

"If we don't leave now, I'll be late." She straightens her long hair and fixes her dress as she turns on her heels and heads for the door. I let her this time, grabbing the handle before she can and opening the door for her. She and Dante had decided on meeting at the restaurant instead of him picking her up. It was my idea. No need for this prick to know where she lives. Saxon agreed with me, so I'll be following behind her Audi in my Tahoe and will be staking out in the parking lot.

We make it to the restaurant, and she gives me a quick mic check as she asks if I can hear her. I give her a thumbs up before she enters the restaurant, alone.

*Stay in the Tahoe. You don't intervene unless she says her keyword, purple, over the mic. Got it?*

Saxon's words fill my head, a reminder that I have to let Sage get as much information as possible, and if she feels threatened or as if she's in danger, she has to say her keyword. Then I'm allowed to bust into the restaurant and retrieve my girl.

"Wow, you get even more beautiful each time I see you." Dante's deep, smooth voice fills my ear piece, and I snarl at the image of him greeting her. Is he hugging her, touching her, kissing her? Fuck, I will kill him. *Keep it together, Saint.*

"You're too kind, thank you, and you're looking handsome as ever." Her response has my blood boiling.

"Your table for two is ready, Mr. Macari." I assume the waiter is bringing them to their table; the sound of Sage's heels is all I can hear. They go through the usual date conversation topics: *How are classes? How's work? I'm sorry for giving you a panic attack at the art exhibit.* Your usual shit. But then Sage says something that has me sitting up straighter.

"How was your friend's service? I'm so sorry to hear of your loss." There is a brief silence, and a shuffling of glasses against the table.

"It was beautiful. He would have thought it was over the top, but it was a nice memorial for him and his family." Another long silence. The sounds of plates being set on the table indicates their food has arrived.

"How long were you friends for?" Sage is wasting no

time in trying to get information, and I smile to myself for her forwardness.

"We went to Berkeley together; he was my first friend in a new state after moving here from Florida. It was strange, though; he never had any enemies, or so I thought, and the day before he went missing, he was acting very strange. He kept saying he felt like he was being watched. Always on edge. I'm still so confused about the whole thing."

"I'm so sorry." Her voice is a mere whisper, as if she truly feels sympathy for the guy. We found out a lot about Damien before we ended his pathetic life. He was the main culprit for locating the Wilder household and relaying that information to the next in line to carry out the plans for the horrific fire. So, Damien located the house, took this information up north to the two lowlifes we interrogated, who then struck the match that ultimately set the house ablaze.

We've been successful so far in following the trail and eliminating those along the way. However, we've yet to find the main perpetrator and mastermind in the murder of Mr. Wilder and the attempted murder of Sage. We are following the right track but still haven't reached the finish line.

"Don't be sorry, beautiful. It is what it is. We'll find out what happened. It's only a matter of time." Dante spoke with such confidence in his statement, it made me feel a little uneasy. Who is this guy? My mind starts to kick into high gear, trying to decipher Dante and how he is connected with all this. As my mind races through all the knowledge I have of this man, his next question has every-thing coming to a fast halt.

"If you don't mind me asking, how did you get the scars on your hands?"

I freeze, awaiting Sage's response and praying to God she doesn't have another panic attack.

SAGE

# CHAPTER 28

## SAGE

*Stay calm, Sage. You knew this question was coming. Inhale one, exhale one. Repeat. You can do this.* Before answering, I take a small sip of my water, trying to calm my nerves as much as I can before I have to explain. Okay, I've stalled long enough. Here goes nothing.

"On my fourteenth birthday, my house caught on fire due to faulty electrical wiring. I was sleeping in my bedroom as the house was almost completely engulfed in flames." I pause, taking a few deep breaths. "My father perished in the flames; I almost didn't make it out." My stomach twists and nausea is fast coming before a gentle hand is placed over mine that is resting on the table. Warmth spreads throughout my fingers and up my arm. Dante's hand is so large it completely covers mine.

"I'm so sorry, Sage. That sounds terrifying. Now I understand what a total ass I was for showcasing my paint-ing. God, I'm an idiot. Please forgive me." Dante's words are so sincere I can't help but give him a sympathetic smile.

He is shaking his head in disbelief, clearly struggling with his embarrassment about his painting.

"It's okay, Dante. Please don't apologize. How would you have known? Your painting is beautiful. You have every right to showcase it in your own exhibit." I remove my hand from the table, allowing his hand to rest against the white tablecloth. As much as this man is kind, generous, handsome, and sincere in his apology, I still don't fully know him. And the moment our skin touches, the only person I wish for it to be is Saint. Which quickly brings me back to why I'm really here.

"Anyway, enough about me. Tell me more about you, Dante. This is the third time seeing you, yet I feel like I barely know you." I hope that question comes out more inconspicuous than it sounded. His eyes soften a bit, and a lazy smile spreads across his face as he raises his wineglass to his lips.

"Well, originally, I'm from Florida and came here after high school to attend Berkeley. Since graduating a couple of years ago, I started the art gallery and have since been sharing my love for the arts with the amazing community of Golden Heights."

"It's funny. I've lived here my whole life and have never seen your studio before, or you for that matter." Okay, this time my tone is a little more suspicious. It's true, though. I've always been in the art community and have never seen his studio, nor him. Golden Heights is a large town, but I feel as though I would have noticed this man or at the very least seen him around.

"Nothing gets past you. Does it, Sage?" There is a weird shift in his tone when he says my name this time. It's lower, deeper, and menacing. It gives me a nervous feeling in the pit of my gut.

"I'm just what people would call observant," I counter. The hard edges of his face and penetrating gaze hold me captive as he tilts his head to the side, inspecting me, or rather, waiting for me to continue. But I don't. I hold his gaze. I'm hoping to make him feel as uncomfortable as I was fast becoming.

"My studio is rather new, only available to the public upon invitation. Similar to the one I gave you and your plus one. Ophelia, was it? Pretty name."

Okay, this conversation is going from sincere and innocent to calculating and prying. What is this sudden shift of personality with him? I can't figure him out, but there is something telling me to press on, to drill him for more. This is my chance to help find my father's murderer.

"Tell me more about your family. I met your brother and his friend at the club. What kind of person was your father? Luther, was it?" My skin heats in an instant. My father's name rolls off his tongue like an old friend, or enemy. I can feel my cheeks heat as my blood rushes to my face and chest.

"How do you know his name?" I ask, my tone flat. I don't recall ever mentioning my father's name to him.

"You told me when you were explaining your scars."

"No, I don't believe I did. So, enlighten me, Dante. How do you know my father's name?" A long pause passes; a silent battle rages between us to see who will break eye contact first. I'm not letting up. My father is a sacred subject for me and anyone who dares speak his name is a threat to me, to my family, and to the club. An evil smile briefly touches his lips, causing me to inhale a calming breath to help me remain composed.

"Ah, I see. Well, I must have heard it in the paper after the fire. It was reported on, wasn't it?"

"It was, but his first name was never mentioned. They referred to him as Mr. Wilder. No mention of a first name for him or myself. So, stop making excuses, please, and tell me the truth." My skin is red-hot. I am surprised I can keep a cool tone at this point. I know without a shadow of a doubt this man has to be connected to my father's murder in some way, shape, or form.

"Well, I feel the air between us has shifted a bit, and—"

"Sage, sweetheart. I need you to come home immediately, please. It's an emergency." I jerk my head to the side as a pair of hands lift me from my chair and assist in grabbing my bag.

"Frankie, what are you doing here?" I ask in a hushed tone. What the fuck was going on?

"Are the boys okay? What's going on?" No answer. Frankie isn't even looking at me. Instead, he pins Dante to his chair with a glare that could make someone internally combust.

"Frankie, long time no see, old friend. How are you?" Dante says, making me stop in my tracks.

"You know my uncle?" I ask, confusion making my head hurt.

"Oh, we go way back. Don't we, Frankie?" His tone is condescending, and it puts me even more on edge than I was before.

"Officer Macari. Yes, it's been a long time."

"Officer Macari? You're a cop?!" I practically yell, the whole restaurant now starting to shift their attention to our table.

"Sage, let's go. I'll explain later," Frankie whispers to me, but I am tired of being confused and left in the dark, and I'm not going anywhere until I get answers.

"No, I want to know now. Please, *Officer Macari*, explain to me how you know my uncle?" I wanted to punch the smug little expression off Dante so bad, but assaulting an officer didn't seem like the right idea in a public place, or in any place, for that matter.

"Ah, what a shame Frankie never mentioned me. We were close for a while, back in the day." My head snaps to

Frankie, who is still looking at Dante as if praying he would disappear. "I was the federal agent assigned to your family's fire, or should I say, the horrific murder of your father." My heart races with this new information and answers the question I've wanted to know the answer to since that fateful day. The feds never truly believed it was an accident either. Had they been investigating this the whole time without my knowledge? Why?

"So, tell me, why don't I know you personally then, if you're the agent assigned to my family? I feel like we should be well acquainted since I, for one, was involved in the fire as well." Dante's eyes shift to Frankie, and I follow his line of sight.

"I'll leave that up to your uncle to explain. It's been a nice night, Ms. Wilder. I hope we can do it again sometime." Dante stands from his chair, tosses cash on the table, and leaves me and my uncle standing alone in a restaurant full of people who are still watching us with utter shock. I'm not ending the night like this. Fuck no. I am going to get my answers, and I am going to get them right fucking now.

SAGE

# CHAPTER 29

## SAGE

I follow Dante out of the restaurant, my uncle spewing some nonsense behind me as he follows close on my heels. The moment I burst through the restaurant doors, I spot Dante unlocking his all-black BMW in the parking lot.

"Dante!" I yell to him, my voice carrying across the lot. He doesn't stop. He keeps fidgeting with his keys, but when I yell his name again and push his car door shut, I know I finally have his attention.

"I wasn't finished. What do you mean you know Frankie? I want to know right now." Dante licks his bottom lip and annoyance finally rears its ugly face.

"Did you really think the feds believed your case was an accident? Who told you that, by the way?" I look at Frankie and am surprised that Saint is now standing beside him, anger evident by the crease between his eyes. I turn back to Dante.

"We've been investigating Luther's death since the day he died. In the beginning, we worked closely with your uncle, trying to identify every enemy he ever had. And let me tell you, Sage, there were many. Frankie was helpful at the start, but soon enough, he stopped cooperating with the investigation and went silent all together. We felt like we were on the right track at one point and leads brought us to Damien's involvement. So, I inserted myself into his life and became friends rather quickly. I was on the verge of new intel, and suddenly he magically disappeared." Dante's eyes meet Saint's, and my chest tightens at the silent communication between the two. Does he know Saint and Saxon are behind his death? "It's all a bit suspicious, isn't it, Saint? All the leads we follow magically disappear or end up dead under suspicious circumstances." Saint lifts his chin in defiance but gives away nothing.

"What are you implying, Officer Macari?" I ask, gritting my teeth in frustration.

"What I'm implying, Sage, is as much as it hurts to lose a loved one, you and your father's club need to leave it up to the professionals to track down the men responsible for his murder. Now that you know we've been actively investigating his homicide, I will keep you updated on any new leads we find. Unlike your uncle, who seems to have lost interest in finding his brother's murderer, I hope you and I can keep this line of communication open. I, for one, know what it's like to lose someone close to you, and I can assure you that I am here to help, if only you and your family will let me." I step back as Dante opens his car door, steps inside, and drives off, leaving me with more questions than answers.

I take a few deep breaths before I turn to face my uncle.

"What the fuck is he talking about, Frankie?" My tone is murderous. I am angry, more than angry. I am irate. How could he stop assisting in the investigation? Didn't he want to know who did this to our family? To me?

"It's not as it seems, Sage," he speaks in almost a whisper, which irritates me even more.

"It's not? Then please enlighten me, Frankie. Help me understand!"

"We need to discuss this at home, Sage. This is too public for this type of conversation. Frankie, meet us back at the house immediately." I've never heard Saint speak to Frankie in such a way. Almost like he is scolding a child, but Frankie doesn't fight back. As we make our way to Saint's Tahoe, leaving my car in the parking lot, Frankie gets on his motorcycle and takes off in the direction of the house.

We follow close behind, not wanting to let him out of our sight in case he takes off.

"He lied to me today," Saint says in a low, whisper-like tone, almost as if he didn't mean to say this out loud. I turn to face Saint, his profile hard and completely focused on Frankie's taillights.

"What do you mean?" Saint's knuckles begin turning white, the squeak of the steering wheel leather beneath his hands showing just how much anger he is holding back.

"Today, in the kitchen, I was looking into Dante's background, and when I asked if he knew who Dante was, he told me no. It makes sense now that he was the agent assigned to your family's case. I thought I recognized him in the club, but I couldn't pinpoint where I'd seen him before." He clenches his jaw so hard, I fear he might break a tooth.

"That was seven years ago, Saint. I can barely remember people's names after five minutes." It's true I am awful at names, but I can see the frustration in the way he narrows his eyes. He is pissed at himself for not remembering. As if it is his responsibility to remember every person he's ever seen or met. Saint's always put the most pressure on himself. He is a perfectionist to a fault. No mistake is a good mistake in his eyes, and when it comes to his family, it's his duty to protect us. This is why Saxon trusts him so much, as do I. He's always looking after others before himself. He is quite literally a man who would take a bullet for you.

"Seven years is a long time," I say. "Why would Frankie lie to us? Or not want to work with the feds to track down Dad's killer?" I can't find a reason why not working with the feds would be beneficial. Chills start prickling my skin, and I try my hardest to force away the thoughts of betrayal, especially when it involves Frankie. My uncle. My last remaining family besides my brother. There is no way he was involved in my father's, his brother's, murder.

"Sax, are you home? We need to talk immediately. Frankie's on his way over as well. You may want to brace yourself. I have Sage." I look over at Saint; I hadn't noticed he had called Saxon. I can hear Saxon's confused and angry tone from the passenger seat. I can't make out what he's saying, just that his tone gives away his mood almost immediately.

"We'll tell you everything in five minutes. We're almost there." Saint hangs up the call and pockets his cell.

"This isn't going to be good," I mumble, knowing my brother's anger is about to reach all new levels.

Saint pulls up right behind Frankie's bike and watches as he enters the house before the pair of us get out and make our way inside as well. The moment I open the door, Saxon's voice booms through the foyer.

"What the fuck is going on, Frankie?!"

"Listen, it's not what it's going to sound like. You have to take my word on this and just trust me."

"Trust you? I don't even know what the fuck is going on. Please enlighten me. Tell me why I get a call from Saint saying the three of you are on your way, and that I better brace myself with whatever this is?" Saxon waves his hands in the air at the mention of "this." Frankie and Saxon are standing in the living room. Upon entering the room, the energy is palpable. So many questions and so many emotions swirl in my gut; I hope Frankie is right, that this is all a misunderstanding. When they see Saint and me enter the room, Frankie puts his hands in his pockets while Saxon immediately asks us what's going on.

Saint gives a shortened brief of my date—how Frankie showed up and dropped a bomb that Dante Macari was actually a federal agent who had been assigned to Luther's murder seven years ago. He also mentions how Dante told us that Frankie stopped communicating with the feds while they were hunting down the murderer.

Then it all happened so quickly. One minute, Saint was talking, and the next, Saxon has his hands clutching Frankie's shirt and is slamming him against the wall. Shit, I knew this wouldn't go well.

"Saxon, stop! Please!" I scream, but I am sure he can't hear me over his own voice, demanding Frankie to tell him if he was involved in any way. I know better than to step in between Saxon and Frankie. When my brother goes into his rage, he sees black, and no one is safe.

"Sax, enough. We need him alive to explain himself." Thank God for Saint and his sheer size. He is able to grab Saxon and pull him away from Frankie. He is still yelling. However, I am able to stand in front of Saxon to try and bring his attention back to me instead of Frankie.

"Sax, please look at me. Just stop—look at me!" I yell. After another few minutes has passed, Saint and I are able to calm Saxon down enough to try and get more information from Frankie. We find it safest to have Saxon be at one end of the room with Saint, while Frankie and I take the sofa furthest in the corner. Saxon can't sit down; obviously, the man is possessed and ready to end Frankie's life if he was involved in the slightest bit in our father's murder.

"Frankie, for fuck's sake, explain yourself from the beginning. Why the hell did Dante make it sound like you were somehow involved.?" I finally ask. The room goes eerily silent after my question. The only noticeable sounds are Saxon's breathing, which is still harsh from his outburst. Finally, Frankie sighs. Rubbing his hands through his hair before he leans on his knees and clasps his fingers together.

"Everything Dante said is true." Fuck, I wasn't expecting him to say that. I look at Saint, who has moved closer to Saxon just slightly, so he can catch him if he rushes Frankie again.

"He's right about me no longer helping with the investigation. And it's not what you think it is. In the beginning, I did everything I could, told them everything I knew about your father and his deals in hopes that it would lead to his killer. Then, suddenly, in the midst of the investigation, I started receiving messages from blocked numbers, letters with no return addresses, even fucking pictures of you and Sax doing mundane things, like eating lunch, going for rides, or going to school. I showed the first few letters and messages to the police, but then I received this one." Frankie pulls out his cell, skims through his photos, and pulls up an image before handing it to me.

I take the phone from his hand and peer down at the image. It's of my father, from maybe eight or nine years ago. His handsome face resembles so much of Saxon, but it isn't him in the photo who I am staring at. It's the woman. A woman I've seen before. I squint down at the image until realization crashes through me like a freight train.

"Is that Mayor Harrison's wife?"

My phone buzzes in my purse that's still hanging off my shoulder. I pull it out to see I have a text alert. Opening the message, I read and reread the text illuminating my cell phone screen.

DANTE:

Don't let your guard down around your uncle. We need to talk again; you and your brother may be in danger. Let me know when you're free as soon as possible.

What the actual fuck is going on?

SAGE

# CHAPTER 30

SAGE

I pocket my cell without responding to Dante. I need answers about the photo that I'm now looking at. Bile churns in my stomach as I look at the far too intimate photo of Mayor Harrison's wife, Gloria. Dad has her held against his chest, their eyes locked on one another so enduringly emotional it feels wrong to be looking at this photo. A private moment captured to expose something that was meant to be secret.

"Wait, was Dad having an affair with Gloria?" I ask in a whisper as I hold back the tears forming behind my eyes.

"It looked to be that way," Frankie says, and my chest tightens while the blood in my veins rushes to my ears. I'm not mad, but I am feeling... something. Confusion maybe?

"Are you saying the reason Dad was murdered was because he was seeing Gloria behind Mayor Harrison's back?" It's the same question I'd already asked, but I'm not sure I truly understand. Saxon comes closer to the couch, his hand waving off Saint as if to say he's fine, and I hold out the phone to him. He takes it and glares at the image with Saint at his side, looking over his shoulder.

"So, you're implying Mayor Harrison found out about the affair and this could be the reason he was murdered in the first place?" Saxon breaks the silence that had fallen over the room. "What were the other messages you received? The letters and stuff you just said?"

"They were all short, nothing that stood out or gave any information about who could have sent them. One said, 'Any affair, by its nature, feels like a spark but ultimately ends in disaster.' It was as if the messages were meant to be for your father, not me. The messages were all phrases that indicated your father was having an affair, but until I received the photo proving his connection with Gloria, I hadn't believed it. The reason I quit cooperating with the police was because if Mayor Harrison is involved, the evidence I would have collected, I would be giving straight to the cops. You three and I all know how the mayor has the police chief in his back pocket. So, I stopped. I started doing my own digging and got close a few times, but every lead I got led to a dead end."

Frankie paused then, standing from the sofa and pacing the room, looking defeated and so alone. As if this whole time, he'd been carrying this burden on his shoulders.

"Why keep this from us?" I ask, watching him pace back and forth.

"Sweetheart, you'd just lost your dad. Why would I tell a fourteen-year-old who just lost their only parent left that he was having an affair that may have caused his death, which almost killed you as well? My only job was to protect you both and make sure nothing else hindered you from having a beautiful, fulfilled life. I couldn't break you anymore than you already were." He looks at Saxon then, his eyes full of sadness and hurt.

"I know you were twenty at the time, but don't forget

you lost a parent as well. I don't care how much of an adult you think you were at the time; you lost a father. You started becoming more and more angry as you grew up. You carried so much on your shoulders from the club, feeling as though you needed to raise Sage, stepping into a role you weren't fully prepared for. The best years of your life were taken from you and forced you to grow up faster than you should have. You should have been out partying, getting in trouble, and chasing girls, instead you quickly became president of The Kings' Aces—the leader of the greatest motorcycle club in the country."

I look at Saxon, whose eyes are fixed on Frankie; his expression is as unreadable as it is most of the time. If he feels broken or distraught, like I am, he never shows it. Instead, he lets out a deep breath and straightens his spine a little more.

"Don't pity me, uncle. I wanted this; I've always wanted this. I missed out on nothing. Now, send me all the messages, pictures, and letters you received from this anonymous prick. Since it's been seven years, and you've still not found the person responsible, I will." Saxon then exits the living room, grabs his motorcycle keys, and speeds down the driveway.

This is how he handles any of his emotions; he never allows others to see him falter or crack. He leaves by himself and deals with it on his own. It's how he's always been.

"I'll follow him," Saint finally says.

"No, don't. Let him allow his feelings to come out. He won't show them when he's around anyone. He won't do anything dumb; he just needs… time." I say, placing my hand on his chest to stop him from leaving. I fix my eyes on Frankie.

"Thank you for telling us, but next time you need to share with us everything you know. I can't afford to lose anyone else." I cross the room and give him a hug; his arms wrap around me and squeeze so hard it feels like an apology.

"I'm so sorry, witch stick. I've only ever wanted to protect you."

"I know." I hug him a moment longer, his embrace speaking so many unspoken words. Frankie kisses my forehead before saying goodnight to the both of us, grabbing his keys and leaving as well. The moment his bike is down the road, and we can no longer hear the rumble of his engine, Saint wraps his arms around me, pulling me into his chest where I finally allow the tears to fall. After I am sure I have no tears left, I pull out my phone and send a message.

ME:

Meet me tomorrow at Green's Café, 7:00 a.m.

DANTE:

Got it.

SAGE

# CHAPTER 31

## SAGE

The next morning, I arrive at the café twenty minutes early. My curiosity is humming at what this federal agent needs to tell me. I haven't mentioned anything to Saxon and Saint about my meeting, but now that I am here alone, I feel like I should have brought someone. The bell on the front door rings, and I can feel the ominous presence of Dante before I even look up from my coffee.

"Thank you for meeting me," Dante says, pulling out his chair and taking a seat opposite of me.

"What do you have to tell me?" I get right to the point. One, because I hadn't told anyone where I was going and two, I am dying to know what the hell is going on. He waves to the waiter and orders a black coffee before settling his eyes on me.

"Sage, the reason I was at the club that night we met was because I knew you'd be there." I furrow my eyebrows. Was he following me?

"For the past seven years, I've been assigned to your

father's case in hopes of taking down the higher-ups in this town who think since they have power, they can do whatever the hell they want."

"Are you talking about the mayor?" The look of shock that Dante gives me tells me he didn't think I knew about my father's affair. Hell, I hadn't known until last night.

"Frankie told me." He closes his eyes for a long while before continuing. He leans closer towards me, and his voice is a mere whisper.

"I wanted to meet with you to inform you that I have been watching you and your brother since the fire, due to many tips that your lives may be in danger as well. The moment Frankie was informed that the pair of you may be targeted next, he stopped all communication with me. I thought that was suspicious on its own because why would he not want to be involved in figuring out this whole mess with your family."

The look on my face must show the same confusion because I can't find the words to ask or explain or even speak, for that matter. So much information is being thrown at me so fast, from last night to now. I can't believe this is my own life and not a movie plot.

"Why did you make yourself known now, after all these years?" I ask. Why target me in the club, or invite me to the art show, or paint a fucking picture of me to showcase at the exhibit? Why now?

"Your uncle had been radio silent for the last six years, but recently, with the help of Damien before his untimely demise..." I look away from him for the quickest moment, unable to hold his gaze. "He informed me that a man he was in contact with wanted him to accompany him on a job that would involve a very high-up motorcycle club. Initially, he didn't want to do it. He said it felt like a suicide mission, but I encouraged him to move forward. That way, when I made contact with you, it didn't look too suspicious." Dante pauses for a moment, taking a long sip of his coffee. His eyes are heavy and dark shadows appear below his eyes. He is tired and rundown by the looks of it. I'd just seen him last night, yet he looks like he aged ten years over night.

"What I'm getting at is, your uncle is finally coming out of the wood works after six years of no activity, and the first thing I hear of is a job that would end the biggest motorcycle club's existence by eliminating you and your brother. I took drastic action and inserted myself into your life as quickly as I could, hoping that your uncle would fear that if I was around, you and Saxon couldn't be touched. We were still working behind the scenes and hoping to get more answers on this job that Damien had coming up, but then he disappeared, and I no longer had my connection."

I inhale a deep breath, not understanding. If this is all true, why does my uncle want to hurt or *eliminate* me and Saxon? We're family. I silently curse my brother and Saint for killing Damien. "What do I do now?" I ask, not knowing what else to say.

"Don't do or say anything, Sage. I will continue to be in contact with you when I know more information. In the meantime, stay with your brother and Saint. I know they can protect you, even though their ways are less than legal. They can keep you safe. I'll message you soon." With that, he leaves me sitting in the café, alone and more confused than I've ever been. I need a nap.

———

I can't sleep after learning everything about Frankie from my secret meet up with Dante. My chest hurt with thoughts that my father was keeping secrets from Saxon and me. My father told us everything, or at least, I thought he did. Knowing that he was having a secret relationship with a married woman feels like a betrayal. Not that my father didn't deserve love or a companion, but with a married woman—the fucking mayor's wife, of all people?

Love is funny. You can't pick who your heart will love, but it's dangerous when it could be someone who is already spoken for. Love is painful, yet peaceful, dangerous, yet fearless. Did my father know the dangers of falling in love with Gloria? Probably. Why else would he have kept such a secret? Love can be our most desired and most troubling emotion, yet it's still something we all crave and want more than anything. At least, I do.

The longer I sit in the library thinking about it, the more I realize my father and I are not so different. He fell for a woman who was spoken for—unavailable. And here I am, falling for someone I know would cause problems between my brother and me. Still, I can't get the image of Saint out of my head. The feeling of his calloused hands against my skin. The taste of his kiss. The presence of him in the room, a dark shadowy pressure, squeezing against my skin and igniting the dormant butterflies in my stomach. I crave his scent, his voice, his touch—fuck—I want him to tell me I am his good girl. I've never had a kink for something like praise, but when Saint says them, it makes me feral for him.

"May I come in?" I startle and drop my copy of *Romeo and Juliet*. I fumble for my book where it now lies face down on the floor.

"Yes, of course," I say as I lean over and retrieve my book. A sudden dark, palpable weight follows behind him as he enters the room, and it presses against my lungs. Suddenly, it's too hot in here. I need to take my blanket off my lap. I watch as he walks into the library, freshly showered, as was I, and the scent of clean soap fills my nose. Crossing the room, he takes the chair across from me, spreading his legs wide and placing his hands on the arms of the chair before asking me, "What are you reading?" I look down at my book. Why, I'm not sure. I know what I'm reading.

"*Romeo and Juliet.*" My voice comes out a little shaky, and I can't help but feel slightly embarrassed.

"Ah, a forbidden romance. Sadly, it ends in tragedy, am I right?" Saint never reads; I am taken aback at how he knows. "Is that one of your favorites? By Shakespeare, I mean."

"I think it is." My voice is small as I turn the book over in my hand again and again. I've never thought about it before, but I guess I do gravitate towards this specific love story. We both fall silent, the grandfather clock in the corner the only noise breaking the painful silence. I finally look up at Saint, his silvery eyes burning into my skin. His hair is still a bit wet, and his lips are slightly parted. He is shirtless, and maybe this is what is making me feel off balance because all I want to do is run my hands down his chest and follow the trail of hair that dips below his sweatpants. Now that I know what's beneath the clothing, I want more of it. I've begun to crave it.

"Do you like what you see, baby?" His voice is sultry and caresses me like velvet.

"I think I do." *Where the hell did that come from, Sage?* I swallow, the room suddenly feeling so small.

"You *think?*"

"Maybe I need to see more to make up my mind completely." The smile that pulls the corner of his mouth up has my heart racing and core throbbing. But when he licks his bottom lip, I crumble.

"Is Saxon back yet?" I pray he isn't, as bad as that sounds, but all my body wants right now is Saint. His only response is a shake of his head.

"He went to Sky's, so that means it's just you and me tonight." Just what I want.

"So, what do you have in mind?" I'm playing with him;

it's evident by the devilish smile he keeps giving me. I need more.

"I have a few things I could think of, however, all my ideas require you to be a lot less clothed." Now it's my turn to smile. I stand from my chair, the rest of the blanket collecting at my feet. Grabbing the hem of my tank top, I pull it over my head, baring my chest to him, as I toss my shirt to the side.

"Like this?" I say in a small voice.

"A bit more, sweetheart." His eyes remain on mine, not once breaking contact. I thread my fingers through my shorts and pull them down my legs, leaving only a small piece of fabric to cover my most intimate parts.

"How about now?" I ask again as I squeeze and massage both my breasts. A guttural growl escapes his mouth as his eyes continue holding mine.

"You're getting warmer." With that, I remove my panties, my final piece of clothing, and stand completely exposed to him.

"That's *my* good girl. Already so wet for me." He's right. I can feel the slickness of my arousal against my thighs, and I can't prevent my face from heating at his discovery. Standing from his chair, he takes one step towards me. The heat from his body coats my skin, causing my nipples to harden instantly. A prominent bulge in his sweats shows just how ready he is for me, and I can't help the small sigh that falls through my lips. Lifting his hands, he cups my face, his thumb parting my lips with a slow caress. My eyes closed at his touch, the feeling so light but so sensual at the same time.

"Look at me, Sage." A soft whisper that touches my lips. His face is so close to mine I can taste his spearmint toothpaste on my tongue. "I want you to see who it is you belong to. So, tell me, Sage. Who owns you?" My breath hitches as I try to contain the swarm of butterflies beating and clawing their way around in my stomach. I pull my bottom lip into my mouth, biting it just enough to bring me back down to earth.

"I belong to you." My words are shaky as I try to breathe normally, but my attempt is futile.

"And who am I?" Our lips brush against each other, the warmth of his skin heating mine.

"Saint. I—I belong to you, Saint." The force with which our lips collide is that of a lion finally catching its prey. Starving and unable to control himself when what he wanted most of all was right in front of him. I lay my hands flat against his abdomen, clawing my fingernails down every delicious dip and crevice of his muscles until I reach his waistband.

I pull away from his hold just long enough to pull his sweatpants down, freeing what I've been wanting this whole time. His impressive length is already fully erect as I coax Saint to sit down once again. He hesitates a moment, not wanting to relinquish control of the situation, but when I grasp his cock in my hand and start pumping ever so slowly, he gives in. Once he's seated, I kneel between his open legs, pushing my hair back from my face and grabbing his length once again. While holding his stare, I spit onto his tip and start working my hands up and down, eliciting a groan from his chest. It only edges me on. The way I am able to pull his pleasure from him is addicting, and I want to give him more. I want to please him.

Letting him go, I place my hands on his abdomen before I lick my lips and dip my head forward. I stick out my tongue, playing with his tip as I watch his mouth part and his abs flex at the sensations I invoke. Then slowly, I take him down, inch by inch, until he is touching the back of my throat. I hum around his velvety smooth skin, his cock twitching in my mouth at the vibrations.

"*Fuuuck*, that's it. Choke on me." His fingers thread

through my hair, his grip tight as he pushes my head further down his length until I gag and tears begin to blur my vision. He holds me there for a moment, listening to me choke and watching my drool drip from the corners of my mouth. It's filthy, and I love every bit of it.

He pulls out of me slowly, smiling at me with admiration.

"You're so fucking beautiful." My stomach heats with his words. Something about the way he looks at me and feeds me compliments makes my chest swell. Our relationship, up until now, had always been insult after insult. A budding game of cat and mouse, where we thrived off badgering each other. I bullied him, he bullied me—it was how we got along. I looked forward to seeing him, just to see how far I could push his buttons. It was like our relationship was a playground crush, and for years, this is how we operated.

So how did we get here? Me on my knees, fully exposed to the man I never imagined falling for. The admiration in his eyes speaks volumes to me. The once playful, annoying bully is now holding me with a lover's touch. Gentle and all-consuming in the way that I crave more and more until he occupies every ounce of my mind. Silvery eyes, calloused hands, a sensuous smile that makes my heart skip a beat. Every ounce of this man has slowly seeped out of the friend zone and entered a zone I am yet to identify. I willingly surrender to this man. He can have me, own me, destroy me in any way he sees fit. I am completely his. Is it because he sees me for me, flaws and all? Every scar, every dent in my exterior, yet he still calls me beautiful.

I've never needed a man to tell me I'm beautiful, but the way he makes me feel like I'm worthy. Worthy of love, worthy of affection and care, is more than any man has ever made me feel. I'm his equal. Rather, I am his queen he sets on a throne, where no one will ever hurt me. No one will ever allow me to feel anything but deserving. He makes me feel more like my previous self, the Sage before the fire. I've missed her.

"Come here, baby." Saint grabs me and lifts me effortlessly into his lap. His hands slide up my sides and pull me to his face. With his mouth on my chest, he gives feather light kisses to each breast. Kissing, licking, and nipping his way back and forth; all the while, his hands are pressed firmly to my back, keeping me against his body. The ache between my legs is throbbing and in desperate need of some type of friction to help alleviate my own pleasure.

I rock back and forth against his cock, spreading my juices up and down his length, dying for more of him. His chest vibrates with desire as he lifts his hips to meet my core.

"Desperate, are we?" His voice is low, and it only intensifies the pressure building in my core. "Tell me what you want, baby." I continue grinding against him, finding a rhythm and tilting my head back. I can't respond. My mind is focusing on finding a release.

"Use your words, Sage." Fuck, the way my name rolls off his tongue is so hypnotic.

"You. I want you inside me, please." I've never begged a man before, but for Saint, I'd beg all fucking night if I had to. Call me pathetic, but I see it as being passionate. The moment the word "please" leaves my lips, Saint grabs my hips and lifts me off his lap, only to set me down gently, penetrating me with each delicious inch of his cock. He lowers me slowly, allowing my walls to stretch and accommodate his length. I can't help the hiss and moans of satisfaction I let slip the moment I'm fully seated on his lap. My hands grip his shoulders as my fingers dig into his skin. Saint is big, and I don't mean regular big. He's the biggest man I've ever been with, both in length and thickness. It's painful at first, but quickly transforms into a toe-curling pleasure that ignites in my stomach and builds with each thrust of his hips.

"Oh, fuck," I whimper, the feeling of being impossibly full takes hold, and I'm an addict for more. I work my hips up and down. The sound of my wetness and our skin slapping fills the room in a chorus of filth and vulgarity.

"That's it, baby. Ride my cock." His words bring a whole new sense of confidence I've never had during sex. I've experimented, yes, but Saint makes me want to show him just how much of a dirty little whore I can be. As I continue to chase my release, Saint tilts his head back in euphoric bliss, allowing me to take control, and I've never felt so feminine, so desired, so powerful. His hands are gripping my ass hard enough to bruise, and I hope it does. I want him to mark me, to show that he is mine and I am his.

He slaps my ass so hard the sound cracks against the air. I welcome the sting and moan as he rubs the pain.

"Oh, fuck, Saint I'm going to—" I'm so close. I can feel my orgasm on the precipice, and I want it to crash through me and consume me in the best way. Our breathing grows heavy, but when Saint reaches in front of me and starts circling my clit with his thumb, I detonate. I moan through the most intense, mind-numbing orgasm that seems to last forever, and I never want it to stop. His hands grip my hips again as his thrusts grow thunderous and relenting. His hips lift and meet mine as the sound of our skin slapping picks up and fills the room. I'm still floating high on my orgasm when Saint finds his own release; his grunt and final thrust that reaches the perfect spot, have me spiraling into another orgasm. My skin is beading with sweat as warmth ignites once again, deep in my core, flooding every available ounce of my being.

Sex with Saint is almost like a dream—a fantasy, even. Men like this only exist in the romance books I read. Women write about men like this. Men who can bring us to an orgasm and suddenly another and another until we're riding a roller coaster of pleasure and euphoric bliss we never thought possible. Saint brings me down from the clouds of contentment, pressing our foreheads together as we catch our breath.

"What are you doing to me?" A whisper against my lips draws me in until we devour one another again; our lips are gentle, warm, and filled with so many unspoken words it's hard to decipher. I don't answer the question because I don't have a good answer. It's not what I'm doing to him, but what exactly are we doing to each other, and how the hell do we plan to allow this *thing* to continue? The plan is blurry, and I start to feel like there was never a plan in the first place. We let the built-up, caged, and wild animals unleash until we collided against one another. And there's no way of ever capturing them again. We had a taste and ate the forbidden apple. There's no going back, and quite frankly, I don't want to.

SAINT

# CHAPTER 32

## SAINT

Last night, the library incident was only the appetizer. Sage and I ventured to her room, then went to the kitchen for a snack. Then we ventured to my room, the shower, the kitchen again until the sun started rising and we realized we'd never gone to bed. I couldn't stop. She's the candy your mom tells you to stop eating after two pieces, but when she turns around, you dive in for more and more until you've developed a sweet tooth, and nothing can stop you from getting your next taste.

I've crossed the line of best friend code, and honestly, it was a long time coming. Deep down in the depths of my soul, I've wanted this. Fuck, have I wanted this. I've dreamed, fantasized, and wished for the moment I could be inside Sage Wilder, and now that I have, I'm never letting her go. We'll have to tell Saxon eventually. There's no hiding this forever, but right now, I'm still floating on the highest of highs, and I never want to come down. Not yet.

I'll gladly live in this bubble of delusion we've created and stay here for as long as I can.

"We have to tell Sax." Sage's voice has me crashing down to Earth faster than I'd hoped for. She's lying at my side, her arm draped over my bare chest and her leg over my thigh. Her nails continue gently trailing over my chest, giving me goosebumps from the tickling sensation. "We can't hide this forever. The longer we do, the angrier he'll be." She's right. The longer this stays in the shadows, the more of a betrayal it will feel like. I breathe in a long sigh, the scent of strawberries and vanilla invading my scene.

"I'll tell him." I wasn't sure when, but I would.

"We should tell him together."

"No, let me do it. I'd rather he be mad at me and take out his anger first before confronting you. I've handled him angry before." I groan at the last bit. We both know a mad Saxon is a dangerous Saxon, and I know the storm that will unleash when I tell him.

"Well, I can't let you take all the blame."

"Yes, you can. Plus, aren't you going to be late for class?" The speed at which she flies out of bed is astonishing. Her muffled curses as she grabs her clothes and looks for her phone to check the time, have me stifling a laugh at how frazzled and chaotically she is moving.

"Fuck, I'm going to be late." Another glance at her phone. "I have to be there in twenty minutes. I won't make it in time." As she is dressing at lightning speed, I get out of her bed as well and grab my clothes.

"I'll drive you. I'll get you there on time. Meet me in the garage in five." I leave the room and hurry to my bathroom to brush my teeth before throwing on my boots and heading for the garage. It's warm outside, even for it being 7:45 in the morning, so I decide to take her on the bike. Plus, I always get to my destination faster on my bike.

Opening the garage, I back my bike out and am not

expecting to see Saxon standing there waiting for the door to fully open.

"Where are you going so early?" he asks, looking like he too hasn't slept all night.

"I'm taking Sage to class. She overslept, and she's scared she'll be late." His only response was a second too long glare as he steps up beside me.

"Right, when you're done I—" He's cut off.

"When are you telling Saxon?" Sage has her back to us as she closes the side door and peers down at her phone.

"Tell me what?" His question is laced with pure venom, his eyes shifting from me and landing on Sage, who looks mortified and utterly terrified at seeing Saxon. Her mouth drops just enough to be noticeable before she slams it shut. Silvery eyes met mine and go back to Saxon in a flash.

"I already told him I'm taking you to class because you can't set your alarm in time to get up for class." I pray that my lie works, but no amount of suspicion eases from Saxon's face as I lift Sage's helmet in her direction.

"You coming, or do you want to be even later than you already are?" She runs to my side, grabbing her helmet and giving her brother a quick kiss on the cheek before throwing her leg over my bike and securing her helmet.

"Saint, come right back when you're done. I have news. And, Sage, I want to speak to you after class." Saxon backs up from my bike, allowing me to start the engine and head down the driveway.

"He knows something's up," Sage says into my ear over the roar of my engine. As we continue to the main road, I reach back and squeeze her thigh.

"It'll be okay, Sage. I promise." I took off down the road, faster than the marked speed limit, but we were, in fact, late as fuck.

After I drop off Sage, she tells me Ophelia will bring her home since they have the same classes today. I watch as she heads towards her building and sneaks into the door before I head back towards the house. I'd be lying if I said I'm nervous about whatever Saxon has in store for me. I'm not scared of him. Hell, we've fought before—all-out fist fights a few times, but I've also never had to tell him I'm sleeping with his sister. That's what made the tightness in my chest more prominent.

When I pull back up to the house, I notice Frankie's bike is in the driveway, and curiosity sparks in my gut at whatever news Saxon has. Fuck, it hadn't even been twenty-four hours since Frankie dropped the bomb on us that Luther was having an affair with the mayor's wife. This can't be good. I leave my helmet on my bike and bring Sage's helmet inside, setting it on the table by the door. Then I follow the voices coming from the kitchen, mentally preparing myself for whatever is about to happen.

"So, you're telling me that someone was sending you these images in hopes that would stop you from communicating with the feds? You see, Frankie, that's where I have a hard time believing all this. My father was already dead at that point, so there was no need for blackmail at all. You knew nothing about his enemies, so why would you talking with Dante expose who the murderer was? Besides, the media stated it was an accident, faulty electrical. Am I right, Saint?" I was leaning against the door frame to the kitchen, Frankie's back to me, unaware of my appearance.

"That's right," I say, allowing Saxon to continue prying for information. Frankie looks back at me and then immediately back at Saxon. However, I can see the worry on his face by the scrunch of his forehead. I agree something isn't adding up. His story is messy and not making any sense. He is keeping something from us.

"Listen, you two, I don't appreciate being ambushed—"

"Then tell me the truth, Frankie!" Saxon doesn't let him finish whatever he was about to say. I cross my arms over my chest, watching the rise and fall of Frankie's shoulders from behind.

"Listen, your father was murdered, I'm assuming, because of his affair. No one knew other than the murderer and then me when I received the photos. I thought the logical suspect was the mayor, and the impossible amount of security he has tailing him at all times. I didn't want the feds finding out about the mayor and his wife's involvement in fear the murderer would retaliate and come after you and Sage. Besides, how do you know you weren't supposed to perish in the house like your father and almost Sage? What if Luther and the two of you were the targets?"

I hadn't thought about that. My blood starts to boil at the image of Sage being freed from the house, and imagining that Saxon could have been inside as well. They are my family. The only two people in this world I care most about. My eyes shift to Saxon. His dark glare still holds Frankie's, but I can tell he's considering what Frankie had just said.

"I was afraid if I continued working with Dante, the murderer would come back and take away the two of you. I figured that's what the blackmail was for, warning me to stay out of the investigation, or so I thought. I couldn't have your deaths on my hands. I wouldn't survive it. I couldn't lose you too."

I guessed that made sense in a way. The murderer, let's say someone connected to the mayor, who is a sleaze and dirty politician anyway, found out about his wife and Luther. They hired someone or sent someone to murder him, and thankfully, Saxon and Sage were lucky enough not to be caught in the crossfire. Barely. Then they threatened Frankie with retaliation if he continued to help the feds hunt down the culprit. Frankie is, or was, Luther's brother. They worked together, so the feds knew Frankie had the most information about who could have possibly wanted revenge on Luther.

"My only question is, why keep that from Saxon, then? Why not tell him, especially last night? Why try to hide it even more?" Frankie turns to face me, his expression shifting a bit, making me feel a hint of unease.

"You know your best friend as well as I do. What do you think is going through his head right now?" His question is clear.

"Find out if the mayor is truly behind all this, slit his throat and watch until the last drop of blood exits his body." Saxon answers for me. His anger is the root cause of Frankie not telling him.

"Exactly my point. Your anger will get you killed, boy. Best learn control if you want to take down the mayor." He's right. If we go after the mayor, we need to do it strategically and quietly. We can't just ride up to his mansion and bust through, guns blazing. We need proof and a solid plan. I watch as Frankie brushes his hands through his hair. A frustrated sigh fills the kitchen as he pulls out his phone and glances down.

"Right, I need to eat and shower. I'll call you later, Sax, and we'll figure something out." Pocketing his cell, he turns his back to Sax and makes his way past me into the foyer. Saxon and I say nothing as he exits the house and jumps on his bike. I enter the kitchen fully then, and sit down at the small breakfast nook table, leaning back and spreading my legs wide.

"What do you think?" I ask, adjusting my jeans and getting comfortable. Saxon looks at me, leaning his back against the island and shoving his hands in his pockets before answering.

"I don't trust him. He's been keeping all this from us for seven years. The only reason he said anything was because he got caught. Once a liar, always a liar." My shoulders stiffen at his comment. I'm not a liar per se, but I am keeping a huge fucking secret from him, and the guilt is strangling me inside.

"Can you get ahold of his phone records from that long ago, so we can pinpoint where the messages were pinging off the cell phone towers?" I am no computer genius, by any means, but I can definitely work my way around a computer.

"Yeah, of course," I answer.

"We'll start there. Maybe that can lead us to something." I stand from the chair and start towards my room, where my laptop is. Saxon's next question causes me to freeze in my tracks.

"Are you messing around with my sister?"

Fuck.

SAINT

# CHAPTER 33

## SAINT

I wanted to be the one to bring up the conversation, not the other way around. Now, it will definitely seem as though I've been lying to my best friend. This is what I get for sleeping with my best friend's sister. Fuck, this is going to hurt.

I turn to face Saxon, his face hard as granite as he pins me with his dark eyes that are now solid black. His eyebrows pinch even harder together at my silence, and before I know it, he's pushing off the island and storming over to me in a tornado-like fury. I close my eyes, allowing and welcoming the pain he is about to give me because, let's face it, I deserve this. The crack of his fist slams into my jaw, causing me to stumble back. I maintain my balance, but when his fist connects with my face once again, the force of his blow knocks my ass on the ground.

"Are you fucking kidding me!? She's my sister!" Saxon's voice says it all. He's more than upset; he's a man possessed, and no amount of friendship will excuse my

"

behavior. I welcome his next few blows over and over again. The metallic taste of blood fills my mouth, and the pain of his fists radiates throughout my skull.

"Fight back, you piece of shit!" I don't. I'll let him beat me for as long as he needs to. Every time I stand again, he throws another punch. My face, my stomach, my sides, I can only imagine how rough I'll look later. Guilt starts to bubble in my chest as I stand once more. Saxon has stopped, his breathing harsh and exhausted, but his expression gives way to more than just anger. He's hurt. This is betrayal at its worst, not only from his best friend, but from his sister.

"Sax, I never planned this. It just happened," I finally get out. Every word is painful from his relentless beating.

"Fuck you, Saint. She's my sister." I lift my shirt up and wipe the blood from my face, the constant drip irritating me.

"She's too good for you. She deserves—" Locks of his hair fall from its bun and he quickly secures it.

"She deserves the world," I finish for him. Lowering my head, I straighten my clothes out from the chaos. He's right. Sage is too good for me. My hands are stained with blood and filth that will never be clean. She's the light God chose to keep on this earth. An angel destined for greatness, who doesn't need the sin of a man like me tainting her.

"You and I both know she's better than us, Saint. She's better than all this." His hands gesture at his surroundings. His words mean more than just this beautiful house she lives in, but also the club, the brutality, and the secrets. "She deserves to marry a gentleman, live in a big fucking white house, have a dog and two kids, and be on the school committee. She's more than this life. She's pure." A long pause settles between us. His face is pained with the realization that Sage was born into this life, and whether he likes it or not, he can't protect her from choosing what she truly wants. I just hope what she wants is me. "We were destined to live this life, Saint."

He leans his back against the island once more, his head tilting back as he lets out a deep sigh. Blood drips from his busted knuckles, and I watch as one crimson drop splatters to the white marble floor. As I watch the blood spread, I can't help but agree with him. I'm the drop of blood, and she's the white marble. She's good, and I'm evil. Hades and Persephone. I'm selfish for wanting to keep her for myself, when in reality, she deserves rich, colorful gardens, not my dark shadowy depths.

"You're right." My voice is so low I wonder if he even hears me. "I'm sorry, Sax. I overstepped. It shouldn't have happened." I can't handle the blanket of regret and guilt that's now draped over me. I head to my room, knowing damn well what I have to do. I should end things between us. As much as I'd rather die than live in a world where she's not mine, I can't drag her down a path that's not meant for her. I can't stomp out her flames with my ashes. She needs the best, and I simply am not that.

"Do you love her?" Saxon's voice stops me once more before I reach my bedroom door. His question is something I've not allowed myself to think much about before. I like her. Fuck, I like everything about her. When she's gone, she is all I think about. When she's near, I want to touch her. I want to fight off all of her nightmares. I want to hold and cherish her. I want to be the person she runs to when she has a bad day, when she's sad, or angry, or happy. I want to be her first thought in the morning and her last thought when she goes to bed. I've always liked Sage. Ever since the first time we met, all those years ago.

The first time I was invited to Saxon's house after school. She was the first person I saw when I entered the doors. She was in jean shorts, a baggy boy shirt, black-and-white Converse, and a backwards baseball cap. A little tomboy, following around her father like he was her prince charming. Something about her energy pulled me to her—a gravitational force constantly surrounded her, and I never wanted to stay away. It was physically impossible. It's clear now: I've always loved her. I loved her then, I love her now, and I'll love her forever.

"Yeah, Sax. I do." I close my door after my confession, not caring anymore about the repercussions of my words. I love her and there's no changing that. I love her so much that I'd be willing to let her go to ensure her future shines as brightly as she does. As much as it would kill me, I know I should to let her go.

I know I should… but I won't.

She's mine.

# SAGE

# CHAPTER 34

## SAGE

"You and Saint?!" Ophelia practically screams on the lawn at our campus. Between classes, we grab our usual café sandwiches that are sold on campus and find a shady spot on the lawn to sit and eat before our next class starts.

"Shhh, O, don't yell," I whisper to her, but I don't miss the heads that snap in our direction at her declaration. Her face is still in shock, her mouth wide open and eyes as round as saucers.

"You know, I shouldn't be too surprised," she finally says, ripping open the Saran Wrap on her sandwich and taking a small bite.

"What do you mean, not surprised?" I ask, doing the same to my sandwich. Chewing her bread, she speaks with her mouth full.

"I mean, it's pretty obvious the way he feels about you. Constantly watching over you, interrupting almost every date you've ever been on, and the way he looks at you… I mean, come on, girl. *The way he looks at you.*" She emphasizes her last statement before taking another bite of her sandwich. I impatiently wait for her to continue. However, she never does.

"How?! How does he look at me?" I finally ask, my sudden outburst making her jump in surprise. She hurriedly starts chewing and swallows her bite.

"You don't see it? Jesus, Sage. The way he looks at you makes me believe in love at first sight. He makes me want that kind of love. The *have you seen the way he looks at you?* kind of love. You know what I mean?" I stare at my best friend for a moment, her eyes going off somewhere far away from here, as if she's trying to manifest this type of love. I watch as her eyes drift further and further away, the pit of my stomach aching for her. I silently pray we both find that kind of love. I know Saint likes me, but does he really love me?

"Anyway." She shakes herself out of the haze she was in and peers over my shoulder. Her eyes grow two sizes by the time I finally turn around to see what she's looking at. If Ophelia's eyes grow two sizes, mine must have quadrupled because it wasn't a what that she saw, it was a who. Dante.

I told Ophelia everything about Dante, Saint, and my uncle; I couldn't keep it from her any longer. Her shock at seeing Dante make his way over to us, dressed as if he were coming from another art exhibit, has her fingers fly over her cell phone screen. I know exactly who she's texting, and I'm thankful for it, Saxon. I don't know if I can truly trust the man. Then again, he didn't have to tell me anything involving my father's case, but he did.

"I just texted Saxon. Should we leave?" she asks, fear laced in every word she whispers. I shake my head. I should leave, but my curiosity and the slightly concerned look on Dante's face have me staying.

"Ladies, it's nice to see you again. Sage, may I have a quick word with you?" I look back at O, and she gives me a tentative look—a silent plea to stay put until Saxon gets here. Call me stupid, but my curiosity wins. I excuse myself from my best friend's presence, and we make our way to a private patch of grass beneath a tree.

"This better be—"

"Sage, listen to me." He cuts me off, his demand a whisper of concern that has my stomach churning. "You and Saxon cannot trust your uncle." I step back from Dante. Suddenly, his body is far too close for my liking.

"What are you talking about? What else has happened that you needed to come here to tell me that? You've already told me this."

"Listen, I know your father was involved with Mayor Harrison's wife. We know the police department has connections and resources that are being provided to the mayor, and we've been trying to weed out those involved with his less-than-legal business ventures." He lifts his head and peeks around, seeing if anyone's listening in, but we're alone.

"Like it or not, your father had a huge target on his back with our agents and once he was murdered, we dove deeper. We found things we weren't expecting. One being the affair he was having with Gloria and now this shit with the mayor and his 'resources.'" Dante uses air quotes when saying resources, and it made him look oddly human. No more the cool, stoic, mysterious art connoisseur, but now the real, gritty, intelligent FBI agent.

"How is this all connected, then?" I ask, a migraine starting to prickle behind my eyes at this whole mess.

"What I've found out so far is your uncle may have a deeper friendship with Mayor Harrison than he's letting on. It's quite possible your uncle is responsible for helping the men who killed your father. We've received intel that something big is about to happen, but we are not one hundred percent sure what. At the moment, you and

Saxon are not safe. I fear you're currently being targeted." The sound of the wind, the rustle of the trees, and the sound of Dante's voice all start to grow muffled, as if I'd just dunked my head underwater. The air is suddenly too thick to inhale, and my skin is hot, as if I'd just stepped in front of a heater. Dante's form is suddenly shrinking before my eyes.

*It's quite possible your uncle is responsible for helping the men who killed your father.*

No, no, no, no. There's no way Frankie was involved; no, this can't be right.

"Sage, look at me. Sage." Dante is talking. I can hear the faint, muted sounds of his voice while his hands rest on my shoulders, trying to snap me out of my soon-to-be panic attack. Then everything changes.

The squeal of tires and the unmistakable pop of three shots fill the air. Then I'm thrown to the ground. A heavy mass lies on top of me. The sudden darkness swirls around me.

"Stay down, Sage!" Dante yells from on top of me. His body is draped over mine as the unmistakable sound of gunshots pierces through the air. I close my eyes, covering my head with my hands as more shots are fired. Seconds feel like an eternity, but in reality, it was all of sixty seconds until silence falls around us.

"Dante? Dante?" He isn't answering me. I try to lift him off me, but he's too big. "Dante!" I scream as crimson liquid starts to pool around me, on top of me, on my hands, in my hair, down my neck. "Dante, wake up!" Scream after scream until footsteps come up beside me.

"Sage, are you okay?!" Ophelia is next to me, her cries frantic as she tries to push Dante off me. After a few tries and working together, we are able to roll Dante off me. A loud thud makes bile rise in my throat as I peer down at the now lifeless body of Dante. Blood is all over him. His eyes are closed without the slightest bit of movement coming from his form.

"Oh God," Ophelia cries, covering her mouth as she drops to her knees. "He's dead." Her cries grow louder and louder. The sound becoming unbearable. I cover my ears and close my eyes as if I could magically teleport somewhere, anywhere but here. I sit there beside Ophelia, hoping and praying this is all a dream, and I am going to wake up any minute.

But I never do.

"Sage! Are you hurt? For fuck's sake, look at me, Sage!" When I open my eyes, my brother is standing in front of me, his onyx-black eyes staring at me, waiting for a response. He pulls my hands from my ears and examines me for any injuries, but I am fine. Not even a scratch from where Dante threw me to the ground.

"Answer me. Are you hurt?" he asks again. I shake my head rapidly before looking back to the ground where Dante lies. Saint is there, checking his pulse, and I notice the deep black and blue bruises across his jaw and cheek. A deep gash slits across his eyebrow, and he has a puffy lip with dried blood crusting his mouth.

"Saint!" I say, kneeling down and cupping his face. "What happened?" He doesn't look at me. No, he looks over me—towards Saxon. I follow his gaze and look down to see Saxon's knuckles look just as bad as Saint's face.

"Did you two get in a fight?!" I blurt out, looking back at Saint, who's now released my hands from his face and stood, leaving me kneeling on the ground.

"We'll talk about this later. We need to go. *Now*." Saxon says, his tone a command, not a request. "Ophelia, ride with Saint back to the club. Sage, you're coming with me. You can shower at the club."

"But I can—"

"Sage, now!" Saxon yells, but when I turned around,

Saint is already leading Ophelia to his motorcycle. He doesn't even spare me a glance as he hands Ophelia his helmet and swings his leg over his bike. Ophelia looks at me with concern, tears, and a puffy face before she mouths the words, *I'm sorry.*

We will see each other in a bit when we get to the club. The sooner the better. Because I intend to find out what the fuck is going on.

SAGE

# CHAPTER 35

## SAGE

We arrive at the club, and Ophelia and I immediately head to the bathroom, where there are two shower stalls waiting for us. We both have Dante's blood all over us, me more so than her. Once we finish, there are two pairs of sweatpants and two white T-shirts folded and waiting for us on the bathroom sinks. The guys always have a change of clothes here for instances like these. Blood is never a good thing to track back to the house. Luckily, these clothes are small and fit Ophelia and me relatively well. They do the job. The moment I dress, I exit the bathroom, hell-bent on finding my brother and Saint.

"Where are you going?" Ophelia's voice calls after me, but I can't answer her. I'm too focused on finding two of the biggest pains in my ass. They are exactly where I thought they'd be—the meeting room. When I burst through the doors, my eyes immediately land on Saint's. Silver irises surrounded by fresh bruises and puffy skin.

"What the hell is going on? Why were you two fighting?" I have an idea of what it was, but I want to hear it from them.

"Don't play dumb, Sage. It's not a good look for you." My brother's voice is dripping with venom. The corner of his mouth tips up in a scowl that gives everything away.

"You and Saint have been keeping some secrets. I merely needed to relieve my stress and confirm my suspicions." I don't speak. I hold my ground with my spine straight and my stare burning into my brother, waiting for him to explode. But he never does.

"You're not to see each other anymore. Do you understand, Sage?" The way my chest hollows and vision turns red scares even me. I've never had a temper, but the sternness of my brother's voice as he makes demands as if I am a child has every drop of my blood boiling.

"You can't boss me around forever, Sax. You especially can't tell me who I can and can't see." Saxon's fist slams on the mahogany table so hard I fear it will splinter. I can't help the sudden jump of my muscles.

"You will do exactly what I fucking tell you to do because I'm the one in charge of you! I'm the one responsible for you!" He's never spoken to me in such a malicious way before; I've heard him lose his temper, but it was never directed towards me. I force down the lump in my throat. I will not cry.

"I'm no one's responsibility. I'm a grown woman, free to make her own decisions—" I stop when he starts taking long strides towards me. I'm not scared he's going to hurt me; he would never lay a hand on me. However, he's also never yelled at me before, or looked at me the way he is now. Like I'm his enemy he's about to eliminate.

"That's close enough, man." Saint's low voice is suddenly incredibly close. I was so focused on Sax, I hadn't noticed Saint moving to my side to stand slightly in front of me, blocking Saxon from getting any closer.

"You think that's wise, Saint?" The room falls silent. The tension, as thick as an electric blanket, makes the room heat to unbearable temperatures. "What? You think I'd hurt my own sister?" Saxon scoffs at his own question. He backs away before he raises his fist and hits Saint across the cheek.

"Sax, are you serious?! What the hell?!" I scream, grabbing hold of Saint's shirt, steading him from the impact. Sax raises a fist again, but I'm quicker. I stand in front of Saint, blocking Saxon from delivering another blow.

"Move, Sage." His words are lethal and laced with so much anger.

"If you hit him, you better hit me too. I'm guilty as well."

"I won't say it again."

"No!" I scream. Energy buzzes through my body; defiance I've never shown my brother makes him tense every muscle in his body.

"I know it was wrong to keep this from you, but you're proving us right. We knew you'd react this way. Always anger, no questions about why or how. Just Saxon's way or no way at all. Have you ever asked me what I want? Who I want? Out of everyone I could be with, I want to be with him." I can't help the shake in my voice. I don't want to cry, but I'm pleading, begging, for him to hear me out.

"He's protected me from day one. He's been there for me when you couldn't. When I was alone and feared the shadows in the night, Saint was there. He's always been loyal to you, doing everything you've told him to do. So now that we've grown feelings for one another, you get pissed and throw a tantrum like a child? You have a role in this as much as he does. What did you expect, Sax!? All the times you told him to follow me, watch over me, stay with me, you thought nothing would happen? He's always been constant for me—Mom died, Dad's dead, fuck, who knows about Frankie, and you… you've been off living your life, trying to find love for yourself, leaving Saint behind to watch over me as if I needed watching. Did he ever tell you no?"

The room is silent. I'm not losing this fight, and I'll be damned if Saxon is going to stand in my way. I finally lower my voice, a sudden wave of exhaustion coming over me.

"You have to see this for what it is, Sax. Yes, I'm sorry for keeping this from you, but I care about him, and I hope he cares about me too. You can't stop me from being with him. You need to push your overbearing, protective, asshole brother role aside so we can work together on figuring out what the actual fuck just happened to Dante."

Oh shit, Dante. He was murdered—in front of me. He died protecting me, shielding me from the bullets of the drive-by. Bile quickly rises in my throat as I look down at my hands. I can still see the blood, his blood, coating my fingers, dripping down my arms. He told me Frankie was involved in some way. Our uncle had a hand in killing our father. My breathing is short and jagged; I can't inhale enough to fill my lungs.

"I-I can't." I grab the table beside me, steadying my swaying body as I continue to try and catch my breath.

"Sage, listen to me. Breathe. Come on, breathe." I can hear Saint behind me, his strong arms wrap around my waist, holding me up. The image of my brother's form blurs in front of me, little black dots speckling my vision.

"Come on, Sage. Breathe, baby, breathe." I can't. All I can think about is blood. So much blood weighs me down, as if Dante's body is still on top of mine. My body is spun around, Saxon disappearing as Saint's face comes into my line of sight. Calloused hands cup my face, our noses practically touching as he coaches me to take in a deep breath. I try, I really do. I'm suddenly sitting in a chair with my brother's hands on my shoulders as Saint kneels in front of me.

"Deep breath, in. Deep breath, out. Good girl, just like that." I copy Saint, inhaling and exhaling on his count until the room stops spinning and finally comes into view. The weight pressing down on my chest slowly eases up. I cling to Saint, holding his wrists as he continues holding my face in his hands.

"That's it, baby. Good job." Saint presses his forehead to mine as the fear and panic seeps out of me. Exhaustion quickly takes hold of me. I need to lie down. I am so tired.

"How do you feel?" Saint asks. My eyes close as I lean into him.

"So tired," I whisper through a yawn. If I don't lie down, I'm sure to fall asleep in this chair.

"We need to take her home. She's about to pass the fuck out," Saint says over my head. But it's Saxon's response that shocks me.

"Go. I'll get Ophelia home." I'm instantly scooped into strong arms, floating through the air as I curl up into Saint's chest.

"And Saint." Saxon speaks again. We stop moving then.

"I'm glad she's got you. Take care of her. Don't fucking break her heart, you understand me?" My heart aches from that blessing I never thought I'd get.

"Always," Saint responds as he carries me out of the meeting room and to his Tahoe. How it got here I'm not sure, but I'm glad it is. I wouldn't have been able to stay awake on his bike.

SAGE

# CHAPTER 36

## SAGE

I wake up in Saint's bed, the space beside me cold and untouched. The faint sound of voices coming from the kitchen draws me from the comfort of Saint's bed. I need to tell the guys about Dante and what he told me. They need to know about Frankie.

I'm still wearing the sweatpants and t-shirt from the club, so I make my way out of the bedroom and towards the voices in the kitchen. When I enter, Saxon, Saint, Finn, and Brooks all stand around the island. Saint sees me first, his eyes a mess of exhaustion and something else I can't identify. The rest of the guys finally notice my presence and turn to look at me.

"How do you feel?" Saxon asks, his tone apologetic but still laced with that deep grumpiness that never goes away.

"Fine. But I need to tell you what Dante told me before I forget the details." Their eyes shift back and forth from one another. I hadn't known if he wanted Brooks or Finn to be aware of the situation, but the subtle nod he gives me lets me know it's safe to talk. The guys are a part of the club as well, so it doesn't surprise me he trusts them to know the details.

"Wait, Frankie, as in Uncle Frankie?" Brooks asks, his eyes landing on Saxon as he gives him a slow nod. I go through everything Dante said from the meetup at the café to his arrival on campus: his warnings, and then the sudden drive-by. I hadn't seen the vehicle or shooter at all. One minute, Dante was talking, and the next minute, I was face down. Saxon and Saint are not too pleased with me secretly meeting up with Dante, and I can't blame them. It was stupid of me to go off on my own, but the desire to know more about my father trumped all my rational thoughts.

"Finn, are you able to pull up security footage from the campus? See if they were able to catch anything—make, model, license plate—that can help us. Whoever did this must have been tailing Dante," Saxon says to the room. My heart suddenly goes to Dante and whether he had a family. Would they know by now? He's dead. I knew the feeling too well—receiving a call that your family member had passed, but to be murdered was a different emotion all in itself. So many questions pour in, and some will never have answers. I ache thinking about it.

"Yeah, no problem," Finn replies. Like Saint, Finn knows his way around a computer. There isn't much Finn can't do. That's what makes him so lethal, dangerous, and terrifying. "Give me a couple hours. Brooks and I will be back with what we find." The brothers say their goodbyes, and they each give me a kiss on the cheek before leaving on their bikes.

I glance at the clock on the microwave and see that it's 7:45 p.m. I had quite literally slept away the afternoon. I was more tired than I'd realized. The high from the adrenaline had quickly subsided after the whole ordeal.

"I'm going to shower. Order some food for dinner. I'm

starving. I don't care what you order, just order something," Saxon says to Saint and me. I watch his back disappear into the foyer and listen as his footsteps carry him upstairs.

The moment the click of the door echoes through the house, I'm moving. I need his warmth. I need his touch. I need... him. He meets me halfway. Strong arms encase me in a shadow of force that lifts me off my feet. My legs instinctively wrap around his waist as I bury my face in the crook of his neck. I've never felt so light in my life. Effortlessly, he holds me to him. Our bodies are pressed so hard together I don't know where he begins and I end.

"Are you okay, baby?" A whisper of a question. So much had just happened in the last twelve hours. Our ruse is up—Saxon knows about us. Saint took the brunt of Saxon's reaction to the news. Dante is dead. Frankie has been a snake in the grass for seven years. Oh my God! Is Ophelia okay? I hadn't even thought about the well-being of my best friend. What does that say about me? My head is swimming with inky black liquid that I can't sort through. It's all so much, too much.

"Sage, talk to me." When I don't answer him, he finally pulls away, setting me gently on the island's surface. The cold of the granite seeps through my body, giving me chills even though I'm in sweats.

"I'm okay. How's Ophelia? Where is she? How are you?" I speak so fast he puts his hands on my thighs, spreading them so he can step closer to me.

"Shh, she's fine. She's with Owen. She didn't want to go home alone, so he insisted she could stay with him."

"What about you?" I ask, raising my hands and placing them gently on the sides of his face. Black and purple discoloration covers his left eye, a cut on his eyebrow has just started to scab over, and the puffiness of his bottom lip is going down. He still looks awful from his injuries. He's still stoically beautiful, though. It almost makes him sexier with his bruises. I'm convinced nothing could make this man unattractive.

"Better than ever." His lips press against mine. Saxon was still visibly angry at our secret, but oddly enough, his comment at the garage makes me feel like he's okay with this. Well, maybe not fully okay, but accepting. We kiss slowly, gently, delicately. Neither of us wants to pull away. Pressing his body against mine, his warmth caresses me like a warm blanket on a rainy day. He compliments me as I do him. My form fits in the pocket of his chest like two pieces of a puzzle, carved to fit perfectly. I've known Saint for the majority of my life. He's been best friends with Saxon since they were twelve and I was six. As far back as I can remember, he's been a pillar in my life. A second protector, always here, always watching, always caring for me as if I've always been his. Maybe it was inevitable we'd find ourselves in this situation. Two people colliding in a world of chaos, providing stability in this otherwise hectic life.

"I'm so sorry," I whisper.

"Don't do that, Sage. I'd go through beating after beating if that meant I got to keep you. I can handle him. What I can't handle is being here and seeing you every day, never having the chance to make you mine." Another soft kiss, and a smile spreads across my lips.

"You know what, you're kind of a romantic, Saint. Who would have thought?" I joke, pressing a kiss to the tip of his nose.

"Just don't tell anyone. I have an image to uphold." His lips curl into a dangerous side smile, awakening the butterflies in my stomach. "Let's order some food, or I might die of starvation." Saint turns to open the drawer with all the takeout menus we have stashed away. Picking up the menu for the Thai restaurant the three of us love, we place an order and wait for Saxon to return from his shower. In the meantime, I cuddle up next to Saint on the couch, no longer afraid anyone will see or catch us. We sit and flip through Netflix, settling on the newest action flick.

For the first time in a long time, I feel content, at ease, and just so fucking happy. Even when the darkness of the truth lingers in the background. We'll have to figure out this whole mess with Frankie, but until then, I allow the fears and darkness to hide in the shadows. I grasp onto the light for as long as I can. This night is mine before chaos is unleashed.

SAGE

# CHAPTER 37

## SAGE

It takes Saxon a few days to warm up to the new dynamic in the house. Saint and I respect him, so we hold off on any PDA in front of him. It's awkward enough seeing his best friend with his sister. I don't want to poke the bear, so to speak. Saint has his own apartment, but he's been staying at the house more days than not. In fact, I can't even remember the last time he wasn't here. I like it that way.

Finn and Brooks were able to extract some of the security footage from campus that gave us a clear image of a license plate attached to the dark blue van that pulled up beside me and Dante before he was gunned down. It was eerie, almost like an out-of-body experience, watching the footage. Dante had seen the van almost at the exact moment it entered the side parking lot. There was no hesitation—he covered me in an instant. I couldn't watch after that. Knowing Dante was taking bullets for me made the guilt unbearable.

The license plate number came back to a man with a bogus name, which led us to yet another dead end. However, I can't stop watching a section in the video where the van window was rolled down. The side profile of a man was faintly visible. Over and over again, I watch, pause, and rewind until I'm able to pause on his profile, where he was most visible.

"Are you able to zoom in or enhance this still shot at all?" I ask Brooks, who's sitting next to me in the meeting room of the club.

"Yeah, of course." I slide the laptop towards him, and he begins typing away. A moment later, he slides it back to me. I study the image, and bile quickly rises in my throat.

"Are you okay?" Brooks asks me, but I'm already up and heaving into the closest garbage can. "Jesus, Sage. Here, take this." Brooks has a handful of tissues waiting for me as he rubs my back with his other hand.

"Sax, Saint, get over here!" he yells for the guys, who had stepped out of the room for some air. We'd been discussing every detail of the fire and anything we may have overlooked during that day and the few months following. I hear the door burst open, heavy footsteps making their way towards me as I heave all the contents of my breakfast into the garbage.

"Sage, what's wrong? What happened?" Saxon's voice is loud, but he isn't yelling; he sounds more concerned than anything.

"I don't know, man. One minute, she's looking at this photo, and the next, she's hurling into the trash," Brooks explains to the guys.

The slide of the laptop across the wooden table fills the room. I finally stop gagging and take the water Saint has waiting for me. I wipe my mouth and down the bottle of water, trying to get the awful taste out of my mouth.

"I don't know what you're seeing, Sage. What's going on?" I step closer to Saxon; Saint follows close behind me, his presence warm.

"Look at the person in the photo."

"I am. Do you know who the driver is?" I shake my head.

"No, not the driver. Look who's beside him, in the passenger seat." Saxon gets closer to the image, squinting at the shadow of a man, sitting without a care in the world in the passenger seat.

"That motherfucking piece of shit! I'll kill him!" Saxon's yell makes my bones shake with unease. Only one thing would come from this type of fury: death. I pity anyone in his path. Well, except my uncle. Anger, sadness, disbelief—so much swirls in my gut as I look at the image of Uncle Frankie sitting in the passenger seat of the dark blue van. The van in which a man I don't recognize shot multiple bullets in my direction. I could have died. If Dante wasn't there, I would have.

"So, it's true. He is connected. In a more sinister way than he's claiming," Saint says to the room. Saxon is vibrating with so much pent-up anger I fear he may explode. I place my hand on his shoulder. He quickly moves from my embrace, storming to the door before I call after him.

"Saxon! We need a plan first. It hurts, I know, but if you want to take him down, we need to be smarter than him. We need to play him at his own game." With both hands on the door, Saxon stops. Saint, Brooks, Finn, and I all watched Saxon's back rise and fall with each deep breath he takes.

"It could have been you, Sage. I could be putting you in the ground beside Luther right now. Who's to say you weren't the target? What if they planned that for you and not Dante?" Saxon speaks with his back towards me. Saint's hand rests on my waist, his fingers curling into my skin at Sax's words. A noticeable growl resonates in his chest.

"I'm aware it may have been targeted at me, but he's obviously working with other players. We need more information before we strike." He knows I'm right. His anger has always been his driving force, but he knows we need to identify the driver. Maybe this will lead us to something more. Something useful.

With much reluctance, Saint is able to calm Saxon down enough to sit down so we can go over a plan. Finn and Brooks work hard on trying to identify the driver with their facial recognition software. While Saxon, Saint, and I all agree, we will play it cool with Frankie until the plan is set. It's inevitable—Frankie is going to pay. I've given him the benefit of the doubt, but when so many red flags have been raised, and my father's life was the price of his actions, I need justice. Seven years. Seven years my father has been gone; my life was almost stolen from this earth as well. The thought of my uncle being wrapped up in all this leaves me not only devastated, but confused. Why? What was in it for him if my father died?

"Look at this. Frankie has been receiving payments every six months since the fire." Saint speaks up from behind his laptop. We had decided to look into Frankie's finances. Why was evil always driven by money? How could money trump your own family?

"Who's it from?" Saxon asks.

"Unknown. I could try and follow the IP address, but the coding on these transactions is pretty tight. It may take me a while to try and decode." Saxon lets out a huff of frustration.

"Just try. Maybe that will be our answer."

"You got it."

I watch as Saint and the boys work tirelessly. Each one enveloped in their work, while I turn my eyes to Saxon.

He's on his phone, the permanent scowl on his face deeper than I've ever seen it. Stressed is an understatement. He's battling something deeper than betrayal. Saxon has always carried the world on his shoulders, and it's starting to weigh heavy on his back. He redoes his usual man bun—his tick whenever his anger is rising.

"Sax, can I talk to you for a minute outside?" I ask. The guys' eyes jump up from their computers. Saxon's eyes find mine and he nods. Standing, I look back at Saint, giving him a small smile of reassurance. I follow Sax outside, the warm breeze hitting my skin, making me inhale a deep breath of calm.

"What is it?" he asks, turning towards me and shoving his hands in his pockets.

"Don't be like that," I sigh.

"Like what?" He raises his shoulders in a shrug, but I know him all too well.

"Don't act like nothing's bothering you. I know you, brother. I know when you're hiding your feelings, and right now, you're holding them back like the Hoover Dam. What's going on in your head? Is it me and Saint?" I'm worried he's still fuming over me and Saint but secretly hope he isn't.

"Nah. That was shitty of you to keep from me, but the more I thought about it, the more I realized he's the only person in this world I would trust with you." I smile at his comment, warmth filling my chest.

"Then what's going on?" There's a long pause between us. I can see the indignation in his eyes. His eyes always gave him away.

"Doesn't it hurt?" he asks, his question throwing me for a loop.

"Doesn't what hurt?"

"The thought that Frankie may have wanted to kill you

and me, as well as Dad? He almost succeeded with you. Thank God for Saint."

"Why thank God for Saint?" I ask, an odd sensation blooming in my gut as I wait for him to answer.

"Thank God for Saint pulling you from the fire. If he hadn't gotten there when he did, you would have died."

You know that feeling when you get out of a hot tub and then jump into a pool, and the water suddenly feels so cold it takes your breath away? The feeling of electricity buzzing through every nerve ending as your skin is introduced to the water. Like your body can't register quickly enough the sudden change in temperatures. It feels like you're glitching.

"He—He did what?" I whisper. The sudden awareness of my brother's expression tells me he has no idea I didn't know it was Saint.

"Sage, Saint was the one that pulled you from the fire. Didn't you know?" I feel my mouth part in shock. I shake my head at my brother.

"He never told me it was him," I whisper again, my voice sounding so far off I don't fully believe it's my own. This whole time. For seven years, I've wondered who saved me, and the answer was always him.

"But I thought he was with you?" My eyes couldn't focus on him anymore; I couldn't focus on anything.

"I was. We were coming back to the house, but I stopped by the store to get you flowers for your birthday, and he beat me there. He saw the fire and ran in before the firefighters could stop him." I'm tracing the lines of my scars across my hands without realizing. Saxon finally grabs my hands and holds them in his.

"Are you okay? I'm sorry. I've always thought you knew it was him. He received some pretty bad burns himself across his back." I'd never noticed. Saint has a huge skull tattoo that covers the length of his back. A pirate hat and half sunken ship mural covers almost every inch of skin. It's beautiful. How had I never noticed his scars?

"Come here." Saxon pulls me to his chest, hugging me hard, as if to apologize for dropping yet another bomb on my life. "I thought you knew," he whispers in my ear. The threat of tears sting my eyes as I squeeze them shut, not wanting the tears to fall. I squeeze my brother back, my only family I have left.

SAINT

# CHAPTER 38

## SAINT

When Sage comes back into the meeting room, her face is flushed and her eyes are vacant. A look of shock coats her face, but when her eyes find mine, a soft smile spreads across her beautiful face. It sends my heart into overdrive—it thumps so loud I fear the guys might hear it. I want to go to her, pick her up, and take her away from the shit storm that is our lives. The lies, the secrets, and most of all, the betrayal from her uncle is no doubt taking its toll on her.

Looking at Saxon, I can see the same. My brother, my family. My parents dumped me on my grandmother when I was two, so they could continue their drug-addict lifestyle without the burden of a child. My grandmother died when I was seventeen, leaving me with no one except Saxon and Sage. Luther helped me in every way he could, letting me stay with them until I was able to get a place of my own. He brought me into the club after my eighteenth birthday, into his family, where I finally had a place in this world, a purpose. That purpose is keeping those close to me safe at all costs.

Now, the two most important people in my life are hurting, each battling the same demon but in different ways. Where Saxon visibly shows his anger, Sage is the opposite. She keeps hers locked tightly away in a box where no one is allowed to see. I would rather her be expressive with her anger, like Sax, because hiding such strong emotions inside oneself for too long is dangerous. It's only a matter of time before she crumbles from the weight of the unshed emotions. I won't let that happen to her. If she crumbles, I will be there before she hits the ground.

For the rest of the day, we all work to devise a plan to unmask and reveal Frankie for who he truly is. Ultimately, we all want to ask him the same question: why? Was money truly the only factor fueling his plot to eliminate his family? I find it hard to believe that money could lead to such greed, to such malicious intents, to such evil. Their pain has me working hard to try and bring them the answers they so desperately need.

Finally, when our efforts start looking bleak, Finn gets a hit.

"Got him!" he announces to the room, his hands clapping together. "The driver is a man named Charles Ledford. He's got a pretty long record as well. Grand theft auto, assault, a few misdemeanors, attempted murder, burglary, and fraud of some kind." Finn reads Charles's profile before looking up from his computer at Saxon.

"Right, so how is he connected to all this? He must've been hired or contracted to take out Dante, so we need to figure out who hired him." Saxon's voice sounds optimistic.

"I may have an answer to that as well. I was checking his bank transactions and there was a $25,000 check deposited by none other than Tim Blanchett. Who is Tim Blanchett, you ask? I'll tell you. Tim Blanchett just so happens to be Mayor Harrison's head of security. Another fun fact about Mr. Blanchett—he is the older brother to a Mrs. Gloria Harrison."

"Got him!" Brooks yelled, slapping Finn on the back.

"Holy fuck," Sage whispers to herself. Her head lowers to the table in utter shock. The mayor of Golden Heights is connected to Luther Wilder's murder. Why? Could it be as simple as the affair he was having with Gloria? But that still brings me to another question.

"So does this mean Gloria is connected to the fire too? That doesn't make sense, though. Why murder the man she was having the affair with? She must have either gone along with it to keep herself safe, or she didn't know their plan until it was too late," I say. The silence in the room indicates that I'm not the only one thinking this.

"He's right. Either of those theories makes sense, but is there more to it that we're missing?" Sage asks. The question lingers in the air with no answer in sight. I feel like we've hit another dead end. We've come so far, following a path of cryptic clues leading to the finish line, only to become entangled in yet another web of chaos. We have so many facts, so many theories, so many clues, yet I feel like we are still at the starting point. Saxon must feel the same way because he finally breaks the silence.

"Okay, let's push the why aside for the moment. We know who the driver is. We know Frankie was in the passenger seat. We know Mayor Harrison, Tim Blanchett, and possibly Gloria are all connected in the grand scheme of things. Let's start by finding Ledford first, see if we can't get some answers out of him." Collectively, the group nods in agreement. Finn and Brooks start typing away almost immediately. I look down at my watch and see that it is now a little after six in the evening before lifting my head towards Sage. She looks tired, beat down, and, all in all, mentally exhausted. Talking about her father and his murder can't be easy.

Saxon nudges my shoulder. Looking up, he tilts his head to the side, indicating for me to come outside with him. I take one last look at Sage, who is typing away on her phone, and stand from my chair, following Saxon outside. The air is cooling off a bit, not cold, but no longer stifling from the sun.

"I need you to take care of her, Saint. I know I gave you shit earlier, but there really is no one else I trust to take care of her and make sure she's okay. She's safest with you." Clapping a hand on my shoulder, he continues. "Know this though—if you hurt her in any way, I will personally remove you from this earth." His dark black eyes pin me with that last comment. There's no doubt that I believe every word he says. He is her brother, her only family. I respect him for caring and watching over his sister for as long as he has. Luther would be proud of him.

"You don't have to worry about me, man. No way will I ever hurt her." There's a long pause between us. Our relationship finally laid out on the table. No more hiding, no more secrets. Now we can move forward. Saxon pulls me into a bro hug, clapping me on the back before pulling away.

"Take her home. She looks exhausted. Plus, I don't want her to hear what we have planned for Mr. Ledford. I'll text you when we have information on his whereabouts. When we find him, it's time to go to work." I smile, the promise of violence waking up the sleeping demon inside of me. The last person we tortured was Damien Devonte, Dante's buddy we'd tossed in the quarry, and I'm due for another session of pain and bloodshed.

SAGE

# CHAPTER

# 39

## SAGE

Saxon insists I go home with Saint to get some rest. I'm reluctant to leave, especially since we are finally getting somewhere. We need to continue this momentum if we are ever going to get to the bottom of this shit show. We need a plan, a resolution. We need the "why" behind Frankie's motivation. With all my concerns and the need to continue, it's Finn who ultimately convinces me to get some rest.

"Witch stick, I promise you the second I find this piece of shit, Ledford, I will personally let you know." Saxon's not too pleased by his promise to include me in whatever the plan will be when they finally track him down, but if Finn promises something he always follows through. "You deserve to be a part of this as much as the rest of us." He shoots me a wink before he turns his attention to Saxon. I suddenly fear for Finn's safety as Saint and I finally leave the garage on the back of his motorcycle. Now, look, I'm not usually the girl to ride passenger on the back of a guy's bike. However, riding on the back of Saint's bike creates a new feeling of security with him, a new sense of freedom from a different perspective, and I admit I love it.

Pulling out of the garage parking lot, Saint takes off in the direction of the house. The warm air suddenly gets colder each time we pass below trees that provide us with shade. The sun is setting, only the last bit of sunlight shining through the trees. I shiver at the sudden temperature change, and Saint must have felt it too. He reaches his hand behind him, grabbing my thigh with his hand and gives me a reassuring squeeze. This gesture right here is the reason I've fallen in love with riding as his passenger. This touch, this sensation he sends throughout my body with a simple squeeze, is enough to make my insides warm. It lets me know he sees me, he feels me, and I'm safe with him.

I savor the feeling of his grip on me. His long fingers curl around my thigh, squeezing and rubbing his palm against the jeans I'm wearing. Wrapping my arms around his waist, I hold his body tighter to mine, the muscles beneath my hands flexing as I glide them up and down his chest. I continue down, past his abdomen, and rest my hand over the bulge in his jeans. I rub his noticeable erection once, and then think twice about starting something that could be insanely dangerous, especially on the back of a motorcycle. But before I'm able to move my hand away, his gloved fingers grab mine, pushing my hand further against his jeans, continuing the motion of rubbing his cock against his jeans.

I can feel the vibration of his moan against my chest. The satisfaction I get knowing I'm making my man feel good is addictive. I want to be his source of pleasure, so I continue rubbing and squeezing him through his jeans. Soon, I become frustrated with the fabric between us, so I make quick work of his button and zipper, allowing my hand to slide beneath the denim and his boxers.

He's so hard, and already, a bead of precum coats his

soft skin. I'm salivating. All I want at this moment is to be on my knees for him, pleasing him until he finishes. I pump up and down his length, feeling every vein and every twitch of his cock against my hand. I'm already soaking wet, this whole ride fast becoming a tease as his engine vibrates against my sensitive entrance as he speeds up with every turn we take.

With every rev of his engine, I pump harder and faster and know he's close when he snakes his hand back around to grab my thigh once again. This time his grip on me is brutal—I'm definitely going to bruise after this, but I gladly take the pain. I love it. Just when I think he's about to come, he pulls his bike off to the side of the road, where there's a hidden parking area for travelers. The second he parks his bike behind a set of trees, he swings his leg off, grabs me by the waist, lifts me off the bike, and spins me around so I'm no longer facing him but facing his bike.

"Saint, what are we—?" Grabbing the waistband of my jeans, he yanks them down my legs, exposing my ass and throbbing pussy to the now cool air. I shiver as a gust of wind hits my skin, causing goosebumps.

"I'm hungry, baby, and don't feel like waiting until we get home." With his hands on my hips, he lifts my ass until I'm forced to stand on my tiptoes. I place my hands on his bike seat so I don't face-plant onto the ground. Just when I'm about to protest and ask what he's doing, warm breath hits my entrance, and I let out a moan of pure bliss.

"So wet for me already." His tongue darts out, licking between my folds, and I lose it. Letting my head fall back, I lift higher onto my tiptoes as his tongue laps up my arousal and continues its torturous assault that has my core heating from desire.

"Oh, fuck. Yes, Saint. Right there," I beg him as his lips and tongue work their magic, curling, flicking, and sucking their way across my swollen pussy. I'm so close, so painfully close, as he eats me like I'm his last meal. Just when I'm about to fall off the edge, he's gone. I go to protest, but I'm quickly met with his cock fully thrusting inside my pussy.

"Fuuuck, yes," he moans behind me, his fingers curling around my hips to hold me in just the right spot. The sound of slapping skin, our moans, screams, and the curses we both let out with each thrust would have been a sight to see if there were any bystanders. Thankfully, we're alone, but I wouldn't have cared if we weren't. The pleasure shooting from my toes through my spine has me seeing stars, and the only thing I can focus on right now is chasing my release. With a few more thrusts, Saint reaches around me, rubbing his thumb against my clit, and I fall to pieces. If his hands weren't holding me steady, and his bike wasn't holding me up, I would be melting into the ground. Saint is right behind me. Holding my hips, he pulls me hard against his body as he reaches his own release. His head falls against my back as he shudders against me.

"Fuck, baby. I needed that," he whispers behind me, his lips kissing my damp neck as he slides himself out of me. As much as I don't want to leave this moment, we definitely have to get home now. If only to wash the mess that's now collecting in my panties.

We make quick work of our clothes, adjusting ourselves and getting back on his bike to continue our way home. Taking the long curvy road up towards the house, I suddenly feel a pit of dread hit the bottom of my stomach like a dead weight. Looking in Saint's side mirror, I see a black pickup truck coming up behind us, and fast. Saint grabs my hands that are already wrapped around his waist and pulls them tighter to his body, telling me to hang on. I look over my shoulder, seeing the truck inching its way closer and closer to our back tire.

"Saint!" I call out to him, but he's already speeding up.

My heartbeat picks up as I continue to look over my shoulder, and when the barrel of a gun peaks out from the driver's side window, I can't help the scream that leaves my throat. One shot, two shots. The unmistakable sound of bullets whizzing by us has me tensing every inch of my body against Saint's. My eyes slam shut as another shot rings through the air.

"Hold on!" Saint yells to me as he takes a corner too fast and my stomach drops at the sensation, like a roller coaster reaching the top before it plummets to the earth. I open my eyes when the bike levels back out. We are so close to the house, we can make it. We just need to get beyond the gate, and we'll be okay. Right?

I can see the road approaching, and I let out a silent sigh of relief. But then it all changes. Everything happens so fast. With a deafening thud, the truck rams the back of Saint's bike, making us fishtail as my body is thrown like a rag doll from the back. Everything is so bright one minute, and the next, I see nothing, feel nothing, and hear nothing. I'm suspended in a moment of time, frozen as the air prickles my skin. Everything is quiet. There's nothing—no noise, no rev of his engine, or screech of the truck tires. It's as if I've been dunked underwater and the quiet muffle of the world has evaporated. It's dark, everything is fading away, and the last thing I remember is someone screaming my name before the darkness swallows me.

---

## SAINT

Someone is pounding on my head with a fucking sledgehammer, and I'm about to lose my self-control. Whoever it is better run now before I get a hold of them. Why are my eyes closed? The once simple movement is now proving to be difficult as I try to pry my eyelids open to see who the unlucky fucker is, and what is that beeping?

"Saint, you alright, man?" Who is talking, and why do they sound so far away? I try to open my mouth, but again, why is this so hard? My muscles ache, everything is strained, and I feel like I'm being held down as someone holds fire over my skin. What the fuck is happening?

"Fuck, dude. Look at him. He's lucky to be alive." Was that Brooks voice? No, it was definitely Owen's, right?

"Have you seen Sage yet? Fuck, man. She's lucky too." What the fuck? Sage? What are they talking about?

"Where the hell is she?" My voice doesn't sound like myself, raspy and constricted like someone is squeezing my vocal cords. I try to sit up, but someone's hand is on top of me before I can rise. Cords, ropes—no, wires—something is attached to me. Finally, I manage to peel my eyelids open and familiar faces come into focus.

Owen and Brooks are standing over me while harsh lights are beaming down on my skin. My skin feels like someone's taken a Brillo pad to my arms and back, leaving my skin raw. It feels like someone's doused me with alcohol —the burn and constant sting is almost unbearable.

"Easy, big guy. It's just us," Brooks says, his hands resting on my chest to pin me down to what I've gathered is a bed I'm lying in.

"Where am I? Why the fuck am I burning?" I turn my head from side to side, but I'm only met with more fiery sensations.

"Listen, Saint. Someone rear-ended you on your bike. You lost control and crashed. We're at Golden Heights Regional. You've got severe road rash man, like a lot of road rash, but no broken bones." Owen always has to see the bright side of things. As much as I'm in pain from said road rash, at least I'm not broken, right? I have to give it to the kid, he's a pretty optimistic son of a bitch. Then it hits me—Sage.

I jerk my body up, successfully sitting up this time, and I'm hit with a wave of pain that instantly makes me nauseous, but I don't care. I need to find Sage. She was on the back of my bike. Was she as bad as me? Were her injuries worse? Was she alive? I ignored the sounds of Owen and Brooks trying to keep me calm, but nothing was going to stop me from getting to her. I promised Saxon I would protect her. I promised *her*.

I rip the cords from my chest, the insufferable beeping now a constant stream of noise. I rip my IV out when I notice I'm dragging a bag of fluids on a stand and yank the curtain open. Owen and Brooks are right on my heels. I'm in a gown, and thick white bandages cover both of my arms and the length of my right side. My right leg is burning. Looking down, I notice it, too, is wrapped up in bandages, but still, I continue moving.

"Where is she? Where is Sage Wilder?" I slam my hands on the nurse's station. It looks to be the ER; several bays have their curtains drawn, hindering me from seeing inside.

"Sir, I'm going to need you to sit—"

"Tell me where she is!" I yell, as Owen and Brooks come up on either side of me. The petrified nurse eyes both my friends, a silent plea for help that never comes.

"Just tell him. He won't stop until he sees her," Brooks says in a defeated tone, but I don't miss the slight annoyance either. The nurse looks back at me, her breathing harsh. I'm probably scaring the shit out of her. Boo-fucking-hoo.

"She's in room six, right there." The moment she says six, I'm already moving. I hear the small apology Owen gives her, but I don't stick around. I make it to room six, taking a deep breath before pulling the curtain back. However, if I thought I was in pain before, it was nothing compared to the pain that ignites in my chest at the sight of Sage.

SAINT

# CHAPTER 40

## SAINT

"Jesus, Saint. What are you doing? You should be resting!" Saxon says, but it's like he's at the end of a tunnel. I can't interpret what he's saying. I'm too focused on Sage. Her eyes are closed. Oxygen tubing is fastened beneath her nose, and bandages, so many bandages, covered her body, leaving me to believe she too had sustained severe road rash injuries. I feel like my ribs are cracking from the tightness in my chest. The pain I once felt with my wounds is now a second thought as I watch the slow and steady breathing of Sage as she lies in a hospital bed because I didn't protect her.

"I'm so sorry, Sax. I don't know wh—It all happened so fas—" Saxon cuts me off, his hand resting on my shoulder lightly so he doesn't hurt me.

"Stop. This is not your fault." I swallow the lump in my throat and welcome the familiar build of rage within my stomach towards whoever the fuck did this.

"Will she be, okay?" I ask, my voice barely a whisper.

"She'll be fine. She has a lot of road rash, as do you, but she hit her head pretty hard, causing her helmet to split in half. They want to keep her here overnight to monitor her concussion. And as for you—you should be in the next bed over, healing as well." I turn my head so we are face to face.

"But knowing you, I doubt that's going to happen." Saxon shakes his head beside me, stepping back and making his way to Sage's side once again. I take up the spot on her other side. Her hands are also wrapped in bandages, so I stop myself from wrapping my hand around hers.

"Has she woken up at all?" I whisper, not wanting to disturb her.

"She did, but they sedated her. She was in too much pain while they scrubbed her wounds. It was too much, so they put her under."

"Fuck, baby. I'm so sorry," I whisper to her. The thought of her being in such excruciating pain that they needed to sedate her. My rage is growing by the minute, my insides vibrating with so much fury that needs released. I look up to Saxon.

"Who the fuck was in the truck that ran us off the road?" The sleeping beast inside is now stretching and yawning, slowly coming to life within me.

"Finn was able to track him down. He's currently in the basement." He gives me a wicked grin before finishing his comment. Roughly four years ago, Saxon, Finn, Brooks, Owen, and I decided we needed a place that was separate from the club. A place where we could carry out our private meetings and such without entangling the others or putting them in danger. It was our place, a place where we did what needed to be done to protect our family. "He's waiting for us to pay him a visit," Saxon continues. As much as I don't want to leave Sage's side, I want—no, I need—to pay a visit to our guest in the basement. He's all mine.

Ophelia arrives at the hospital moments later, rushing to

Sage's side with tears and snot streaming down her face. The guys had brought me clothes, so I dress as quickly as possible, pain radiating with every move I make. I don't give a fuck. Saxon, Brooks, and I leave the hospital, leaving Owen and Ophelia to watch over Sage and inform us as soon as she wakes up.

The drive to the basement is quiet. The three of us fuming in our own pits of rage. Sage could have died. The thought alone has my blood boiling, my skin instantly rising in temperature. I'm in no fit state either. Thick white bandages cover both my arms and a majority of my right side. Some white patches have turned a slight shade of red from my wounds oozing. As much as my body is screaming at me to let it heal and rest, nothing was going to stop me from doing what I was about to do.

We decided the basement would be best kept past the wood line on Saxons' family's property. We had an underground room, essentially, created beneath a secret door in the soil. A flight of stairs leads to another door that opens up into a ten-by-fourteen-foot concrete room. It was times like now that I appreciate having this space. Lucky for us, not so lucky for the guests we bring down there.

I exit the car first, slamming the door behind me before a shock of pain radiates through my body. Fuck, road rash sucks. I groan to myself, forcing my body to move towards the wood line and seek out the secret door. My body is buzzing with pent up aggression. The need to cause physical pain is overpowering my own pain, which continues to rise with every step I take. I reach the door first, but the sound of Brooks's voice has me stopping before I kneel to the ground.

"Don't, Saint. I got it. Jesus, even after crashing your bike and skidding across the pavement, you're still going." He kneels and grabs the handle, lifting the door with a grunt due to the weight and letting it fall to the ground.

"I didn't crash my bike; I was run off the road. Big difference," I say, descending the stairs first with Saxon following close behind.

"Well, excuse me. Just remember, you're technically supposed to be in the hospital still. Don't go getting an infection or some shit." Once I open the second door, Brooks closes the first one, keeping our secret hideout hidden from the rest of the world. Stepping into the open room, the sound of Finn's music hits me with a deafening force.

That's one thing about Finn—whenever he's torturing someone, he likes his music blaring to drown out the screams of his victims. Finn's back is to us, a rag soaked in blood dangling from his back jeans pocket. He's twirling a kitchen cleaver in front of our guest, who is tied to a chair in the middle of the room. His arms are secured behind his back, and his legs are tied to each chair leg; his eyes give away his fear as he eyes the three of us as we enter the small space.

Finn turns around, following the man's gaze,

"Ahh, there are my friends. Now the real party can begin." Finn speaks loudly over his music, so we all can hear, barely. *You're Going Down* by Sick Puppies is blaring so loud I can hardly hear my own thoughts. Saxon lifts his hand and indicates to Finn to turn the music down. Finn does, and the sound of whimpering fills the room. The piece of shit excuse of a man is crying in the chair, his eyes leaking with tears at the image of the four of us standing in front of him.

Sitting in the chair before me is none other than Charles Ledford himself. The man responsible for killing Dante, and almost killing Sage, not once but twice now. There is no force great enough to hold me back; my body is already moving. I can hear Saxon say something, but my fist is already raised, my vision already obscured by red. I land blow after blow, bones crunching and blood shooting from his face, putting me in a frenzy of wrath and destruction. Charles Ledford deserves every broken bone, every ounce of lost blood, every bruise, and every cut I deliver to his face.

"Saint, easy man. We can't have him dying on us before he gives us the information we need." One of the guys says behind me, as hands and arms wrap around my body, yanking me off Charles. Once the guys successfully get me cooled down, my skin and wounds are burning. It feels like someone is ripping my skin apart inch by inch. However, I'm not going to give Charles the satisfaction of knowing he hurt me by ramming my bike off the road. No. I will stand here and be his own personal devil. By the time I'm done with him, he'll beg for death.

Charles coughs and spits blood from his mouth while his nose produces a constant stream down his chin and neck. His nose is broken, not only by evidence of the blood, but by the oddly shaped way it's now sitting on his face. Good. I hope it fucking hurts. Once the room settles down and Charles catches his breath, Saxon approaches the chair, kneeling down to his level like he's about to scold a child.

"Now, you're lucky I pulled him off you. I could have very well let him beat you to death, and I wouldn't have cared one fucking bit. However, I need something from you first." Charles isn't looking at Sax. His head is bowed like the coward he is. "Hey, I'm talking to you!" A shrill scream pierces the air as Saxon drives his knife into Charles's calf. I smile in satisfaction, welcoming his pained cries.

"Now that I have your attention, answer me this." Saxon stands from his kneeling position, straightening out his shirt before continuing. "Why did Tim Blanchett hire you to kill Dante?" Charles doesn't answer. His sobs are the only noises coming from his mouth. "Not going to talk? I'll fix that." Another stab of his knife, this time to his thigh. More screams. "Come on Charles, don't make this more complicated than it needs to be." The moment Saxon lifts his knife from Charles's thigh, he finally speaks.

"Okay, okay! Please, I'll tell you!" Saxon pats his hand on Charles's cheek, as if he's praising a dog.

"That's it. Good boy. So, tell us. Why did he hire you to kill Dante?" There's a pause before Charles finally answers.

"I wasn't hired to kill him; I was hired to kill the girl." Saxon turns his head, and we locked eyes. We both knew exactly who he's referring to. Sage. Before I can reach Charles once again, Finn and Brooks each grab my arms and hold me back.

I watch as Saxon steps behind the chair and leans down so his mouth is by Charles's ear, his knife now placed tightly against his neck.

"Why did he want you to kill my sister?" If Charles wasn't already scared, the change in Saxon's voice would have done it. There's one thing about Saxon that makes the hairs on my neck rise. Whenever he is truly enraged, a black veil slips over his soul. It drapes over the part in his brain that differentiates between good and evil, and evil always wins. His voice, his posture, his energy—it all changes into the world's apex predator and ninety-nine percent of his victims don't make it out alive. I've seen him do some fucked up shit, and the worst acts were always done to those who hurt his family. Saxon had just shifted into his beast form, patiently waiting for Charles to answer his question.

"I-I was hired because the other guy couldn't follow through with it. He-he said he couldn't be the one to pull the trigger." Another glance from Saxon, his eyebrows furrowed in confusion.

"Who is this other guy?"

"I don't know his last name, just his first name. He wanted to come with me the first time to ensure it was done, but then that guy showed up and blocked my shot."

"Who is the other guy?!" Saxon bellows in Charles's ear, making him flinch.

"Frankie! His name's Frankie!"

SAINT

# CHAPTER 41

### SAINT

We knew he was involved in some way, shape, or form. However, we were not prepared to hear that Frankie was the mastermind in trying to kill Sage and Saxon. Once we get Charles to talk, he sings like a canary. Charles never stood a chance. We all know damn well that this man's going to die in our basement. However, he doesn't need to know that. We promise multiple times he'll be released if he gives us all the information we need. After a few fingers are removed with Finn's bolt cutters, he gives us one more shocking piece of information that ultimately ties this whole mess together.

Charles informs us that Mayor Harrison, Tim Blanchett, and Frankie have been conspiring against Luther since before his murder. He also informs us that Frankie has been harboring hate for his older brother for some time. When asked why Frankie hated Luther so much, all he says is Frankie was jealous of Luther for the life he had. Which is strange because, although Frankie was not the leader of The

Kings' Aces, Luther never asserted dominance or power over his brother. Luther always treated Frankie as his equal. The men's relationship started when Frankie got the suspicion that Luther was sneaking around with someone. So, he decided to tail Luther one day, and, to his surprise, he discovered the secret affair Luther and Gloria were having. He snapped a few photos and took them to the mayor, who showed his head of security, Tim. With help from Frankie, they plotted to eliminate Luther, but Frankie was adamant that he wanted Saxon and Sage in the house when it burned as well.

"Take his body to the hole and dispose of him," Saxon informs Finn and Brooks, to which they gladly oblige.

"It doesn't make sense, man. Why does Frankie want you and Sage dead too? There has to be something, right? We have to be missing something," I say to Saxon as I clean up my hands with a cloth, meticulously removing all of Charles's blood.

"Fuck, man. I don't know. Why agree to raise us after Luther died, but then conspire to kill us later?" The look on Saxon's face as he speaks is twisted in pain and hurt at the thought of his uncle planning to not only kill your father, but you and your sister too. What the hell would he gain by doing such a horrific act, and against his family, no less?

"I have a fucking headache." Saxon brushes his hair back with his hand while removing his cell from his pocket. "Let's check on Sage and see if she can be discharged yet. I don't trust leaving her alone right now." I agree, we need to all stay close, especially knowing what we know now.

"Owen, how's Sage doing? Is she awake yet?" Saxon speaks into his phone as we ascend the stairs from the basement. There's a long pause. When we finally reach the top of the stairs, and I successfully closed the hidden door behind us, I turn to face Saxon, who's now looking as though the vale to his darkness has swept over his whole being again. I furrow my eyebrows in confusion as to why he's suddenly enraged. I motion for him to put the call on speaker phone, which he does.

"Yeah, man. Frankie showed up about thirty minutes after you left. He said he would take her home when they discharged her and set her up with the home care nurse that will be changing her bandages every other day." Owen speaks so nonchalantly, and it occurs to me that he doesn't know what we know now about Frankie. We are both silent, the realization of the danger Sage is now in, hitting us like a ton of bricks.

"Sax, man, are you okay? How did the base—"

"Where did Frankie take her?" Saxon's voice is lethal, dripping with so much murderous intent I know tonight is about to turn into even more of a blood bath.

"Uh, he said he was going to take her home. I assume your house. Sax, is everything okay?"

"Get to my house now. We're on our way. Frankie's not safe. We'll fill you in when we get there." Saxon hangs up the phone, and we take off to the house. We are far into the woods behind his property, so it takes some time for us to finally see the glowing lights of the house shine through the trees.

"Text the twins and tell them to get here ASAP," Saxon tells me, but I'm already sending the message. When we finally reach the house, we storm in, calling to Sage in the hope she's here, but there's no answer. I knew deep down she wouldn't be here. That would have been too easy.

Five minutes later, Owen comes running in through the front door.

"I'm so sorry, man! I didn't know. I—"

"It's fine. We learned some things from Charles. The biggest being that Frankie wants Sage and I dead. Did he say anything else that would indicate where he was taking her?" Owen runs his fingers through his hair, guilt plastered all over his face.

"Nah, he came to the hospital. Asked how she was doing. Sage finally woke up about ten minutes after you all left, said she was in pain and the nurse gave her more pain meds. Frankie then left and spoke with the nurse about discharge. The nurse said she wouldn't be discharged for another couple days, but Frankie was insistent that it be tonight. I remember he looked flustered and in a rush of some kind." Owen takes a deep breath before continuing. "Then he demanded that he take her home. He wanted her comfortable in her own space and had to fill out a form that stated he was going against hospital recommendations. But then the doctor came in and said she is legally an adult, and she has to make the decision herself."

"What did Sage say?" I ask.

"Well, at first, she was hesitant and wanted to stay in the hospital due to her pain level, but then Frankie sat on her bed beside her and whispered something in her ear. After that, she agreed and said she wanted to go home. Ophelia and I tried to talk her out of it due to her state, but she was adamant that she needed to go home. Fifteen minutes later she was wheeled down to Frankie's car, and they left."

"That motherfucker." The backdoor suddenly bursts open and the twins rush in, looking like they just played around in the mud. Technically, they did, while disposing of Charles.

"What the fuck is going on?" Finn yells, both twins breathing heavily as they just ran from even deeper in the woods than Saxon and me. Saxon quickly gives Owen a rundown of what happened in the basement, while I inform Finn and Brooks about what happened at the hospital. The longer we take explaining this shit show, the more danger Sage is going to be in.

"Right, let's check Frankie's house first. See if he's dumb

enough to go there," Saxon says and starts for the front door. However, I have something that no one knows about: I had placed a tracker on Sage's phone a while back in case she found herself in danger. I knew it was wrong and an invasion of her privacy, but right now, I'm pretty fucking thankful I had.

"I put a tracker on Sage's phone." The room falls silent as Saxon gives me a hard look.

"In any other situation, I would beat the fuck out of you. For now, I have to say, smart move." I pull out my phone and click to my tracker app. Sage's icon pings almost immediately. I look at the location and see that she's currently moving. It looks like she is heading towards the hills. "She's headed towards Ruhn Canyon on the outskirts of town." I say, lifting my head from my phone.

"Fuck, and guess who lives by Ruhn Canyon? Fucking Mayor Harrison," Saxon says as we make our way to the front door. I grab the knob and swing open the door, and freeze. The last person on earth I'd expect to be standing on the porch is now standing face to face with me, hand raised as if he was about to knock on the door. The rest of the guys also freeze behind me. Five sets of eyes trained on the person we thought had died, now alive and well, staring back at us.

"Dante?" I ask in utter bewilderment.

"Yeah… we need to talk."

SAGE

# CHAPTER 42

## SAGE

My whole body is screaming at me; my skin still feels like someone is holding a torch too close to me. The burning and stinging sensation travels through my whole body, and I can't help the silent tears sliding down my check. Frankie is driving, but he won't tell me where to. While in the hospital, he insisted I come home with him, but I knew my body was not ready to leave the hospital. I hesitated at first, especially after seeing that Frankie was in the van that tried to kill me. I wanted to oust him right there, expose him for who he truly is. Then he told me something that quickly changed my mind.

*If you don't come with me right now, Saxon and Saint will be dead in the next hour. I'll make sure of that. So, I suggest you act normally and sign this release paper so we can leave. If you make a scene, they're as good as dead.*

I immediately signed myself out of the hospital against the doctor's advice. There was no amount of pain that I could be in that would make me stay and take the chance of my family dying. Leaving the hospital, Frankie pushed me in my wheelchair to his waiting car. Putting me in the passenger seat, he then proceeded to place zip ties around my bandaged wrists.

"Is this entirely necessary? I mean, look at me Frankie," I winced as he'd tightened the zip ties around my badly torn up, and heavily bandaged, wrists. He hadn't answered me. Hell, he hadn't even looked at me.

"Frankie, what's going on? Why are you doing this?" I pleaded, as he got into the driver's seat, starting the engine, and pulling out of the parking lot. Again, no answer, not even a small glimpse out of the corner of his eyes.

"Where are you taking me? Where are the guys?"

"Shut up, Sage. Please, just shut up." His voice was pained, as if he was conflicted about what he was doing. A tone that displayed so much emotion, yet so little at the same time.

"Uncle Frankie, please. Are you in some type of trouble?" I'd lowered my voice in hopes that my smaller, child-like voice would crack the stone that had encased his once gentle heart. He didn't answer again. I'd stared at the side of his face, his profile looking so much like my father's it triggered a sharp pain in my chest.

"I can help you if you are—if you'd just tell me what's going on?"

"Shut up!" he'd yelled, making me flinch in my seat. Gone was the calm, silly, caring, and generous uncle that briefly raised me. In his place sat a stranger, unrecognizable and tormented by his own actions. I wondered if who he was before was an act this whole time.

We have been sitting in silence since that outburst. I glance at Frankie again and try once more to get some answers. "Are you going to hurt me, Frankie?" I turn my head back to the front, staring out the windshield at the darkness outside. We are traveling towards the hills.

Towards the canyons near the quarry. The one I loved to visit as a teen. I don't know where he's taking me, or if he'd truly going to hurt me. I have to assume yes, or why would he be doing this in the first place?

"Did you try to kill me that day? I saw you in the passenger seat of that van." The air suddenly shifts; the weight of the world feels like it's crashing down on me as the inside of the car begins shrinking around us. I know his answer, but when he finally speaks, it becomes so much more real.

"Just know, this is all your father's fault. You can thank him soon enough." I can't form another question, a response, a retort—anything. I am completely speechless. What was my father's fault?

We finally reach the end of the road at the top of Ruhn Canyon. A massive white, Mediterranean style mansion, with beautiful arches and gardens filled with luscious flowers of every color that line the exterior, comes into view. Greenery expands the length of one side, the vines climbing the architecture so perfectly it looks like this house is straight out of a magazine. The house is absolutely breathtaking, and I can't stop staring. I don't even notice the man who opens my door until it's swinging open so abruptly, I jump in my seat.

Rough hands grab my shoulder, my skin burning beneath his grasp, and I groan in pain as he drags me out of the car.

"Don't fucking touch her, Tim. I can get her." Frankie's voice comes from around the car. As the man drops his hands from my shoulders, I inhale a few deep breaths until the pain begins to subside a bit.

"Bring her inside," Tim orders; my uncle gestures for me to follow the guy I know to be Mayor Harrison's head of security. I follow slowly, taking in my surroundings and looking for any and all exits. Three men are positioned around the front of the home: one at the front door and the other two near the driveway. With the house sitting on the hill, there's only one way to enter the estate, and that's through the driveway. It would be fairly easy to see someone entering from quite a ways away. I can see the guards each have a pistol attached to their hips, and Tim has a small pistol tucked into the back of his pants.

I follow Tim into the open and elegant foyer, through a series of long hallways adorned with Mediterranean style decor and plush runner carpets that look to be brand new. We finally reach the end of the hallway that opens up into a massive conservatory-like room. The whole room is constructed with windows—the walls, the ceiling, every-thing. It allows me to see the night sky, which is speckled with bright, beautiful stars. I can't help but admire it.

"Sit down." Tim's grumpy voice draws me from my trance. Annoyance quickly takes over my senses, and I give him a disgusted look.

"Watch yourself, girl." I do as I'm told, taking a seat in one of the many plush white chairs that fill the room. Frankie walks up beside Tim and both of them start whis-pering so low I can't hear. This only irritates me more.

"Why don't you share with the room what you have to say, Frankie?" I know I'm playing with fire, but with the pain and the pure exhaustion, my attitude is harder to conceal. Both men look at me. Frankie gives me a look that screams "Shut the fuck up," while Tim gives me a look that says "Your time is coming." Like I said, I'd reached my limit of fucks to give the moment we left the hospital. Now, I'm just vexed. Pure rage and wrath course through my veins as I stare at my so-called uncle.

Without answering me, both men leave the room, leaving me alone with my hands still zip tied together, rubbing against my bandages, which inflames my road rash even more. There's a door that leads to the back of the house from the conservatory. However, one of the men from the front of the house is now standing in front of it, looking out to the forest. That exit is a no go. I scan the room to see if there is anything I could use to free my hands or use as a weapon, but the room is fairly empty except for the six chairs that are placed sporadically throughout. There are two ways to enter or leave the room: one door at the far end of the room and another located at the opposite end. Large arches frame each opening, and I can't help but admire the beauty of this home.

While searching the room, something catches my eye at the opposite entrance that we had entered previously. Not something, but someone. It's a woman. A gorgeous older woman, with dark auburn hair, bright blue eyes that shine against the moon's light, and her complexion is utterly flawless. She gestures for me to be quiet with a delicate finger pressed against her soft pink lips. She's hiding from someone, no doubt Tim and Frankie, but then she lifts a piece of paper up with a black bold message written in smooth cursive.

*They're coming to rescue you. Stay calm. Everything will be okay.*

I read and reread her message over and over again, hope suddenly restored with a simple message. I can't help the small smile that touches my lips as I look back to the beautiful angel of a woman, and then it dawns on me.

"Gloria?" I whisper to her. She responds by nodding once and giving me a sympathetic smile that warms me from the inside out. No wonder my father liked this woman. I don't even know her, but her presence alone makes me feel calm, serene, but most of all, safe, under the circumstances. I stare into her eyes for a long moment before she turns the paper over and starts writing another message on the back. Muffled noises fill the hallway where Frankie and Tim had disappeared to, and she writes faster.

Finally, she caps her marker and turns her paper around for me to read.

*I won't let anyone hurt you. I promise.*

I can't help the tears that fill my eyes. I believe her. I've never met Gloria, or even knew of her existence, yet I believed with all my heart she would do anything and everything she could to protect me from her brother, my uncle, and possibly her own husband. As a single tear falls down my cheek, Gloria gives me a reassuring smile before the sound of footsteps reenter the room, and then she's gone. Frankie, Tim, and Mayor Harrison are now in the room with me, staring down at me as if I'm a disease they don't want to get too close to, for fear of contracting it.

"How much longer do you think it will be before he shows up?" Mayor Harrison says in his condescending, arrogant politician voice of his that makes my skin crawl.

"I'd assume not too much longer; they are insanely protective of her," Frankie says, lifting his wrist and checking the time.

"Yeah, so protective they left her unguarded at the hospital, and that kid just let you take her. Some crew you got there, Frankie." Tim cackles as he eyes me. I look at Frankie and can't believe the man I've trusted my whole life is letting some hired security guard talk down about his own family. But he isn't family, he's a traitor, and I pray the guys show no mercy to him. Blood or not, he is no longer an uncle of mine.

"How long will it take after they're both dead for the funds to hit the account?" Mayor Harrison asks, his question directed to Frankie. This time, he pulls out his phone and starts scrolling before he answers.

"It takes roughly three weeks after proof of death." Putting his phone back in his pocket, I can't help myself anymore. I need to know.

"Why are you doing this? What's in it for you?" Tim's

and the mayor's laughter fills the room while I wait impatiently for an answer. Is the answer that obvious, and I'm just too dumb to realize?

"The fact that her father never told her makes this whole situation that much more comical," Harris says between laughs. "Go on, tell her, Frankie." I turn my head to Frankie, the threat of tears stinging the back of my eyes, but I won't let them fall. I won't give them the satisfaction of watching me cry. Frankie clears his throat and takes a step closer towards me.

"Your father created trusts for you and your brother. A hefty 1.5 million dollars to each of his children the moment you turn twenty-eight years old. Once you reach that age, your trusts would be handed over for you to do as you wish."

"So that's it? It's all about money to you?" I yell, unable to control my anger.

"NO! It's not just about money, Sage! Your father left me nothing! Absolutely fucking nothing. His will stated that I was to be your legal guardian and take over the responsibility of raising you two. I was only twenty-eight years old! He gave me nothing but the burden of his kids. I was given nothing, not the house, no money, nothing to do with his estate, and he expected me to just raise both of you, out of the goodness of my heart!" I've never seen Frankie raise his voice like this, anger seeps out from every pore. Anger that has been built up and stored for so long, and he's finally letting it go.

"Your father came to me before he died and expressed his concerns about the possibility of someone murdering him. He said he had a feeling he was being tailed and had a gut feeling something bad was going to happen." Frankie laughs—an evil, sadistic sound I've never heard him make before; it makes the hairs on the back of my neck raise. "He was right because once I learned of his little affair, I told my two friends here. Lucky for me, they have connections that could make it look like an accident. Luther told me about his will and the trusts he had set up for you and Saxon. So, we made a plan, burn the house down with all three of you inside, and, *poof*, the money would be mine."

"But Saxon wasn't home that night," I whisper.

"Imagine my anger when I learned that you were saved and Saxon wasn't even at the fucking house!" I wince at the sound of Frankie's outburst. My gut churns with the realization that my uncle killed my father and tried to kill me and Saxon too. Our own uncle wanted us all dead, for money. For a fucking paycheck. I can't look my uncle in the eyes anymore. He looks like a monster, a demon, a wolf in sheep's clothing—the person responsible for taking my father away from me. He's a stranger I've never seen before, a man fueled by his own greed, who is willing to go to extensive measures to get what he wants.

"Why?" I still can't comprehend all this. "Why did you hate Dad so much? Your own brother?" From the outside, my father and Frankie had a wonderful sibling relationship, always close and communicative. There was never any sign, to me at least, that either one hated the other. It was never even a thought in my mind that they had any animosity towards one another. It doesn't make sense.

"Ah, yes, your father, my brother. The picture-perfect man he was. Loved by the club, by the citizens of this town, even winning the nickname 'The Real Mayor of Golden Heights.'" I look to the real mayor at this comment. His face twists in annoyance and anger. "Your father was the golden boy of Golden Heights. Always the light of our mother's eye, and when your grandfather, my father, handed over the club on a silver fucking plater to Luther before his own death, I knew where I stood in that family. As if he didn't have another son standing beside him on his death bed. Like I was a shadow of his favorite son." Frankie's gaze drifts off somewhere outside of the room we all occupy. As if speaking of his past magically teleported him back in time.

"You always said you didn't want to the responsibility of being in charge of the club. If you truly wanted more responsibility, you never did a damn thing to show it," I say, my chin lifting high with defiance. "This is all to do with jealousy, then? You couldn't bear the thought of others seeing you as a lesser man than my father? Do you know how childish that sounds, Frankie?"

"No, my dear. This isn't about jealousy; this is about stepping into the shoes that were mine from the start. It wasn't until I found out about his little affair that the wheels started turning in my head. I knew everything needed to look like an accident, especially if I wanted to gain the spot of president in the club. Which I deserve.

"These fine gentlemen here were all too excited to assist me with my plan, especially the mayor. You see, he couldn't have his wife murdered. No, that would look too suspicious if Luther and Gloria just so happened to turn up dead. So, I enlisted their help with the promise of a nice hefty amount of the money once it was delivered. You see, I would have killed you both a long time ago, but since this all had to look like an accident, I needed more time to reconvene, replan, and ensure the steps were precise and measured so they'd never lead back to me. Plus, it would have been too suspicious if the pair of you died immediately after the fire. You know what I mean?" The smile Frankie gives me sends chills down my spine. Evil, complete and unequivocally evil.

How had I gone all these years thinking Frankie was anything but a demonic being walking this earth? Walking plainly in our lives? Playing this character of loving and present uncle, while all along, he was a wolf in sheep's clothing. A phony, masquerading around as a heartbroken brother who lost his sibling in a tragic accident. Had I been so blind to miss the signs? Racking my brain, I can't even remember there being any signs to see.

I can't hold back the choke and shakiness of my breathing. It feels like an elephant has just sat on my lungs, and my world is spiraling around me. Since my father was murdered, I've been living with pure evil. A man who wanted me and my brother dead. Everything feels like a movie; this couldn't possibly be my own life. It all sounds so insane, so far-fetched I can't quite wrap my head around it all. While I'm sure I'm about to have a panic attack, their laughs fill the room once again as they stare down at me. Their psychotic and deranged hyena laughter makes bile rise in my throat, but when I look up again, my racing heart begins to slow, and I inhale a few deep breaths to bring me back to center.

They are here. They are here to save me.

"What a riveting story you have there, Frankie," Saxon's voice silences the room, and all heads snap to the archway. "You made one mistake with your plan, I'm afraid. You thought you were on the same playing field as us, but damn, how you are so very, very wrong, Uncle."

SAGE

# CHAPTER 43

## SAGE

Two shots pierce the air. My eardrums feel as though they've just exploded in my brain, and the only sound left is a single ring carrying on into eternity. My eyes had slammed shut at the sound of the first shot, my body tensing on its own. The second shot had me flinching in my chair, my brain ignoring the pain of my road rash and shifting into survival mode. When the room falls silent, I peel my eyes open to the sight of my brother holding his smoking pistol, now trained on an equally shocked Frankie.

My eyes dart to the two men lying motionless on the floor before me. Tim and Mayor Harrison lay in pools of their own blood that are rapidly expanding beneath their still bodies. I don't know when my jaw fell open, but seeing my brother take the lives of two of my captors so fast, so instantaneously, with no remorse, is something I wasn't entirely prepared for. My brother is ruthless, I know this. We all have an image of our loved ones, but we never imagine them being a cold-blooded killer. Saxon is unflinching, calm, and fixated on our uncle with pure savagery etched across his face. If he wasn't my brother, I would fear the man standing before me.

"Listen, Sax, we can talk about this," Frankie pleads, his voice laced with fear and regret as he takes a step back from my brother. Saxon, however, matches his every step. When Frankie takes one, so does Saxon. Until he is flush against the window and the barrel of Saxon's pistol is pressed firmly against Frankie's forehead.

I'm so fixated on my brother and uncle I release a small squeal when someone comes up beside me and holds my wrists.

"Oh God, Saint. You scared me." I whisper as I watch him carefully cut the ties from my wrists. As soon as they hit the floor, he scoops me into his arms and presses me into his chest. The warmth and security of his hold sweeps over me, encasing me in all that is Saint. Home.

"I hate to admit it, but you had me fooled. Who would have known, Uncle Frankie? The man who took us in after the tragic loss of our father turned out to be the darkness plaguing our world all this time." I turn to my brother, watching his towering rage encompass my uncle. Frankie's frame grows smaller and smaller by the minute. For a brief moment, I feel sorry for him. Briefly. Until the memories of all he's done swarm into my mind once again. No amount of pity will be wasted on this pathetic excuse of a man.

"You know what, I was going to arrest you and save you from these boys' barbaric and torturous ways, but hearing you confess to all you've done, well, I've changed my mind." My head swings around, not expecting to hear the once familiar voice, and my eyes collide with a very alive Dante. I noticeably gasp, not expecting to see him, while Saint and Saxon seem abnormally calm by his presence. Lifting my head to look at Saint, he gives me a reassuring smile.

"We'll fill you in later," he whispers to me, kissing the top of my forehead.

"What, you can't—" Frankie stutters over his words.

"He's all yours, boys. I'll have this cleaned up by morning," Dante says, before making his way over to stand in front of me.

"Are you okay, Sage?"

"Yeah, I'm fine, but how did you—what are you doing here?" I ask, confusion starting to make my head hurt. He smiles down at me as I fumble with my words.

"Like I said before, we've been investigating your father's case since the beginning. It wasn't until we received help from an unlikely source that we were able to connect all the dots leading straight to Frankie."

"Unlikely source, who was—?" Gloria walks in through the archway, looking elegant and classy as she glides through the room. Coming up to me, she throws her arms around my neck, embracing me as if I was her own daughter. Saint lets me go, and I return the gesture.

"I'm so very sorry, Sage. I'm so sorry this had to happen to you and your brother. I never wanted any of this to happen." Her hug grows tighter, my skin burns with her embrace, but I don't show my pain. She needs this as much as I do. "When Frankie approached my husband about his plan, he was all too happy to oblige. All because of our relationship. I can't help but feel responsible for everything." I stop her right there. Pulling away from her embrace, I look her in the eyes. They are so blue, so beautiful.

"This is not your fault, Gloria. None of this is anyone's fault but those three men right there." I don't have to turn to see the men I'm referring to. Gloria's eyes fill with tears that quickly cascade down her cheeks. She was a prisoner to her husband for seven years, living in this home with the man that helped kill the man she fell in love with. She lost her love and her brother, Tim Blanchett. I lost my father and my uncle. So much loss, so much pain fills this room around us.

"When I overheard the plan to try to kill you and Saxon, I couldn't let that happen. I snuck out that same night and ran straight to Dante. I knew he was the main agent on Luther's case, and I told him everything." She looks to Dante, who places a hand on her delicate shoulder.

"The moment she came to me, I knew you both weren't safe. I headed to your school to inform you and then the drive-by happened. I was wearing a bulletproof vest, but one of the shots hit my shoulder, and I took the opportunity for them to believe I was dead." I let out a breath. My body slowly begins to ease the tension I've been holding this whole time. Exhaustion is quickly taking over.

"After I heard about the motorcycle crash, I knew we couldn't wait any longer. He was getting too close to you, and we needed to take action."

"That's when he showed up at the house, right before we were on our way here to get you," Saint says beside me.

"Wait, how did you know where I was?" I look up at Saint, who looks at Sax, who continues staring at Frankie.

"Don't be mad, babe, but I installed a tracker on your phone." I pull my phone from my back pocket. It's dead now, but the thought of Saint putting a tracker on my phone should infuriate me. However, I'm glad he had.

"Thank God you did," I say, tucking my phone back in my pocket. Tension visibly releases from Saint's shoulders at my reaction. He must have thought I'd be pissed, and normally, I would have been, but at this moment, I'm grateful. I yawn into my elbow, my eyelids becoming increasingly heavy.

"Get her home. My guys will have this cleaned up, and we'll talk when you've all gotten some rest," Dante says to the room. I can't just leave. I need to talk with Gloria more; I need to know about her and my father's relationship; I need to talk with Saxon. I need so many answers, but my body is betraying me. Slowly, I'm becoming drained from being in fight-or-flight mode for so long, and my need for rest is triumphing over everything else. While two police officers enter the room, they head over to Frankie where they proceed to put him in handcuffs, allowing Saxon to finally come over to me. I swing my arms around his neck, a small sob leaving my throat as he wraps his arms around me. I notice a small tremble in his arms as he holds me for a long moment.

"Are you okay, witch stick?" I let out a small chuckle at his nickname for me and nod against his shoulder. "Everything will be okay now. Go with Saint and get some rest. You both need it." He kisses the top of my head before pulling away from me and giving Saint a bro hug.

"Take care of her," Saxon whispers, but I hear him. I smile at his acceptance of me and Saint. I watch the two men I care most for in this world; the fragments of my heart mold back together and warmth radiates within my chest. Saxon walks back to the two cops and speaks with them about taking over Frankie. Finn, Brooks, and Owen enter the room on cue and take Frankie away, and I know at that moment, I'll never see my uncle again. Good riddance.

SAINT

# CHAPTER 44

## SAINT

After leaving Mayor Harrison's house, Sage and I head home while the guys take care of Frankie. They are taking him to the basement, and I know the next twelve hours will be the last and worst hours of his pathetic life. I wanted to be there with Saxon, but he insisted on me staying with Sage, and I didn't argue. I much prefer that option.

The ride home is quiet. I hold Sage's hand while she lulls in and out of sleep. She is exhausted. From the motorcycle accident, to being taken from the hospital and held hostage by Frankie, I would be surprised if she wasn't tired. When we finally get home, we make our way inside and straight to my room. I help her change out of her clothes carefully so as to not disturb her bandages and dress her in one of my oversized shirts. I also get her a couple of ibuprofens, since we hadn't filled her medication prescription yet, and help her into my bed.

I quickly changed from my clothes as well and slide in beside her. Her warm body presses against mine, and I wrap my arm around her waist, holding her against me and never wanting to let go. We lie there in silence for a long while, allowing our hearts to calm down from the night we just experienced.

"How did you get past the guards at the mayor's house?"

"Dante had over a dozen agents stationed around the house. Once they took down the two guards, Gloria let us in right through the front door." I kiss her forehead, her eyes flutter shut, and she inhales a deep breath.

"I can't believe it was Frankie all this time. I mean, we thought he was involved somehow, but I guess I wanted to believe he wouldn't do such a thing." Her voice is pained as she speaks. Besides Saxon, Frankie was her last living relative. Her last sense of family. It hurts knowing she's lost so much in her short life. I want to say something, comfort her in some way, but I don't have the words. What does someone say in a situation like this? But then, I'm not expecting her next question.

"Why didn't you tell me you saved me that day from the fire?" My hand that's rubbing circles on her back suddenly freezes. I honestly don't know why I didn't tell her, other than the fact that I didn't want her to see my true feelings for her at that time. She couldn't know that I'd loved her since day one. I couldn't give into temptation with my best friend's little sister, it was wrong. Plus, she hadn't loved me the same way I loved her. She'd loved me like a brother, and I loved her in the worst forbidden way. I, for so long, hid my feelings from her. When sometimes a crack in the shield would show, I quickly hid behind the denial that I tried so terribly to portray.

"I didn't want you thinking of me any differently." It's a lame excuse, but it's true. I didn't want the idea of a heroic action to somehow change her perception towards me. Sometimes people fall for the hero simply because they've done something great. However, I'm no hero. I can be dark, brutal, barbaric, obsessive, protective—everything that makes up a villain. I wanted her to fall in love with me for who I truly am, and I'm no hero. I don't know how to explain myself in a way that makes sense, so I say what I've always known to be true: "I love you, Sage Wilder. I always have and always will." Her eyes fill with unshed tears, and before they can fall, I tip her chin towards me and kiss her with so much assurance, so much honesty, that there is no doubting my love for this woman.

----

## SAGE

The next few days are filled with absolutely nothing but rest and recovery for both Saint and me. We end up having a home health nurse come by and show us how we need to remove, clean, and redress our wounds. Luckily, neither of us sustained any infections from our quick departures from the hospital and other activities. Surprisingly, we are both healing quite well. The nurse only has to come to the house twice before we both feel comfortable enough to do it ourselves. Saxon is against it at first, saying we are both so incredibly stubborn, and we should have the nurse come by some more before writing her off, but like he said, we are stubborn. No more stubborn than him, might I add.

Dante comes by a few days after the incident to inform us of the reports about the mayor being murdered.

"It's being reported that Mayor Harrison was involved in a secret organization that went haywire, leaving him and his head of security murdered in his home. Gloria was 'out of town' during the act and was left unharmed. She has been playing the grieving widow role quite well." Dante smiles.

The living room where Saint, Saxon, and I sit with Dante falls quiet for a brief moment before Dante asks the question he is clearly dying to ask.

"Is he taken care of?" Meaning, was Frankie now dead and disposed of?

"He's taken care of. No worries there," Saxon answers, looking at Saint with a devilish grin. I don't know what they did to him, and honestly, I don't want to know. All I'm aware of is that he's gone and never coming back. That's good enough for me. I do, however, have a question that I've been racking my brain over.

"What was your connection to Damien Devonte? Your real connection?" I ask Dante, and a playful grin splays across his face as he looks at me and then at the guys.

"Well, I was investigating him due to his involvement with the Hellstorm club. As you all know, Frankie hired two men from their club to start the fire that killed your father. Mayor Harrison was known to be friendly with their president for some time. Damien Devonte was the man that was responsible for locating your home and passing on the information to the club. He was involved with their club for years and this task alone gained him the title of an official member of their club, an initiation, if you will, until his untimely demise." He smirks at the guys for a moment, making me think he knows it was them that killed him. "I have no idea what you're talking about," Saxon answers with an equally mischievous smirk. I can't hide my small smile as I cuddle into Saint's side.

"Upon speaking with the Hellstorm's president, he denied having any knowledge of the two members who started the fire. Although he denies the friendship he had with Mayor Harrison. He stands by his word of not being involved with Luther Wilder's death."

"Anyway, Damien's death had me going over the case all the way from the beginning, and I soon found the trusts that your father created for you two." I straighten up when he mentions the trusts. My father never once mentioned anything to me or Saxon about the trust funds he set up us.

"That's another question I have no answer for. Your father had the trusts made, but only to be released when you each turn twenty-eight. I guess I'm just stumped as to why he chose twenty-eight instead of, let's say, twenty-one or even eighteen." Dante looks at Saxon, but it's me who answers this question.

"My father's favorite number. For many reasons, actually." I take a deep breath. His love for symbolism was always something I loved about him. He wasn't a superstitious man, per se, but he did believe in deeper meanings, especially signs that were placed before us. "In Chinese culture, the number twenty-eight is associated with easy prosper and good fortune. My father was also twenty-eight when he met and married our mother. She was twenty-six. She got pregnant when she was twenty-eight and birthed Saxon on October 28. Then I was born six years later, on August 28. Believe it or not, even Saint was born on April 28. See the pattern? The number twenty-eight is very important to my father because everything he loved most circled around that number." I hadn't noticed I was crying until I feel Saint's thumb brush away a stray tear from my cheek.

"There's no doubt our father chose that specific birthday for a reason." Saxon says from beside me, nudging my shoulder and smiling down at me. I hadn't seen Saxon smile so genuinely in so long, it inflates my heart with so much love and contentment that I know at this moment, we will all be okay.

SAINT

# CHAPTER

## 45

**FIVE WEEKS LATER**

**SAINT**

"Say it again," Saint whispers in my ear, giving me shivers down my spine.

"I love you, Saint. So, so much." I kiss his nose first before he captures my lips with his, kissing me like I'm his last breath on this earth. Our wounds have almost fully healed. All that's left is the slightly pink hue of freshly regenerated skin where our bandages once sat. They still hurt at times, especially after showers, rubbing a towel over them or even rubbing my clothes too roughly against it. Even now, as I press my body against Saint's, never fully feeling like I'm close enough to him. I always need more, more of him on me, around me, inside me. He's the best kind of addiction that I never want to be free of.

Tyler Saint Bones slipped into our lives years ago, forever a constant presence in our world from that moment on. From a protective teenager when I first started dating to an even more protective man who's always been in the shadows of my life. He's looked out for me, guarded me, stood up for me—hell, he's even beaten other men for me when they've done me wrong. He's always been the guardian of my heart. Whenever he saw me hurting, he would destroy the cause of my pain. Whenever he felt someone did me wrong, he would teach them a lesson. Whenever I was being too critical of myself or my scars, he would know exactly what to say to make the constant inner dialogue I'd create disappear into thin air.

When we grew up, his attentiveness towards me changed to something more emotional. From the bickering helicopter brother type, to a man who saw what he desired in life and did everything in his power to win me over. Even when he knew it would take patience and time, he never stopped. He never gave up on the idea of us, and I'm so happy he didn't. I've always loved Saint. From day one, he was my second brother, but as time went on, my love for him grew into something more zealous.

Slowly but surely, he slipped past the walls I built around my heart. My carefully constructed barriers had small cracks where Saint was able to sneak in. I started to notice the smaller things I once saw as annoying and began to see his soul. When I used to get mad at him for disrupting my dating life, I now see how he was protecting me from those who never deserved my time, or love, for that matter. He saw my worth long before I saw it myself. When I thought I would never be given the love and affection that other women got, simply because of my flaws, he saw them as symbols of survival.

My scars were once my biggest insecurities, and though I hadn't believed him at first, Saint confessing he saw my scars as beautiful changed everything.

*Whenever I see your scars, I smile. I know you hate them, but I'm thankful you have scars and not a tombstone beside your father. Every time I see them, I thank God he let you stay on this earth another day. Your scars are the symbol of survival. You fought that day and kicked Satan's ass. You're beautiful, Sage, and no amount of scars will ever make you anything less.*

It was in that moment I knew Saint loved me, every piece of me, even before he spoke the words. He loves me, and I love him, all of him: the good, the bad, and the ruthless. I am his and he is mine, always from this moment on.

Straddling his waist, I begin rocking my hips against him, needing that friction, needing his touch to soothe the ache building between my legs. We are already naked, the sound of my arousal slick against his groin. A deep moan comes from his chest as his hands grab my waist, holding me still.

"So needy already, are we?" Our lips are still brushing one another's, his words seeping into my mouth as I smile against his.

"I always need you," I whisper. His teeth grab my bottom lip and pull it towards him. The sting of his bite has me moaning against him. The pain mixing with pleasure is something I've only ever experienced with Saint, and I love the roughness of his hold, only to quickly be replaced with a smooth gentle caress.

"Come here, baby." Saint flips me around so fast I can't help the small squeal that comes from my throat. Lying on my back, he hovers over me with his thick, strong legs straddling my waist as his cock teases my entrance. I tried lifting my hips to meet him, but he forces me back down.

"Ah, not just yet. You need to tell me how much you want me first." I smile up at him. His bedroom banter always makes sex so much more explosive from him building me up, teasing me, or holding off as long as possible before giving me exactly what I want most.

"Please, Saint. I need you inside me. Pretty please." He groans as he leans his head back, his large hand slowly pumping his veiny and already slick cock. It has my hips rising towards him once again. He pumps his hands a few more times before looking back down at me.

"Because you asked so nicely." Moving at the speed of a snail, he teases my entrance with his head and the small touch alone has my core heating from anticipation. Rubbing his head up and down my pussy, coating himself in my juices, I groan at how much I need him to ease my ache.

"Please, Saint, please." I am begging now, my hands grabbing hold of his thighs as I dig my nails into his skin. Inch by inch, he presses inside me, my walls stretching with every inch he gives. It's always a bit painful when he initially pushes himself inside. His length and girth are enough to hurt. But he always gives me time to adjust, and soon, the pain turns to satisfying fullness that has my eyes rolling back in my head.

Our hips finally press together as he pushes himself to the hilt. Our eyes connecting as he gives me another moment to adjust. He leans down, his lips pressing against mine in a slow, delicious kiss that has me melting beneath him. While he kisses me, his hips rise just a little and lowered back down. Again and again, he repeats his thrusts, pulling back more with each movement. Soon his hips are pumping in and out at a faster pace, the sound of our skin slapping together filling the air around us.

He grabs my wrists that are still against his thighs and lifts them over my head, pinning them to the bed with one hand. With his other hand, he finds my clit, making circular motions with his thumb against my most sensitive spot.

"Oh God, yes," I moan, my eyes falling shut as he keeps thrusting in and out, creating a euphoric build of sensations that traveled from my pussy through my core.

"You take me so well, such a good girl." I can't hold off any longer. His deep sexy voice has me chasing my orgasm. I never want this feeling to end. More and more, he thrusts inside me. Faster and faster until I'm swept up in a cloud of blissful pleasure that has me screaming his name. A tsunami of ecstasy crashes over me, my whole body tensing at the sensation. I lift my hips to his again, praying it will never stop.

My body is tingling all over just as Saint thrusts a few more times before reaching his release as well. Just when I thought I was coming down from my high, his lips find my clit, and I flinch at the overwhelming sensation of being overstimulated. At first, it is too much too soon, but then he enters a finger inside me. The build of another orgasm quickly starts forming, and I relish in his need to make me come again.

It doesn't take long, with my fingers threading through his luscious hair, I hold him at the right spot as wave after wave of pleasure soars through me once again. Perfection, magnificent, sublimity, there is never a word accurate enough to explain the way Saint brings me to orgasm. I moan through my climax, coming all over again—all over his face. It is filthy, it is dirty, it is exactly how we like it. He lifts his head, and I let my hands fall from his head as I slowly came down from another beautiful climax.

Opening my eyes, I see Saint is smiling back at me. His lips are a mess from my arousal as he licks his lips clean. Leaning down, he kisses me softly. I can taste myself on him, and it just makes everything so much more, well, us. A beautiful, chaotic mess of perfection.

"Say it again for me," he whispers beside me. He lays his head on the pillow we're sharing and pulls me into his chest.

"Only if you say it back to me," I tease, kissing him again for good measure.

"Always."

"I love you Saint." Another kiss, his hand cupping my check before pulling back and staring into my eyes.

"Now it's your turn. Tell me your love is like a burning flame." I giggle to myself.

"No Sage." My eyes shoot straight open in shock, as I wait for him to continue, or rather, hope he continues. "My love for you will never be described as a fire because eventually fire burns out. My love for you is more like the steadiness of a gentle river. It's forever flowing and never stopping. Even when it reaches the sea, it still flows. Forever moving and never stopping—that's my love for you, Sage. Eternity." My eyes fill with tears, my eyelashes pushing them down my face as my bottom lip trembles.

"Saint," Is all I can say. He captures my mouth with his and shows me just how much he is meant to be mine.

SAGE

# EPILOGUE

## THREE YEARS LATER

### SAGE

I'm running late, as always, but I can't find my wallet anywhere.

"Has anyone seen my wallet?!" I yell down the stairs to Saxon and Saint, who are impatiently waiting for me to finish getting ready so we can meet Gloria for dinner. It's my twenty-fourth birthday, and since that awful night, I've become so close to Gloria. She's made me feel so close to my father, even though I never knew her while they were together. She's kind, caring, and saved mine and Saxon's life when she herself was a prisoner to the same monsters.

I also invited Mira to come to dinner, but she's secretly been seeing someone, and I couldn't be happier for her. At first, I could tell she felt guilty for having feelings for someone other than her husband. When he died, she vowed to never love again, but the heart wants what the heart wants. Besides, no one should have to walk this earth alone. When love finds you, embrace it and cherish every moment you have together.

"It's down here. Now hurry up!" Saxon calls to me as I roll my eyes and head down the stairs to a waiting pair of silver eyes. Saint is dressed in an all-black ensemble; his hair is a perfect, messy style, emphasizing his gentlemanly appearance. It should be illegal for any man to look this handsome. My black heels click with every step I take, my red spaghetti strap dress hugging my body in all the right places. The high slit on the side gives Saint something to look at as I take the last few steps.

"You look absolutely stunning, babe." I rise to my tiptoes to give him a kiss. Even though I'm in three-inch heels, he still towers over me. I love it. He makes me feel feminine when I've always felt like a tomboy. Extending his hands out to me, he hands me a little package I hadn't known he was holding.

"What's this?" I ask.

"Not sure. It was left on the porch with your name on it." Saint shrugs but places the package in my outstretched hands. Rolling my eyes, I know it's another birthday present from only God knows who. Opening the package, I tear away the simple black wrapping paper and lift the lid off the box.

"What's it this year?" I hear Saxon ask from the front door. Peering inside the box, I see a delicate piece of jewelry. A white-gold necklace that has a pendant hanging from the middle. Lifting the velvet jewelry holder from the box, I see the pendant is an emerald stone sitting in a circular setting. It's beautiful, stunning, actually.

"It's a necklace, with an emerald pendant," I whisper to the guys. My eyes examine the jewel and its beauty as I hold it between my fingers. The golden evening light that shines through the windows bounces off the stone, causing a ray of green strikes of light fill the foyer.

"Oh my gosh," I whisper. I'm taken aback. A gift like this must have a cost a pretty penny. Saint gently takes the necklace from my hands and indicates for me to turn around. I do so, and allow him to place the necklace around my neck where it sits across my collar bones. I can't help touching the stone once he's done.

"Will I ever find out who keeps sending me these incredible gifts?" I ask to myself, not really addressing the question to anyone, rather, the ghost of my secret gift giver. Saint rests his hands on top of my shoulders, and his lips brush my ear, warm breath fanning across my skin as goosebumps rise across my body.

"Maybe the person has been right in front of you this whole time." His voice is a whisper, his lips kissing my neck, and it finally hits me.

I spin around so fast I practically collide with his chest.

"It's been you this whole time?" I ask, my eyes wide. I can't believe I didn't see it before. He doesn't answer me right away, his lips turning up into a small smile.

"Damn, man. Who would have known old Tyler Saint Bones was a freaking romantic at heart? You two make me sick," Saxon mumbles behind us, opening the front door and rushing us to head out. Before either of us can move, I throw my arms around Saint's neck and kiss him with so much love, I feel as though my heart may explode.

"Thank you, Saint. I love you so much."

"I love you too, baby."

Saxon makes a pathetic gagging sound behind us, and I can't help but laugh at his childish ways.

"Right, let's go. We'll be late," Saxon says as he unbuttons the sleeves to his black button-up to roll them up to his elbows. He too, is wearing black slacks. His hair is pulled back in a slick man bun, but he stops dead in his tracks when he fully sees what I'm wearing.

"Sis, I love you, but what are you wearing?" he says,

eyeing me in disapproval, playing the big brother role far too well.

"A dress. Now let's go. *We're going to be late,*" I say back to him in a mocking tone. I walk past the guys, but don't miss the remark from Saint that has me laughing to myself.

"So little faith in me, Sax. Do you really think anyone will get away with looking at her the wrong way? You must have forgotten who we are." I look over my shoulder at the bro hug they give each other, and my heart warms at their friendship. The thought of it being ruined because of me makes me physically sick. I couldn't live with myself, knowing I was the cause of a bond being shattered.

We all ride in Saint's Tahoe to the restaurant, my favorite one in town, Raul's Seafood. I'm flipping through my class schedule for my senior year on my phone, not fully comprehending that I'm starting the last year of college already. The painting of my parents on their wedding day is still not fully complete. It's still hiding away in the private room in the library. This painting has been my work in progress during my whole college career, and I can't help but feel nervous to present it as my final project this year. However, since finally opening up my custom paint shop beside the garage, my confidence in my work has skyrocketed, simply because of all the work I've brought in and five-star reviews that have been published so far. Sage Customs is flourishing. Suddenly, a blindfold is placed over my eyes.

"Saxon, what are you doing? You're going to ruin my makeup," I groan, but let him tie the fabric over my eyes.

"It's funny how you are so particular about your makeup all of a sudden," he jokes from behind me.

"Shut up," I groan again, tucking my phone into my purse.

The Tahoe slows down and takes a turn, I'm guessing, into the parking lot before we stop completely. Saint turns off the engine and informs me to stay put while he exits the vehicle. A moment later, the passenger side door opens and strong hands help me out of the vehicle. I take small steps as Saint wraps an arm around my waist to steady me.

"That's it, one step at a time. Here's a step up, be careful," he instructs me until I feel the cool breeze of the air conditioner in the restaurant. We finally stop as the fabric around my eyes loosens. As soon as it leaves my eyes, I'm greeted with a thunderous,

"Surprise!" I jump at the sudden hollering, and my eyes quickly adjust to a room full of all my friends. Ophelia, Bristol, Frieda, Owen, Brooks, Finn, Skylar, Gloria, Mira and a gentleman I assume is her new friend, Sam, Dante, and all the club members are standing together holding a large banner that reads, *Happy Birthday Sage!*

My hands fly to my mouth at the shock and utter disbelief. I grew to hate my birthday due to the loss of my father, but within the last few years, Gloria changed how I saw things.

*Never stop celebrating you. I know your father would be looking down at you with sadness at the thought of you forgetting about your birthday. Another year on this beautiful earth is a day worth cherishing, and you, my dear, are someone worth celebrating.*

I scan through everyone here today, and my eyes fill with tears with so much love for each and every one of them. These are not just my friends; this is my family.

A soft sob, or laugh, I can't tell which one, leaves my mouth, and I turn to see Saint smiling down at me.

I look at Saxon on my other side, who pulls me into a hug, whispering, "Happy birthday," in my ear. I give him a quick kiss on the cheek and turn back to Saint, wiping my eyes at the same time. When I turn, I look up, expecting to see Saint's handsome smile, but I'm confused when I see him below me. He's on his knee, and as if my heart couldn't feel any fuller, he says to me, "Sage Wilder, will you marry me?" A gasp is all I hear. The room has suddenly become painfully silent. No more cheering, no more "happy birthdays," just the sound of my breathing, and the pounding of my heart. I can't speak. The only word I manage to get out is "Saint." That's all he needs to hear. He lifts me up into his arms, spinning me around as I hold on to his neck, smiling and laughing down at this beautiful man who stole not only my heart, but my entire soul. The room erupts in applause as he stops spinning us, and I can finally kiss the man I will spend the rest of my life with.

"I love you, Sage Wilder."

"I love you too, Saint."

"So, is that a, yes?" he asks with a sheepish grin.

"Of course, it's a yes!"

### The End

# THANK YOU

Thank you for reading Secrets Unveiled, book one in the Kings' Aces series. If you enjoyed this, please check out more from Rebecca Hamby

# ABOUT THE AUTHOR

Rebecca is a newly published author who lives in North Carolina with her husband, two kids, and four-legged friend. You will usually find her escaping into her writing where her deepest and darkest thoughts are created for others to enjoy. When she is not writing she is either exercising, listening to audiobooks, playing with her kids, watching true crime documentaries or zoning out while thinking of all the ways to torture her characters. As most of us authors nowadays say, check trigger warnings before diving in. Thank you for being here!

Learn more about Rebecca Hamby at www. rebeccahambyauthor.com
Join her newsletter to receive updates, teasers, giveaways, and special deals!

# ALSO BY

## THE DARKNESS TRILOGY

The Shadows Book 1

The Abyss Book 2

The Awakening Book 3

---

## THE KINGS' ACES SERIES

Secrets Unveiled Book 1

Book 2 (Coming Soon)

Book 3 (Coming Soon)

Book 4 (Coming Soon)

Book 5 (Coming Soon)

# ACKNOWLEDGMENTS

Firstly, I need to thank my amazing editor, Maddi Leatherman, for helping develop and edit this story into what I feel is the absolute best version it can be. Your suggestions and commentary helped me expand Sage and Saint's into so much more than I could have imagined.

I also want to thank my amazing cover designer and formatter, Abigail, with Pink Elephant Designs. You never stop amazing me with how you can take a few of my ideas and transform them into nothing short of a masterpiece. Thank you so much!

Of course, to my readers, because let's face it, without the love and support of all of you, I wouldn't be able to share these characters stories with all of you.